NOT IMMUNE TO DEATH

RUBY DAKOTA COZY VETERINARY MYSTERY SERIES

ANNIE MOORE MARTIN, DVM

DISCLAIMER
This is a work of fiction set in the very real — and very wonderful — town of Hays, Kansas. While the author's experiences there shaped this story, all characters are fictional. Names, personalities, and circumstances are products of the imagination. Some dogs, however, are entirely real and deserve full credit.

Publishing Coordinator & Book Designer – Sharon Kizziah-Holmes
Cover Design – Sweet 'n Spicy Designs

Paperback-Press
an imprint of Paperback Press, LLC
Springfield, Missouri

ISBN -13: 978-1-970560-40-4

DEDICATION

To John, the love of my life

After 51 years of marriage, you know me better than anyone. Somehow, you still believed in this book even when I wanted to quit. You encouraged, you pushed, you guided. Consider this yours. The Lord knows you earned it.

ACKNOWLEDGMENTS

John, my husband of fifty-one years, co-editor, and the most patient man I know—none of this happens without you.

Finley Williams, my 12-year-old granddaughter. After many months of agonizing over the right title, I gave her the book's premise. Without a moment's pause, she replied, "Not Immune to Death." Maybe I'm not the only writer in the family anymore.

Adrienne Brodeur, who in Kauai, gave me the courage to write.

Adriana Trigiani, whose Master Class, "Writing with Humor," changed everything. She was the first to tell me I write funny and that I should consider performing stand-up comedy. Bless her!

Nicholas Delbanco, whose four-day Master Class taught me how to improve and revise my manuscripts with intention.

Ruth Ware, whose Master Class showed me how to craft a page-turner.

William and Lara Bernhardt, outstanding instructors at their Writercon Retreat, who pushed me further than I expected.

Barbara Kuert, who was always there with a listening ear.

Robin McGee, who once again brought her considerable talents to cleaning up my writing.

Deb Witcraft, my college roommate and forever friend, who, early on, offered to peruse the manuscript for errors.

Marcia Lawrence, my editor, whose sharp eye for detail improved every chapter of this book.

Jaycee DeLorenzo, for a creative cover design delivered beautifully under pressure.

Sharon Kizziah-Holmes, Paperback Press, LLC, for patiently guiding me through the publishing process—and for not giving up on me.

Prologue

The bullet shatters the clinic's plate glass window and whistles past my ear just as I bend down to wipe a puddle of dog urine left by my last patient. The sound hits me before I realize what is happening—a deafening crack followed by the tinkling of glass raining onto linoleum. I drop to my knees, heart hammering against my ribs like a trapped animal. Years of veterinary training kick in, not the part about dodging bullets, but the instinct to stay calm during life-threatening emergencies. My hands tremble anyway. Someone just shot at me. At *me*, Dr. Ruby Dakota, a veterinarian whose most violent encounters until now involved angry cats and an occasional snapping dog.

Broken glass crunches under my palms as I crab-crawl across the clinic floor, the sharp edges biting into my skin. The antiseptic smell of the clinic mixes with the metallic tang of my own fear. A second shot punches through the display of dental chews, sending plastic packaging flying in an explosion of color and noise. Whoever is out there isn't giving up easily. I taste copper as I bite the inside of my cheek, trying to control my breathing. My mind races through possibilities. A disgruntled client whose pet didn't survive surgery? A drug addict desperate for the controlled substances locked in the safe? The IRS finally coming after the questionable deduction I claimed three years ago?

None of those explanations feels right. But as I drop lower to an army crawl, the linoleum cold against my stomach, I know exactly when the countdown to this moment began: at sunrise, when two men in black suits appeared at my clinic door.

CHAPTER 1

Two Days Earlier

The prairie sun peeked over the horizon, casting a soft glow on the blonde brick facade of my life's work. The plastic sign above the entrance read, "Pediatrician to Pets Veterinary Clinic, R.A. Dakota, D.V.M." To the people of Hays, Kansas, their four-legged friends were no less than family, a sentiment I'd honored in my practice for the past 34 years.

Elizabeth Custer, the wife of George Armstrong Custer of Little Bighorn fame, once said after visiting Fort Hays, "There was enough desperate history in that little town in one summer to make a whole library of dime novels." I'd lived out my own dime novel here. At 62, I found myself broke, a little arthritic, and without a social life.

First, let me properly introduce myself. I'm Ruby Anne Dakota, but the last person who called me Ruby is still limping. Everybody calls me Dakota. I'm a small package, standing at four-foot-ten on a good day, with the fierce attitude of a Doberman Pinscher. I do love my R.A.D. initials. This name thing started when my grandparents christened their daughters Pearl, Goldie, and Sylvia—even worse than the name Ruby. This *is* the Midwest, after all.

The Pediatrician to Pets Clinic, nicknamed Pee2Pee, truly encompassed my entire world. I performed a juggling act daily from eight a.m. to six p.m. Surgeries, where I removed body parts from male and female dogs and cats to prevent unwanted animals from ruling the world, filled my mornings. In the afternoons, I bounced between exam rooms to diagnose, treat, and vaccinate against diseases I might never encounter. Most evenings and weekends were extensions of this nerve-wracking schedule.

There was precious little "me" time as I toiled away under the critical eye of my corporate boss, Dr. Jake Morgan. He was also my first boss right out of veterinary school, when I was a starry-eyed new graduate ready to save Iowa's pet population. That's right. My old, overbearing boss was now my corporate boss. Little did I know when I sold my clinic to Pets Buy that Jake would come along with the deal as my regional manager.

Jake was a blond-haired hulk of a man, the size of a Kansas City Chiefs tight end. He had a blue-eyed stare that could melt granite and a smile that belied the mean spirit behind it. His obsessive-compulsive tendencies forced us all to behave like "Cats on a Hot Tin Roof." He was a living, breathing nightmare for a veterinarian like me who suffered from panic attacks.

Before each day descended into chaos, I cherished my early morning solitude. I felt a certain calm in my surgery room, despite the faint odor of anesthetic. Or perhaps that's *why* I felt so calm.

"It is six a.m.," the Christian radio station murmured in the background, a soundtrack to my daily devotional, *My Utmost for His Highest*. The stainless-steel surgery table, usually reserved for more clinical procedures, now served as my breakfast nook. Wielding an unused scalpel, I sliced through the flaky crust of my cherry turnover. The scent of warm fruit and buttery dough comforted me against the impending bedlam of the day.

"Breaking national news!" The KPRD radio announcer's voice jolted me as if shocked by an electric cattle prod. "A rare disease previously found only in African baboons is responsible for the death of two lab workers at the Center for Emerging and Zoonotic Infectious Diseases, CEZID, in Manhattan, Kansas."

I paused, scalpel hovering over my pastry, a strange chill running down my spine. I knew that facility. I had colleagues there. And something about African diseases made my stomach clench in a way that had nothing to do with my cherry turnover.

The sharp rap of knuckles against the glass front door startled me out of my reverie. My pulse quickened, another early morning emergency. I bolted up from my stool, nearly toppling it in my haste. Coffee sloshed over the rim of my mug, and adrenaline surged as I darted toward the front door. My mind cycled through the potential casualties that could befall Hays's pet population at sunrise, along with appropriate medical interventions.

Instead of Mrs. Schmidt with Bizzie, her bellyaching poodle, two men who looked like they'd stepped out of a "Saturday Night Live" skit peered through the glass. The duo stood at attention on my All Pets Welcome mat, their Ray-Ban aviators glinting despite the pale dawn light, their black suits creased sharper than a Schnauzer's ear.

It seemed too early for the IRS to appear on my doorstep. Had I accidentally booked a Blues Brothers tribute band? I eyed them back through the door. I'd dealt with IRS agents before. I owed back taxes from previous years, but they'd never dressed like this. They always looked like they shopped at Accountants R Us and wore khaki slacks, button-down collars, and poorly fitting suit coats. Business casual. These guys were anything but business casual. They were no-nonsense, business serious.

"May I help you, gentlemen?" I called out through the doorbell speaker, my voice hitching a bit higher than usual.

The shorter one, built like a fire hydrant, leaned into the Ring doorbell. “We’re with the FBI, ma’am. We need to speak with you,” he replied, his voice devoid of emotion. This was not a social call.

“FBI? Would that be the Freakin’ Barking Investigators?” I quipped.

No response. At the same time, Chui, my pint-sized chiweenie, pushed against my legs, determined to claim his spot at the door. Chui barked his little apple-shaped head off with Rottweiler ferocity, nudging my leg to remind me he was ready to defend his territory—or die trying.

With a resigned huff, I punched in the alarm code and twisted the double deadbolts. The security helped keep out drug seekers targeting veterinary clinics. My hands hovered over the door handle as my mind raced with questions and scenarios. I was a dog and cat doctor, not someone who would interest the FBI. Perhaps the IRS had merged with the FBI, and my arrest was imminent. Seemed like overkill. For heaven's sake, they could have just sent another red-lettered URGENT notice.

As the men entered, Chui launched himself like a fuzzy missile at the taller agent’s polished wingtip, latching onto his shoelace. His bark was mighty, but his bite... not so much.

“May I see your badges?” I asked, aiming for nonchalance but coming out more like a nervous squeak.

I had no idea how to verify a badge but asking seemed appropriate. Mostly, I was stalling to mentally prepare for whatever charges they might bring. The two men reached into their jackets with synchronized precision like two choreographed hand models, flicking open leather wallets to reveal gleaming badges.

“I'm Agent Thompson, and this is my partner, Agent Johnson.”

I nodded, though their names had already slipped from my memory. I had what I called human name amnesia.

Recalling an owner's name was difficult, but this didn't apply to animals. I always remembered their pet's name, history, and favorite treat.

"Oh, thank God you're not from the IRS," I replied. "Whew! What a relief, but why are you at my door at six in the morning?"

"Sorry. That's classified, ma'am," Agent Whoever replied. "We have orders to escort you safely to an interview that concerns national security. Grab your toothbrush and a change of clothes. You're coming with us."

"Classified?" I echoed my relief at their non-IRS identity, but it was short-lived. "That sounds... ominous." I raised my eyebrows with a blend of curiosity and concern.

"Ma'am, it's imperative we leave now." His voice was as firm as a drill sergeant to a recruit.

"Right now?" I asked as I squinted at the clock on the wall. "It's 6:15 a.m. and barely light out. My staff isn't here yet. I haven't even put on my makeup."

Just kidding. I don't wear makeup.

"Ma'am." There was a hint of impatience in the agent's tone.

I suspected arguing with the Bureau was about as effective as trying to convince cats to swim. I glanced down at Chui, defending his territory one shoelace at a time. Although he was primarily a Chihuahua-dachshund cross, he must have had some rodent-destroying terrier in his lineage. He continued to growl through clenched teeth and remained attached to his prey. The prey, Agent Whatever, slid his foot in a circle and shook him around like a whirligig.

Chui is the Swahili word for leopard, pronounced "Chewy." He was unaware that his height, weight, and tiny brain disadvantaged him. He weighed in at a pitiful five pounds, which probably kept the agent from pulling his weapon.

“Ma’am, could you detach your dog from my shoelaces?”

“Chui!” I admonished, though I couldn't help but admire his lionhearted spirit. “Let go, buddy. The man's not a walking chew toy.”

The valiant defender momentarily paused his assault, brown eyes locking onto mine in confusion. Taking advantage of the ceasefire, I knelt and pried Chui’s jaws free from his leather-laced quarry. I scooped up the pint-sized warrior and tucked him beneath one arm like a furry football.

“Sorry about that,” I muttered, directing a sheepish grin at the men. “He's got a powerful will for such a pint-sized pup.”

“Clearly,” the agent remarked dryly, attempting to straighten his now-soggy, dangling shoelace with as much dignity as he could muster. At the same time, the chunky agent stood as stoic as a statue, a statue that was about to break into laughter, no doubt mentally adding this encounter to his list of embarrassing assignments.

“Please hurry, Dr. Dakota,” Agent Whatever called after me.

“Just give me ten minutes to pack,” I replied.

Chui’s blonde hair formed unruly spikes that made him look perpetually startled. I tried in vain to smooth them and rewarded him with a small corner of my cherry turnover as we passed the surgery suite.

“You sure showed them who's boss. Now, back to your luxury condo,” I said with a chuckle, shifting him to my hip like a child. We navigated through the maze of examination rooms until we reached Chui's kingdom in the kennel room. The chain-link gate of the dog run gave a familiar squeak as it opened.

“Here you go, buddy,” I cooed, setting him down on the cool surface. His toenails made clicking sounds as he trotted over to his bed, a plush fleece-lined number from

L.L. Bean that cost more than some of my own furniture. A small Persian throw rug covered the floor next to his bed. Chui snuggled in beside his stuffed toy giraffe, Lola. Chui loved Lola. Who would've thought a tiny dog could live in such luxury?

But then again, he was my only living family member.

Chapter 2

The clinic had been home for six months, ever since the landlord sold my rental house out from under me. My nonexistent savings and disastrous credit left me with the clinic as my only housing option. The upside: no rent and plenty of roommates. The downside: those roommates sometimes produced odors that would make a coroner gag. Often, they howled late into the night. Any sound outside the clinic sent them into a cacophony of squeals, yips, and barks. Coonhounds and beagles were incredibly vocal and might occasionally receive a light sedative wrapped in a dog treat. I mean, I had to sleep sometime, didn't I?

Living at the clinic meant all my clothes were already here, one small benefit of this housing disaster. I wore scrubs day and night, sometimes changing them in between when I remembered. I had one pair of tennis shoes for work and play, though I'd forgotten what play was. As a solo veterinary practitioner, I was on call 24 hours a day, seven days a week. Hays was not big enough to support an all-night emergency clinic. There was no passing off patients who needed round-the-clock care at the end of the day. After-hour emergencies meant meeting terrified clients at the door, reassuring them that yes, their Pomeranian, Bob

Barker, who had finished off a box of Russell Stover chocolates, would survive.

Last night was blessedly quiet. A whole night's sleep dramatically improved my attitude. I managed to cooperate with the agents while keeping my snark to a minimum. I mean, they *were* wearing guns. I did fail to ask the obvious question though. Why would the FBI want me, a small-town veterinarian with more debt than savings and more animal friends than humans? Of course, I was always up for an adventure and longed for a much-needed vacation, even if it meant being kidnapped by federal agents.

I pulled my cell phone out of my crossbody pouch. I used to keep my phone in my back pocket, but it kept ending up in the toilet or the washing machine. The pouch saved my staff from spending half their day calling my phone to locate it.

I called Harley's number. Harley was my able and ample-bodied veterinary technician who lived in a trailer behind the clinic. Harley could wrestle down the toughest dog on the block without spilling her coffee.

"Harley, I need you to come to work early. Two FBI agents are here. They've demanded I go with them for an interview." I still assumed it was related to some current or bygone IRS infraction, of which there had been many.

"Oh, no!" Harley gasped. "They found out about my backroom sales of Mellow Fellow?"

Mellow Fellow was Harley's homemade calming pet food invention. Sales had soared since the arrival of a fireworks factory on the edge of town. Harley had developed a secret recipe that chilled out even the most anxiety-ridden canine companion. Even I was unaware of the specific ingredients. Perhaps a sudden increase in the controlled substance orders had triggered an investigation by the DEA.

"Or maybe they are on to the dog shelter kickback scheme… Oh, Doctor, we could all go down for that one!

Wait. I know what it is," Harley continued. "They've been to the pet cemetery and discovered not all the graves contain a body."

Harley was known for her unorthodox, mostly compassionate side hustles, some of which bypassed her boss's scrutiny.

I struggled to keep my composure as I pressed my fingers to my temples. "Harley, stop jumping to conclusions."

Like I wasn't.

"I need you to walk the boarding dogs and follow the charted medical treatments for the hospitalized animals. Cancel my appointments."

"For how long? When should I reschedule them?" Harley asked, her voice tinged with concern. "Should I come visit you in prison?"

"I can't answer that," I replied, my voice steady but my mind filled with uncertainty. "I could be away for a while. The FBI agents asked me to pack my toothbrush and a change of clothes. Call Dr. Miller if my absence is prolonged. I'll keep in touch."

I hoped I sounded reassuring, but the situation was far from ordinary. I could feel my respiratory rate increase.

Dr. Miller was a tall, silver-haired, mixed-practice local veterinary colleague who took pity on me when I was away for a continuing education meeting, a rare occurrence. His calming demeanor reassured clients they were in capable, steady hands. Sometimes, my hands weren't that steady. I always risked losing clients when I referred them to him.

Since my social life was nonexistent by choice, I required no extra help on weekends. I had no time for frivolous pursuits. My patients were my life. This pressing situation might mean a more extended leave, though. I couldn't help but feel a pang of guilt for dumping my circus into a colleague's lap.

I made a second call to the Belladonnas, my professional support group. Although I probably needed therapy, this group was not that. It was an alliance of professional women and close friends who supported each other. We kept our phone numbers on speed dial, which gave me options when I felt overwhelmed by my circumstances.

This elite club included Emily, a medical doctor to humans, and Kit, a Ph.D. pharmacist to humans as well as to animals. The third member, Rhonda, was perhaps an unlikely but infinitely more valuable member because of her skill set as a semi-retired dispatcher for the sheriff's department. Rhonda was also a part-time tax preparer for Frontier Tax Professionals. Unlike the other group members, she was good with computers, relatively normal, and well-adjusted. She also shared the ability to wake up at a moment's notice to offer down-to-earth advice to a struggling group member. I rounded out the quartet.

We called ourselves the Belladonnas because, in Italian, it translates to "beautiful ladies." It was also a deadly plant. Yep. That was us. We looked harmless and elderly, but no one messed with us. Whether we tried to solve each other's current life situation or discussed the most recent crime spree in Hays or elsewhere, each brought their unique expertise: Emily with her medical knowledge, Kit with her pharmaceutical insights, and Rhonda with her police dispatch connections and financial experience. None of us had any spare time, but by cultivating these friendships and working through crime puzzles, we eliminated the embarrassment, expense, and inconvenience of a nervous breakdown.

This unlikely union had three commonalities: one, we were all older than fifty with plumpish but still, in our opinion, attractive bodies; two, we were all tired of taking guff from people incorrectly placed in authority over us; and three, we were all currently single, perhaps due to commonalities one and two.

I speed-dialed Rhonda. "Sorry to wake you. I know you worked the night shift at the station, but I need to tell someone that I'm getting into a black Chevrolet Suburban displaying Washington, D.C. plates with two men in suits who have not disclosed our destination."

Just in case I didn't return, I wanted someone to know where to look for the body.

"What? Are you being kidnapped? Should I put out a BOLO or a missing person report? Put up your best fight. I'll get my Smith & Wesson and be right over."

Rhonda's Smith & Wesson Model 10 was a 6-shot .38 Special double-action revolver that she inherited from her father, who was an MP in the Army.

"I'm bringing Rennie too."

Just as dangerous as her revolver was her straight-from-Germany German Shepherd named Rennie. Rennie did not speak English.

"Rhonda, hold on for a minute. I wasn't calling for the cavalry. I wanted to inform someone in the group that I may be unavailable for a day or two. I'm sure it's a misunderstanding over my unpaid taxes."

As I hung up on Rhonda, the more sinister looking of the two agents grabbed my bag, escorted me out of the clinic, and opened the door of the Suburban. He hoisted me and my short little legs into the back seat, tossing my bag onto the floor. The tinted glass was so dark I could barely see Harley waving an anxious goodbye through the clinic's front door.

As the other agent climbed into the front passenger seat, I questioned the wisdom of my actions, quickly concluding that I'd made a grave mistake—poor choice of words. My breath quickened as I groped for the door handle that wasn't there.

My anxiety wasn't debilitating. After all, I'd made it through vet school, didn't I? Sure, the occasional trembling hand meant a few self-inflicted needle sticks while wrangling fractious cats, but who's counting? Copious sweating was normal. Right? Even when surgical gloves practically oozed with perspiration by the end of the surgery. Still an excellent surgeon and an incredibly astute diagnostician, even if I said so myself.

Agent Number Two, the sinister but sultry one, twisted in his seat until he could observe my nervous coping techniques. I took deep breaths, counted my fingers, hunched and relaxed my shoulders, all the tricks I used to calm myself.

"What in the heck are you doing, ma'am? This is not a kidnapping. After all, we're the U.S. government."

That did not instill any comfort, given my knowledge of the U.S. government and its dealings with people overseas.

The ride only took 15 minutes, but it felt like an hour. "Whoa! Why are we at the airport?" I fought off stomach contents that forced their way into my mouth. I was quite sure I was going to die, just not sure how it would happen: heart attack (I had palpitations), a car wreck (the agent drove like a maniac), or starvation (I didn't finish my breakfast).

There was little chance that the last one would happen soon. I can always call on my extra abdominal fat in an emergency.

A Gulfstream G550 waited for us on the tarmac. This situation must have been more critical than I'd imagined, since, in my experience, only high-ranking officials had access to such luxurious transportation. Agent Whoever became frustrated with my slow progress on the steep steps. He grabbed me under my soaked armpits and whisked me up into the plane. My feet never touched the ground. When he let me down, a flight attendant nodded at me. There was no "Thanks for choosing FBI Airlines." Guess most criminals abducted on this jet did not deserve a welcome.

The luxurious lounge surroundings came as no surprise. My tax dollars at work. I tried not to pass out on the champagne leather seats. C'mon, Ruby, hold it together. You've been through much worse. These guys were just escorts. No bag over my head. No handcuffs. Already been there and done that in my youth, although at the time, my wrists were tiny enough to slip free. The agents sat near the back, silent, no explanation, no small talk. Was Guantanamo my next stop? I needed a mojito even though I didn't drink.

My mind again scanned through all the possible reasons for this seizure, the FBI one, not the physical one I was on the verge of. Did someone discover my stash of expired antibiotics I kept around for myself in case of a nuclear attack? Did someone turn me in for using my script pad to write a doctor's note so my neighbor's kid could skip school? Was my time overseas with my parents a possible source of answers? My parents had allowed me to tag along when there was no gunfire involved.

I closed my eyes and prayed that there would be no gunfire at the end of this flight.

CHAPTER 3

Forty-eight minutes later, the jet touched down in Manhattan, Kansas, with nary a bounce. Good thing because I had to pee. No way would I be able to squeeze this chubby sixty-plus-year-old body into that terrifying small locker of a toilet that threatened to whoosh me out of the plane upon flushing. Still panicking, I was not going to risk it. Even if I'd convinced myself there was plenty of room in that toilet, my many long overseas flights still lingered in my olfactory memory. I'd seen hundreds of passengers return from African safaris with assorted intestinal disasters—diseases, parasites, food poisoning—all competing for the four toilets at the back of the plane. That memory kept my hand off the door handle.

The pilot announced we were in Manhattan, Kansas, but I already knew. From the air, it looked like a town carved out of limestone. It was affectionately known as the Little Apple. Another black Suburban met us on the tarmac. No traipsing through Arrivals at the airport for us. Didn't the FBI understand everyone knew that a president, an agent, or a rock star was inside those vehicles? You'd think they'd opt for a few camo Hummers or red Jeep Grand Cherokees for a diversion.

It didn't take long to arrive at the Kansas State

University campus. Could I exhaust the oxygen content in a car by hyperventilating? This was getting weirder and weirder. The Kansas State Center for Emerging and Zoonotic Infectious Diseases, CEZID, was near my vet school. I called it the country-western version of Plum Island.

When Plum Island moved to Manhattan, Kansas, the Little Apple welcomed it with open arms. I thought the citizens might protest against this facility, but perhaps they thought harboring a few infectious diseases from around the world within their city limits wouldn't be that bad. After all, in Civil War days, the people there had survived typhoid, dysentery, and pneumonia. These people were tough. Plus, it was good for the economy.

I felt the color draining from my face as nausea embraced me. Our Suburban had just pulled up to the CEZID security checkpoint. The agents handed the armed guard some paperwork. The bar rose, and we drove to the Employees Only side of the Level 4 biocontainment facility.

CEZID did research, but did I *look* like a lab rat? I worked part-time with lab rats and monkeys during veterinary school. For that job, I had to be TB tested. Apparently, the monkeys had standards. I always tested positive after Africa but never had the disease. At some point in my African sojourn, I'd come into contact with TB-positive people, and now that little red bump at the injection site showed up every time. It always spiked the health department nurse's blood pressure when I returned for a reading 48 hours later. Maybe that triggered something at CEZID.

After traversing several layers of security checks, I found myself alone in a room of white ceramic tile and stainless-steel fixtures. Early Antiseptic. My flushed face was the only splash of color in the room. A young man, who looked like a teenager, dressed in a white lab coat, entered and asked me to roll up my sleeve. The red name embroidered on his chest read "Infectious Disease Specialist Intern."

Good grief. I was in a research facility. I had nothing infectious; if I did, I sure wouldn't want an intern for my physician. Or were they going to inject me with truth serum? From my pharmacology training, I knew they used to inject sodium thiopental intravenously, but I thought that tactic went out of favor decades ago. Thiopental would have helped my anxiety, but only God knew what I would reveal to them. I had my secrets.

"Shouldn't you read me my rights? What about a lawyer?" I queried the technician. He ignored me, swabbed my arm, threw on a tourniquet, and cranked it down. I now knew this was a blood draw, not an injection. Thank goodness. They can have all the blood they want… well, up to a certain amount.

At four-foot-ten, I didn't have a lot of blood to spare.

After filling an excessive number of multi-colored stoppered tubes with my blood, he pulled the needle, taped a cotton ball in place, and cranked some stretchy Coban™ around my elbow. "So, what's next?" I called after him as hc abruptly left the room. "Food, water, a sucker, an explanation… anything?"

I was alone again with my thoughts and my panic. We were well acquainted. I began to wish they'd given me the sodium thiopental. At least I would have slept while I awaited the next assault on my body. I could have screamed, but that would only increase my anxiety level. Was the door locked? I could run, but where? And besides, I was a doctor in a facility full of doctors. That required me to maintain some semblance of decorum.

My mind needed something else to focus on, like what could've gone wrong at the clinic in my absence. The ticker tape in my head never ran out of material. Stress hormones flooded my bloodstream daily. If there were a Mr. Olympia

Fitness and Performance title for adrenal glands, mine would have won hands down. If I wasn't worrying about a dog recovering from a complicated surgery or walking through multiple diagnoses for a cat with chronic diarrhea, I was obsessed with how I might have hurt someone's feelings by being too blunt. Worrying about the clinic right now seemed to be an effective diversion.

Without me there, my receptionist, London, would have arrived at the clinic at exactly 7:30 a.m., already flawless in whatever color Ralph Lauren button-down she'd chosen for the day with appropriate jewelry. Her black slacks never wrinkled, never attracted a single strand of pet hair. The pumps matched her belt, which probably matched something else I was too fashion-blind to notice. If I dressed like that, I'd look like I'd rubbed up against an alpaca by lunchtime.

For me, button-down and ironed quickly became missing a button and wrinkled. Jewelry? Not a chance. I could lose a ring finger caught in the collar of an ambitious Labrador retriever. A necklace could get tangled in the mane of a Chow, where no one wanted to be. And footwear? Since hitting fifty, I'd refused to wear heels, mostly because I was a little unstable and tended to fall off them. That could be problematic for some short women obsessed with their height, but I was beyond caring about looking like a runway model. I was primarily concerned with keeping myself upright.

My mind continued to race like a greyhound after a rabbit. There was a reason that I lived in scrubs and tennis shoes. Scrubs had replaced "butcher aprons" worn by surgeons back in the day, which might have been a comment on their surgical technique. Scrubs were easier to clean and more hygienic. At first, they came only in white, which caused eyestrain in the bright lights of the surgical suite. Oh, and they also showed blood.

Medical apparel companies began making mint green

and light blue scrubs and eventually introduced other colors and patterns. Now I could wear ones covered in dogs, cats, or pawprints that disguised the pus, poop, or pizza that landed on me during a typical workday. My scrubs came out of the laundry ready to wear. I never touched an iron.

Scrubs were the perfect pet-doctoring apparel for a woman my age. The pants were loose-fitting, with a drawstring waistband that allowed for expansion. Pet hair didn't stick to them, and there was never any need to tuck the top in. I didn't want to subject anyone to the sight of my backside bending over their beloved Scooby Doo as I listened to his chest.

With her precision haircut and manicured nails, I knew London counted out the money to start the day and cut up a wide variety of fruit for Ramos's breakfast. London handled front desk duties with help from Ramos, a double yellow-headed Amazon parrot. She also helped Harley feed and walk the boarding dogs in our employee parking lot.

The Pediatrician to Pets Veterinary Clinic didn't have much grass for the dogs to potty. The clinic sat in the heart of town, flanked by a carpet center and an insurance agency. Male dogs used my fake fire hydrant, which looked real enough to fool the occasional firefighter. Though the neighboring carpet store had offered to install artificial grass, I'd read too many horror stories about the smell. You had to keep it hosed off or the ammonia would make your eyes water. I chose natural waste composting in the dirt, gravel, and cement.

Mornings at the clinic were always bustling. At least the staff would not have to assist me in surgery today. Without surgery on the books, the day might stay at a manageable simmer. About now, Harley would try to stuff a pill down a reluctant cat's throat. If unsuccessful, she'd hide it in a small ball of cat food. She'd hook up an IV to the arm of an elderly cocker spaniel who was flirting with kidney disease and reward him with a bowl of commercial kidney diet pet food that smelled awful and tasted worse.

I knew. I'd tried it.

Gertrude, the groomer, whose name in German meant "spear or strength," would take in her furry clients for the day. She had been grooming animals for a quarter of a century. It was hard to tell her age. Years of bending over a bathtub and hoisting dogs onto a grooming table had permanently curved her spine. Her face constantly wore the kind of "don't even consider biting me" look she reserved for every customer. She was a skilled groomer and an excellent employee. Plus, she understood my jokes. I'd never heard her laugh out loud, but a cute little smirk on her face said she got me.

My anxiety had now decreased considerably. I pondered whether it was more stressful to run a hectic small animal clinic or to sit in this sterile room, which smelled of lab alcohol, with no clue why I was here. They were both stressful. I still awaited answers from either the staffers or the men in black who'd deposited me here. They all seemed to have forgotten me. Or perhaps that was part of their game. They might have been letting me sweat, hoping to get a confession. I wouldn't have known where to start and would probably have implicated myself in a crime in which they weren't even interested. Perhaps my blood contained unique genetic information to help track other tax dodgers.

Okay, that was crazy thinking.

Chapter 4

A pasty guy in black-rimmed military eyeglasses eased the door open and eyeballed me as if I were a lab rat. "Good morning, Dr. Dakota. I'm Dr. Hans Leakey. You must be quite confused as to the reason for your hasty relocation."

I adopted a squished-up threatening facial expression and blurted out, "You're not experimenting on me, buddy."

What I didn't say was that if I didn't get to a bathroom soon, he was gonna have to clean up after my urinary urge incontinence.

"Now, Dr. Dakota, just settle down." He spoke to me as if I were a child. I might have been the same height as a child, but really?

"You're here because of the time you spent with your parents in Uganda," he continued.

"What? That was a long time ago. How do you even know about Uganda?" I asked.

"While there, your parents submitted some articles to the *Journal of Immunology*. One of our graduate students uncovered their research while working on his doctoral thesis. Your name came up in their notes. You may not remember, but you came into contact with several viral diseases during your time there. In the Ebola outbreak of the 1970s, 80 to 90 percent of the people infected died. You, your parents, and a small group of aid workers from other countries survived. We need to know why."

"But how does that explain why I am here? My parents have both passed away, not from viruses, though." Tears welled up in my eyes.

"There has been an incident in our lab recently that we must handle discreetly. I cannot express how pressing this situation is. As a veterinarian, I assume you understand the importance of confidentiality in these matters."

"Oh, you mean the two lab workers who died?"

He looked taken aback. "Where did you hear that?"

"Heard it on the radio this morning," I answered.

Small beads of sweat appeared on his upper lip. He stabilized himself by holding onto the lab table.

"I don't know how the press found out. That's classified information, not for the general public."

"Oh, you mean you don't want the general public informed that half of them may suffer hideous symptoms and die soon?" I quipped.

Funny thing. I had panic attacks over the slightest perceived danger, but when it came to medical issues, I preferred to make jokes, sometimes bad ones.

He seemed to regain his composure. "This is a dangerous situation, Dr. Dakota. CEZID is interested in your DNA and the antibodies in your bloodstream that helped you fight those deadly viruses. We need to know what makes you special."

"I'll tell you what makes me *special*, Mister, Doctor, or whatever kind of mad scientist you are. I am a 62-year-old, worn-out single woman with bilateral knee replacements, lens implants, and bulging discs who still gets up at dawn to run a solo veterinary practice. I plow through surgeries on pets that, in human medicine, would require a team of nurses and doctors. I can prep the patient, administer anesthesia, remove a plastic army man from an intestine, put the bowel back together, and look good doing it. What's your talent, buddy?"

"I'm sure that's impressive, Doctor," he said, "but our lab needs to identify this new virus and facilitate the vaccine development as soon as possible. I apologize for our unorthodox tactics, but this involves something much bigger than any of us. We need your help!"

I was all about helping others. That was my profession. I spent much of my time in veterinary medicine educating and consoling pet owners. I loved people, but I loved their pets more.

"If I can help others in a crisis, sign me up. If you need my blood, it's yours."

"We appreciate that, Dr. Dakota." He addressed me with more respect than I had afforded him. "We'll call upon you occasionally as we pin this virus down and work toward a treatment or vaccine. Please understand, however, that we might not be the only players interested in obtaining a sample of your blood… willingly or unwillingly."

"That sounds ominous," I said, as a knot tightened in my stomach.

Dr. Leakey continued. "Our government facility would like to provide some security for you when you return to Hays."

"Nope, no way are you going to invade my privacy by sending a couple of Blues Brothers to shadow my every move. I don't need extra security. Between my chiweenie and my friend's bite dog, no phlebotomist in the world could successfully tap my veins. Are you sure it's a virus? Is it related to Ebola or Marburg?" We had studied these diseases in virology courses, but I was the only veterinary student who had seen firsthand the devastating effects of a human outbreak.

"I'm unable to share much of what we know so far. This is a national security issue."

Oh, brother. I'd heard that before. However, his tone

suggested he was not merely being evasive. He was genuinely concerned for Americans and the world.

"Are we finished here then? Am I free to leave? I have a hot date with a basset hound that needs a facelift." Veterinarians perform some plastic surgery procedures, reconstructive, not cosmetic.

"Yes, you are free to go, Dr. Dakota. We'll drop you at the bus station here in town, where you can catch a bus back to Hays."

"Are you kidding me? You disrupted my entire day, kidnapped me in a fancy jet, offered me private security, and now expect me to ride a Greyhound bus home?" I snapped.

"Sorry, Doctor, but we don't have funding for private jets here at CEZID. Only the FBI does that. See you in a few weeks."

If I had to ride a bus home, I'd keep my blood to myself. If they wanted it, they'd have to play nice.

CHAPTER 5

The Greyhound bus ride stretched to four hours, passing through familiar Kansas landmarks: Junction City, Abilene, Salina, and Russell, each with its claim to fame. Hays already had Wild Bill Hickok. Now it could add "home of Ruby Dakota, government lab rat" to its welcoming sign.

The bus deposited me at the station on Vine Street. It was within walking distance of my clinic, but I called Harley to pick me up on her motorcycle. Perhaps some fresh air and a bit of speed would improve my mood. I immediately regretted my decision. Harley slid into the bus station parking lot and skidded to a stop inches from my leg.

Ugh! Thrill-seekers.

No ride with Harley was ever routine; she turned every trip into an adventure. Truthfully, I knew she wanted an excuse to escape the clinic as much as I did. She preferred bugs in her teeth and hair flapping in her eyes to constant barking, unremitting pressure to perform, and sometimes argumentative clients.

"Hey, Doc, the cavalry has arrived," she shouted over the rumble of her bike, a Harley-Davidson Iron 883™ SuperLow®, "Twisted Cherry" in color. Perfect for her personality.

"Thanks, Harley. You are not going to believe where those men took me."

"Sure I will. I believe the government is capable of anything these days. Just glad you made it back with all your fingernails."

Who knew what theories she had concocted? I'd learned not to explore the darker corners of Harley's conspiracy-obsessed mind. I once read an article about obsessive individuals. It attributed this "I see conspiracy in everything" behavior to the brain's pattern recognition power.

When functioning normally, this pattern recognition helps people survive by spotting real threats. When this power goes into overdrive, the person joins dots in random data, and two plus two suddenly makes five. Harley would have said it equals ten. Some people turned to conspiracy theories to fulfill deprived motivational needs, which I suspected was the case with Harley. I was concerned that the more time I spent with her, the more sense her theories made.

I glanced at my watch; what had seemed like an eternity was only seven hours. This day started with the six a.m. knock at the clinic door, followed by a plane ride, a bloodletting, and a bus ride home. London had rescheduled my afternoon appointments. I was back to my real life. I waited until we returned to the clinic to fill Harley and London in on my forced excursion to the Manhattan-Plum Island-wannabe site. The arrival of an Afghan, not a person, or a knitted lap throw, but a hound, interrupted this informal debriefing. His twin accompanied him, a skinny little man with long brown hair and a Roman nose.

The clinic maintained a hidden collection of photos that showed the uncanny resemblance between owners and their pets. At the top of the board was a photo of an English bulldog beside his owner, who also had a jutting lower jaw, flab rolling over his collar, and a dumpy body shape, the human version of his beloved Winston. We kept this board in the kennel room to cheer us up on a challenging day and to give the boarders something fascinating to look at. This location also allowed us to laugh our heads off without offending our clients.

Research suggests that people gravitate toward pets that mirror their own appearance. The 'mere-exposure effect' states that because we spend a lot of time looking at our faces in the mirror, we prefer pets that give us the same familiar feel. My pet, Chui, looked like a hair dryer had dropped in the grooming tub during his bath.

What did that say about my appearance?

Another theory suggests that we choose our dogs because we've evolved to seek mates who resemble us, ensuring we pass those genes to our offspring. Romantic partners also tend to share a high degree of resemblance. However, since I had no romantic partner, this theory remained untested.

This client and his 10-month-old Afghan Hound would soon be on that board. "Good afternoon, Mr. Willis. Hey, Lennon, how are you doing today, boy?" I left Lennon on the floor as a nod to the Fear Free method. Also, my back didn't feel like hoisting 50 pounds of leggy dog onto the table. This dog's legs were as long as mine.

Let me explain Fear Free. Marty Becker, D.V.M., developed the Fear Free method. It is a concept based on recognizing and taking steps to reduce fear, anxiety, and stress in pets during clinic visits, resulting in a better experience for all involved.

The technique requires the veterinarian to sit on the floor at eye level with the patient to avoid appearing threatening. Oh boy, that wasn't working well for me. For one thing, I could no longer get up off the floor without help, if I could even get down there in the first place. For another, getting down to eye level with an aggressive dog was a great way to come up missing a nose. My reflexes weren't what they used to be. I needed a head start. I loved Dr. Marty, but I didn't think he'd considered that not all vets were 27 years old.

You can't fool an agitated dog. He knew some pain would be involved. In my experience, the dog would rather *inflict* the pain than be the recipient. Did Dr. Marty really think I wanted to go eye to eye with a mastiff who had a head the size of a beach ball while my technician snuck up behind with an injection?

"Mr. Willis, what seems to be Lennon's problem today?" I asked.

"He limps on his front legs. Sometimes it's the right leg, and sometimes it's the left."

I performed an examination and found tenderness over the right humerus. I suspected panosteitis, commonly referred to as growing pains, given Lennon's age and the shifting leg lameness.

"Mr. Willis, I'd like to take an X-ray of both Lennon's legs."

"Fine by me, Doc," he answered. Harley took Lennon to the back.

Popping over to the next exam room, I could hear the pathognomonic snorting of a Yorkie. That's the medically precise way of saying that the symptom displayed was characteristic of the condition. It sounded like an old man startled in the middle of a snore: snort, snort, stop, snort, snort. As I entered, I saw little Petunia, who had an actual petunia clipped to her topknot, pulled so tight that her eyes slanted. Occupied with trying to get her elongated soft palate back into place, she snorted so hard that her little body lifted off the floor. It looked painful and was distressing to the owner, who had misinterpreted this activity.

"Petunia has something lodged in her throat," Mrs. Schultz offered.

I used to roll my eyes at the client's interpretation, but I was older and wiser now. Too often, after I elegantly explained the anatomy of a dog's soft palate and that nothing was lodged in its throat, the dog would hack up a Lego on the exam room floor.

I gently placed Petunia on the exam table. Yes, the table. “Hey, Petunia, nice flower. You are a sweet little baby, aren't you?” Holding her gently, I listened to her chest, checked her eyes, ears, nose, and throat, and looked for other abnormalities. Because I once owned Yorkies, I knew that even though the owner wouldn't admit it, Petunia peed on the floor whenever she wanted, *didn't you, you cute little thing*? Yorkies were notorious for resisting housebreaking. I assured Mrs. Schultz that Petunia would live another day. Her condition did not yet warrant surgery.

Harley instructed the owner on methods to reduce the attacks and scheduled a follow-up appointment. This malady often responded to dietary and stress-reduction measures, which might not be possible in a Yorkie.

Chapter 6

I snuck back to the lab for another Diet Dr Pepper. I popped the top of my caffeinated 'friendly pepper-upper,' and chugged it. In the 1920s, Dr Pepper used the advertising slogan "10, 2, and 4." It was based on a study showing that people experienced dips in blood sugar levels around 10:00 a.m., 2:00 p.m., and 4:00 p.m. The company encouraged customers to drink Dr Pepper at those times for an energy boost. Now, over one hundred years later, I consumed them much more frequently than those scientists intended.

I stared straight ahead at my combination office, laboratory, and pharmacy. Everything was in a bit of upheaval: bills to pay, stool samples to examine for parasite eggs, prescriptions to fill, and tubes of blood to submit to the local clinical pathology lab. I was quite sure my workspace was approaching critical mass.

Most people don't realize that veterinarians also serve as pharmacists licensed to prescribe, fill, and manage the inventory of medications for dogs, cats, gerbils, parakeets, and other species.

Get a grip, Ruby. I took a deep breath. I'd just survived a kidnapping, a bloodletting, and an end-of-the-world, death-by-hideous-disease message unrepeatable to anyone, not even to Chui. It was the craziest day of my life, and now a messy office overwhelmed me?

As I observed what was a complete breakdown of my administrative duties, an ache developed in the pit of my stomach. My respiratory rate climbed without my permission. If I were charting my own vitals, I'd write down tachypnea. Anxiety roiled up in me the way it always did, uninvited, unstoppable, and unimpressed by my attempts to reason with it. I forced myself to move to the next exam room, where a new patient suffering from God-knows-what awaited me.

I masked my inner turmoil with a forced smile and cheery voice as I introduced myself to Mrs. Dreiling. Salt-and-pepper hair drawn up in a meticulous bun thing, flowered pedal pushers, white cotton ankle socks inside black running shoes that looked to have their original tread. She was probably my age mate.

That was terrifying.

"Hello, Mrs. Dreiling. Who do we have here?" I asked as I tried to keep the chart from shaking.

"Her name is Merry Puppins, Doctor."

It must have been Yorkie Day.

"Hey, great name." I didn't know who was trembling more, the dog or me. Little Merry shivered so hard that her topknot resembled a twitching feather duster. At that moment, my eye caught sight of a cobweb. I briefly considered holding her up to whisk it away.

"What's going on with Merry today?" I was still trying to hold it together.

"Whenever a storm hits, Merry shakes uncontrollably and bolts under the bed. Nothing I do comforts her. She does the same thing when she hears fireworks. That new fireworks factory has her in a tizzy. Even the sound of the weekly trash truck coming down the road brings on her tremors."

In a flash, a thought crossed my mind. In this moment, I

was Merry.

Many of my patients experienced these symptoms regularly. Separation from their owners, fear of fireworks or thunderstorms, and, for some little dogs, fear of large dogs all triggered a cascade of terrifying symptoms.

I could relate to the fear of large dogs. Whenever six-foot-four, two-hundred-fifty-pound Dr. Morgan showed up at the clinic, old memories of my first boss flooded in. After 34 years, I'd hoped he'd mellowed. Unfortunately, he was still Jake the Snake, and around him, I reverted to the intimidated, insecure vet he'd shaped. Like little Merry, I trembled, paced, panted, and hid. I often felt like rolling over in a submissive pose and peeing on myself.

"What causes Merry to do this, Doctor Dakota?" Mrs. Dreiling asked. "I can't stand to see her so frightened."

After an initial exam revealed no physical problems, I put on my doggy psychiatry hat and informed the owner, "Mrs. Dreiling, this response may be due to inadequate socialization at a formative age, or it could be learned from an unpleasant experience." I then gave her my list of behavior modification techniques.

"After an attack, when the fear passes, give Merry something she loves, like a treat, to help her associate the calm behavior with a reward."

In my case, every time my trigger, Dr. Morgan, showed his face at the clinic, I should eat a piece of Key lime pie. I liked this technique.

"Next, desensitize Merry Puppins. Gradually expose her to levels of the trigger that barely evoke anxiety. Small steps at a time. Perhaps play a short clip of a thunderstorm or a low-volume sound of a firework exploding."

In my case, I could have London spray Dr. Morgan's pungent aftershave into the air several times a day. That would also help cover up the clinic's disinfectant smell.

"If none of these techniques work, I suggest Mellow Fellow for Merry. It is a dog food with a mild relaxant to relieve her anxiety." It lived up to its name. I'd tried it… more than once.

"I choose the sedative," Mrs. Dreiling demanded too quickly.

Could it be she planned to add Mellow Fellow to her own morning smoothie?

After I left the room for Harley to finish, I began practicing calming techniques, just as I'd done during the FBI abduction. I first counted my fingers, a technique unavailable to most dogs.

As I began to settle down, Harley rushed in with an emergency. Somehow, emergencies always focused me. Good thing. No one wanted a sniveling, sweating, hyperventilating vet attending to their pet suffering from an HBC, Hit by Car.

Harley and I kicked into action, assessed the injuries, stabilized the patient, and proposed the way forward to the rattled owners. Was money an issue? Did they even want to proceed with further treatment, or was their answer the one I always dreaded: euthanasia? Thankfully, X-rays showed it was only a fractured pelvis from which this dog could recover with bed rest.

Oh sure. Like that was going to happen.

They often *did* heal without surgery. I dished out instructions and medications to the owners in the hope that they'd comply. My chest tightened as I left the exam room. I couldn't get enough air. It was as if I were breathing through a tiny straw.

I needed the Belladonnas. This day would be stressful for most people, but it was debilitating for me. I called Emily because she was always calm. "Emily, help. I need to talk. Can the Belladonnas meet tonight? I'm on the verge of a full-blown anxiety attack."

"We're here for you, Ruby," Emily responded.

Our group often spent our time together grumbling about bosses, business, clients, and human and non-human patients. It helped to vent to people who wouldn't take your business all over town.

"Emily, the Belladonnas are my inner circle. I trust you guys. Plus, I might need to be committed to an institution if I don't vent to someone soon."

"Okay, we'll meet at Hickok's Steakhouse at six p.m. Bye," Emily hung up.

I was still holding the phone to my ear. I started to de-escalate. My heart rate was still high, but my breathing was slowing down. Everything would be fine once I was with my friends.

After closing the clinic, I pulled on a clean scrub shirt with a black-and-white cow motif and headed for the restaurant. A steakhouse was a necessity for a town of any size in Kansas. We raised beef. We ate beef. We didn't care about cholesterol. It was too late for that.

We used to call ourselves the Silver-Haired Sleuths, but none of us would admit we had gray hair. My hair color was an 8G Golden Blonde, which I achieved with a L'Oreal box mix. Emily was a light blonde but could afford to go to the salon every month. Kit had a neighbor with a shampoo sink and a hair dryer in her basement. They exchanged beauty services for medication. Now, Rhonda, I wasn't sure about. Her hair has been the same color since she was a teenager. It looked a little muddy, with some silver streaks mixed in. Not stunning, but it fit her down-to-earth personality.

Hickok's Steakhouse was bustling. It wasn't as busy as a Saturday night, but it was still loud. Clinking beer mugs, heated conversations, and brassy laughter, all fueled by alcohol. It smelled of stale beer, charred steaks, and French fry oil overdue for a change.

"Hey, silver foxes," I greeted them as I slid into the curved corner nook and avoided disappearing into the sinkholes in the Naugahyde. "What's happening tonight? Any new romances? Any bosses that need to be eliminated? Any new alcohol concoctions that need a taste test?"

Just kidding. Most of us didn't drink. Some of us have had issues with that addiction; been there and done that for a time in college. Still miss gin and tonics. Emily enjoyed wine with a meal. Kit always made healthy life choices, and Rhonda was on anti-seizure meds that precluded her from drinking.

Kit responded, "Why don't you let us in on that secret trip, the one where someone kidnapped you? Seems like you'd want to share those details with us first." Kit was putting the pieces in order. She hated disorder. However, unlike me, she seemed able to focus, organize, and prioritize. Her motto was "A place for everything and everything in..."

Blah, blah, blah. If she said it one more time, I'd coldcock her.

Kit pressed, "Rhonda won't tell us anything, and that's not fair to Emily and me. We're your friends too. Spill it."

Rhonda had been faithful to our unwritten confidentiality agreement. Our professions required it, and our friendship survived because of it. We didn't gossip with others, and we respected requests for confidentiality even within our group. In my case, with something like my abduction, I thought Rhonda was the one to approach first. She maintained a level-headed and calm demeanor during a crime, even when it involved her good friend.

I recounted the entire story, including the blood draw, attributing it to some research project. I avoided the part about a deadly disease since the nerdy Dr. Leakey at CEZID asked me not to make that fact known.

While we awaited our order, we disagreed on the motive behind the abduction. "Perhaps the IRS wants your DNA to track you and enlisted CEZID to help," Kit joked.

"I don't think they'd spend thousands of dollars to recoup back taxes," Rhonda jumped in. "Nor do I think they'd kidnap you."

"Okay, I agree. Let's assume the IRS is not involved in this."

Since they weren't.

Chapter 7

Day of the Shooting

The Belladonnas' support had calmed me enough for a peaceful night's sleep. No emergencies. Routine surgeries and vaccinations made up most of the day's schedule, with only a few minor illnesses. My life had returned to its chaotic normal. I watched my employees head home as the day wound down. I was already home and anxious to get Chui out of confinement.

Walking through the lobby, I took a mental inventory of the brightly colored bags of prescription diet pet food on the shelves. The evening sun highlighted the pet hair left from today's patients. I grabbed the cleaning spray and paper towels. Several male dogs had engaged in territorial urine marking, each trying to outdo the previous pee-er. I bent over to wipe up the dried urine.

That was when the shot rang out.

The front window exploded inward. I dropped and scrambled toward the back. Another shot punched through something behind me. My ears rang. Glass crunched under my palms. Then my brain caught up with my panic.

Rennie!

Rhonda had dropped Rennie off while she went to the

hair salon. He'd be on my bed, not in the kennel. I could hear the front door shatter as I reached my room. My hands shook so badly I could barely turn the knob.

Rennie was already on his feet, ears erect, every muscle coiled. This retired police "bite dog" had instantly morphed into Officer Rennie mode, proving my theory that a German shepherd with an attitude was the only thing scarier than a perp with a gun.

I remembered Rhonda had given me two commands in German: "Fass!" and "Aus!" One meant attack, and the other meant release.

I prayed I'd get the right one.

"Fass!" I shouted, my voice cracking with fear.

Rennie bolted past me, a blur of fur and muscle, headed for the intruder. His rabid barking magnified in the narrow hallway. The kennel choir of a dozen dogs joined in, also frantically barking, "We don't know what's going on, but we're helping anyway."

Shrill human screams filled the clinic, primal and terrified, followed by growling and what sounded like fabric tearing. Heavy objects crashed to the floor. The screaming intensified.

Good Me hoped Rennie wouldn't kill him. Bad Me wanted to let Rennie chew on the maggot a little longer.

I hesitated for a second about giving the off command. What if the shooter still had his gun? What if he shot Rennie? But the screaming sounded more like genuine terror. I gave it anyway.

"Aus!"

Rennie went silent. Not understanding German, the boarding dogs continued their vocal support. Rennie trotted back to my side, looking pleased with himself. A piece of black fabric hung from his teeth. He cocked his head and stared at me expectantly, waiting for his reward. The only thing handy was a dirty sock at the end of my bed.

"Good boy, good boy!" I screamed in a high voice as we

engaged in a tug-of-war.

I cautiously peeked down the hall just in time to see a silhouette in a black hoodie and sweatpants disappear through the hole in the door, limping badly and clutching one arm.

I couldn't tell if he was young or old, tall or short, fat or thin. I was in shock and only saw him for a fleeting second.

I immediately called 911, which I should have done much earlier. I usually handled crises on my own. My second call was to Rhonda at the hair salon.

"Rhonda, I have some bad news and some good news," my voice shaking. "Someone just tried to shoot a hole in me, and Rennie chased off the perp."

"What's the good news? What do you mean Rennie chased the perp off? Rennie never loses his man, ever. Did you use the two words I told you never to use?" Rhonda's voice rose with each question. "You only use the off command when Rennie is 'detaining' an innocent person. Not when you have an actual criminal."

"What was I supposed to do? Let that guy shoot me? Rennie was the only weapon I had," I whined. "I'm still in shock."

"Rennie is not a weapon. He is a deterrent. He holds them until his handler arrests them. Again, why isn't the scumbag still yelling in pain in your clinic? You didn't give Rennie the Aus command, did you?"

"Rhonda, I only know those two words in German, and the off command seemed appropriate at the time. I didn't want to negotiate with the shooter while Rennie was trying to rip the guy's arm off. I just wanted him out of the clinic."

No hero here.

"I understand your anxiety issues, but really? Did you even get a look at him or recover a gun or anything useful to the investigators?" Rhonda scolded. "That's the last time I ask you to babysit Rennie. He might have been injured or even killed when the guy escaped." I could hear Rhonda's voice tremble.

"Oh, I didn't think about *that* happening. I would never intentionally put brave Rennie in danger," I replied, as I tried to hold back my tears and soothe her fears.

I knew Rennie was retired—retired without a pension. The odds of him surviving long enough to retire had not been good. He'd beat the odds and drawn Rhonda as his new owner. He was a blessed dog. I'd almost ruined his perfect service record.

"I'm so sorry, Rhonda. But I think he did get a good bite in. The perp screamed like a little girl!"

The voice of a lone police officer rang through the clinic. "Police Officer. Put your weapon down and your hands in the air."

"No weapon, Officer. Just my cell phone," I raised my hands. The officer cautiously peeked around the corner, gun drawn.

"Whoa, there, partner. I'm not the enemy," I quipped in country western fashion, even though my anxiety level was at an all-time high, combined with an adrenaline rush that would cause my blood pressure cuff to explode. "I'm Dr. Dakota, the owner of this clinic and the target of the shooting. This is Rennie, a retired police bite dog, so don't make any sudden moves, officer." I was just playin' with him.

"Hey, Rennie. How ya doin', boy? How's retirement treating you? Looks like you put on a little weight. What happened here, Doc? Your entryway is a mess."

My tension subsided when I noticed that this police officer was attractive for his age in a chubby, rugged, belly-over-his-belt kind of way. If women had muffin tops, was there a name for a man's bulging waistline? My muffin top was approaching the size of a giant croissant, but it's hidden. Yet another reason to wear scrubs.

At that moment, the back door exploded as the SWAT

team yelled, “Hays Police! Anybody inside? Make your presence known, or we’ll release the dog!”

Several officers entered and systematically cleared every room. They were in full gear, wearing helmets and bulletproof vests, led by a Belgian Malinois dragging an officer behind him. Rennie jumped to attention and gave me an eyeroll. I suspected he knew this doggie replacement wasn’t half the dog he used to be. After all, Rennie had already done all the hard work.

After countless hours of training, the Hays SWAT team had few opportunities to kick in doors. My predicament gave them just the scenario for which they had prepared. It seemed like overkill, but I was happy to have them surrounding me. I thought it was always better for them to err on the side of caution, especially when my life was involved.

As the bite dog systematically searched the clinic looking for the shooter, the boarding dogs piped up again. Ramos, the parrot, oblivious to the men with guns invading his space, gave the performance of his life, breaking into a chorus of “Singin' in the Rain.” I’d taught him to sing this during his spray shower. As he sang, he lifted his little wings so my spray mist could clean underneath his wing pits. Here, he appeared to raise his hands in response to the SWAT team's command. It was usually hilarious—just not now.

“Ma’am, you can put your hands down and tell your bird to shut up and put *his* wings down. Are you sure there’s no one else in the clinic?” the leader of the posse asked. Tempted to correct him, I instead held my tongue. To insist that he use “Dr.” seemed like an opening for an eyeroll.

I stuttered, “Yes, sir. I mean, no, sir. I, I, I’m here alone.” Rennie nudged me. “Oh, I have Rennie here, some patients and boarders in the kennel, and a parrot singing at the front desk. Just no other humans.”

"Are you hurt?" the hunky, husky old guy inserted himself into the conversation.

"Only a few shards of glass in my hair and hands. That bullet was close," I replied.

"Perhaps we should take you to the ER to get you checked out," he suggested.

"Seriously, this clinic *is* an ER. It may be an ER for dogs, but the same principles apply," I snapped back, insulted.

He immediately replied, "A physician who treats himself has a fool for a patient."

Good one. He quoted the father of modern medicine, Sir William Osler. I kind of liked this cop. The name on his uniform read Officer Wassinger, a good, solid Hays name.

Chapter 8

The suspect remained at large, and the disappointed SWAT dog returned to his air-conditioned van. I suspected Rennie was laughing at the rookie Malinois. The team filed out, a little disconsolate as well. Bite dogs and sniffer dogs performed for the joy of the toy. They only wanted to find the person or the contraband, alert others, and then receive the reward. When the dog succeeded, his reward was a tennis ball or chew toy and high-pitched praise from his handler. It was hilarious to hear those girlie squeals, "Good boy! Atta boy!" coming from well-muscled and otherwise intimidating handlers. This is what I'd tried to duplicate with Rennie.

Harley, my tech, was outside yelling my name. She'd just returned from happy hour at the Handle Bar. I gave the officer at the door a nod, and she entered the clinic. "Hey, Doc. Zup?" She nearly knocked me down with her breath.

Whew! It must have been a doozy of a happy hour.

She continued, "First, the FBI. Now, the SWAT team. What have you done? What have *I* done?" Sometimes, Harley talked too much. She had no filter. Full-blown opinions flew out of her mouth at lightning speed.

"What's up? What's up?" I responded angrily. "I've just been the target of an unknown assassin. You look terrible,

Harley. Are you sure you should be here with law enforcement?" I tried to discourage her from adding to the chaos.

"Just as long as they don't check my blood alcohol, I'm good," she slurred.

Oh, boy.

I explained to Officer Wassinger that this was Harley, my trusted and sometimes uninhibited vet tech. Officer Wassinger placed himself strategically between Harley and me. He smelled good. I was not an expert on men's cologne, but I thought it was Armani, perhaps Emporio. I only knew this because I preferred men's fragrances to the foofy women's scents. Weird for an old lady, but I'd always been more of a dirt-and-spice kind of person, far from flowery.

"You're a lucky lady, Doc," Officer Wassinger said, looking down at me.

"I don't believe in luck, Officer. I'm blessed. I believe in a God who directs my every move."

"Did God direct that guy to shoot you?" he asked.

"He directed me to avoid taking a bullet to the head," I retorted.

I did not elaborate on that subject, as expressing my faith in God in words was a challenge for me. Such a serious conversation dampened my attraction to this guy… a little. My heart rate soared, but that must have been due to the near-death experience.

All three of my companions, the Belladonnas, burst through the back door and interrupted our conversation. Rhonda immediately wrapped her arms around Rennie's neck.

"Well, let's just make it a party," I quipped.

"I'll second that," Harley saluted, and headed for the bathroom.

"What happened, Dakota? Kit and I were getting ready to watch a movie when Rhonda called. She just told us to get over to the clinic immediately. That there'd been a shooting. Are you hurt? Do you need medical care?" Emily, the M.D., asked as she quickly assessed my condition.

"I'm more concerned that you watched a movie without me," I said. "What's up with that? What really stings is that you didn't include me."

"Oh, don't get your feathers ruffled," Kit chided. "It was a movie you've already seen, and we know you never watch movies a second time. Could you just tell us what happened here? What did the shooter want from you? Was anything stolen? I can quickly inventory your controlled substances locker if needed."

Kit routinely helped me with my clinic pharmacy when she could no longer stand the chaos I lived in. She came in after hours to label, organize, and list what I needed to order for the week. Without her help, I would have routinely run out of stock, which is a problem in a veterinary clinic. There were no veterinary supply houses near Hays. I couldn't just run across town to restock from a warehouse.

"No, that's okay. He didn't stay long. Rennie chased him down. I'm sure he's dealing with a few punctures from the bite inflicted on him."

"Why didn't he hold him down until the police came?" Emily questioned.

"Uh, I might have given the off command by accident," I answered sheepishly.

"You only use those commands in an extreme emergency!" Rhonda reiterated through clenched teeth.

"I thought this *was* an emergency," I answered. "Rennie saved my life."

Rhonda grabbed Rennie by the collar and stormed off to the kennels. Boy, she was as mad as a wet cat.

"I want you guys to meet the officer who was the first to respond to the scene." I tried not to blush.

"I'm Officer Hayes Wassinger. Your friend here had a close call. She was pretty lucky, I… uh… mean blessed." Hayes corrected himself.

Kit and Emily snickered. They knew I'd already schooled him on the use of the word "lucky."

"This clinic is now a crime scene," Officer Wassinger instructed. "The CSI team will be here all night collecting evidence: bullets, shell casings, fingerprints, and DNA. They'll secure the scene and protect your clinic. But you need to contact your insurance company and arrange for someone to repair your door and window. Dr. Dakota, you must come to the station tomorrow for a statement. Okay?"

"But this is my home," I protested.

"No, you cannot remain here tonight. Do you have a place to stay?" Officer Wassinger asked.

Rhonda rejoined the group. "She sure does—a secure place. I'm registered for concealed carry, although we no longer need that in Kansas if you're over 21, and I'm way over 21. My home has an arsenal and a bite dog looking for entertainment." Rhonda didn't usually divulge much about her weapons, but she tried to impress the officer.

Back off, Rhonda, this one was mine. Wait. What was I saying? Have my hormones found another production unit? My ovaries were long gone. They had no dog in this fight. Where was this estrogen surge coming from at my age?

Kit asked for a broom to clean up some shattered glass.

"Don't touch anything. It's evidence," Officer Wassinger commanded.

"Sorry, just trying to help." Kit and Emily headed for their respective homes.

I collected Chui from his run. He'd missed the whole thing, although his fur looked like he'd seen a ghost. Rhonda grabbed Rennie, and the four of us put Harley to bed in her trailer.

"She won't be much use to me in the morning with a hangover," I bemoaned.

Rhonda and Rennie jumped into her Jeep. I climbed into my Land Rover. Chui rode shotgun. Every bone in my body ached. I wasn't used to ducking and running so much. Upon arrival, all four of us hit the beds, twin beds for Rhonda and me, and dog beds for the canines.

I was dog tired.

Chapter 9

Upon my arrival at the clinic the following morning, I observed the CSI team concluding their work. Although it was not within their responsibilities, they'd kindly cleaned up the shattered glass on the floor. The Pane in the Glass Company had repaired the door and front window overnight.

Saturday mornings were typically busier than a three-legged cat in a litter box, as many clients scheduled appointments on their day off. Illnesses ignored for several days earlier in the week often seemed urgent to pet owners by Saturday. I wasn't sure I could pull off balancing last night's trauma with being present and professional this morning.

In a small town, news traveled fast. Every client would ask about the shooting before we examined their pet. I wanted to hide under the exam table, but the professional in me had to face the madness.

Of course, Brock Benton decided to visit my clinic amid this hectic atmosphere. Brock owned a fly-by-the-seat-of-your-pants vaccine company on the outskirts of Hays. Their motto: "You got a disease. We got a vaccine."

During the parvovirus epidemic in the 1980s, his father was famous for discovering a vaccine that saved thousands of dogs. However, Brock differed from his father. Not exactly a chip off the old block. He lacked his father's love for animals, gentle nature, kindness, and humility. They were both brilliant, but Brock was mad-professor quirky, forgetful, always disheveled, and a little lonely. He did not own a pet and was annoying as heck.

All that said, he was still my friend.

Brock strove to develop the next vaccine for an upcoming but unrealized veterinary disease epidemic. He'd gotten his hopes up when the recent dog influenza hit. However, someone had beaten him to the punch. Researchers developed a vaccine to prevent H3N8 equine influenza and H3N2 avian influenza strains that had adapted to infect dogs. Poor Brock, living in his father's shadow with unfulfilled ambitions.

"Hey, Brock. What's happening at the virus factory? Any new epidemics on the horizon?" I asked.

"If there were, I wouldn't tell you guys."

He thought he was so clever. A vet should be the first to receive this information if something was coming down the pike. It wasn't like I would steal his glory, royalties, or whatever he got for coming up with a new vaccine.

"What brings you here today, Brock?" I asked, not really wanting to know.

"I heard you had some trouble over here last night," he responded. "Was it a robbery? Did they catch the guy?"

He casually helped himself to a cup from the counter near the sink and filled it with coffee, unaware that it had previously been used to collect a urine sample from a litter box.

Oh well, it probably wouldn't hurt him.

"Yes and no. Rhonda's dog, Rennie, caught the guy and then released him." I wanted to ask Brock to pour me a cup, but I was suspicious he might slip in some new oral vaccine he's running trials on. He wasn't picky about where he got his clinical trial participants.

"You released him? Are you crazy?" he exclaimed.

I tried to refrain from sarcasm. Who was the crazy one here?

"No. At the time, I didn't want to converse with a crazed assassin who still had a few more rounds with my name on them. Hey, Brock, I need to get back to my scheduled appointments if there's nothing else you want. When you finish your coffee, please place the cup in the plastic basin containing the green sterilizing fluid. Thanks."

London had all my charts for the morning neatly lined up on the counter. "What's with Brock coming over here all the time? He acts like he's into you," London teased.

"Eww!" I cringed.

I checked in on Harley, who'd had a liter of Normal Saline spiked with 1 mg of B-12 infused into her veins. It was our old vet school hangover cure. She was now up and performing her morning duties. While reviewing the charts, I noticed several vaccination appointments. Additionally, London scheduled a poodle for suture removal after its owner learned the hard way why professional groomers exist. Nothing inspiring this morning.

That was good. I'd had enough excitement last night for a lifetime.

After administering several vaccinations, I took a call from Kit. "Hey, Doc! Let's get together tonight. We all want to brainstorm over who your hitman could be. Each of us has our own ideas. What about you? Who do you think it was?"

"Kit, I have no idea. Maybe we should ask Rennie. He got up close and personal with the guy."

"That's it!" Kit responded with excitement. "We should have swabbed Rennie's mouth for DNA."

"Kit, I have to go. Carry on, and I'll see you guys tonight for dinner at Hickok's."

The clinic closed at noon on Saturday, but we were never out of there before one p.m. That didn't leave much time before I returned for evening treatments. Harley would join me to walk and feed the inmates at five p.m. I headed back to my bedroom with Chui to steal a nap together. There was nothing like pulling up a warm little wiry-haired body while baseball played on the TV.

Nothing put me to sleep quicker.

I woke up just before five p.m. My nervous system must have needed recharging. After I helped Harley medicate and clean up after the captives, I headed for Hickok's. No clue as to any connection between the two crimes against my person. Being snatched and shot at in the same week was unusual, even for me. My life was relatively uneventful. Yes, I might suffer a laceration from an outraged Siamese and a perforated thumbnail from an agitated Chihuahua in the same week, but they weren't connected. As I entered, I saw the Belladonnas at our booth.

The bar should install a plaque with "Reserved for Belladonnas" on it.

Emily jumped straight to business. "Dakota, sit down with us so we can figure out who's trying to kill you."

"Whoa, give me a minute to settle in. The police are working on it," I replied.

"Says who? We need facts to help crack the case," argued Kit.

"Yeah, I need a detailed description of the perp, type of gun used, fingerprints recovered, the vehicle, and motivation," added Rhonda, true to her profession.

"Rhonda, don't you have access to all that?" Kit asked.

"Nope. I'm just the dispatcher," she replied, "But I know people…"

Emily remained thoughtful. "I'm just glad he missed. It was a he, wasn't it?" she asked.

I stopped to think. "I don't know the answer to that question, Emily. I just assumed it was a man."

As bad as it was for me, this event seems to have

rejuvenated the Belladonnas. Petty crime happened in Hays all the time, but this one was major and personal. Perhaps it gave them a purpose, a distraction from their often-demanding jobs.

Kit, Emily, and I were all employed by commercial enterprises. Kit worked for ScriptSure Pharmacies, a chain store, and Emily worked at an Urgent Care clinic owned by a conglomerate. I worked for Pets Buy, a pet products supply company that ran veterinary clinics like mine and sold dog chew toys, among other things. That was humiliating. Rhonda did whatever she wanted all day, although she often filled in as a sheriff dispatcher. She and Rennie had both retired at the end of their careers with the sheriff's department. Rhonda put in 25 years. Rennie, not so many.

"What can I get you to drink, ma'am?" the server interrupted.

Ugh. There it was again—ma'am. It reminded me that my life was circling the drain, and it felt like I hadn't even flushed the toilet yet.

I ordered water with lemon, to which I added a sweetener. That's what my parents called missionary lemonade. That's what I called cheap.

"Okay, girls, here's the story." To the best of my memory, I reenacted the previous night, leaving out how the weird attraction to a pudgy police officer blocked my attention to detail. Didn't think these women needed to know that. I'd never hear the end of it. Plus, I didn't like the way Rhonda looked at him.

"OK, ladies, let's work on motive." Emily was the cerebral one and wanted to understand the driving force. "Why would anyone want to kill Dakota? I mean, she's not rich. There's not much cash in the clinic, and I don't think sex was a motive. I mean, it's Dakota."

I think I should have been offended by this last comment.

Rhonda defended Emily's idea. "He shot at you before he even got into the clinic. Do you think he wanted to assault a dead old lady with a hole in her skull?"

Rhonda always got right to the point.

The server interrupted us again. "Whatcha' goin' to have tonight, girls?"

I was beginning to dislike this woman.

I ordered my usual ribeye, cooked medium-well. Every time I ordered a steak, I thought of my dad, who would order his steak so rare that it was still mooing. He'd direct the chef to quickly lay it on the grill, warm it a little, and flip it over. I couldn't get past my parasitology professors who'd warned us against meat that wasn't thoroughly cooked. The pictures of those tapeworms had made me gag. Although at this weight, I could have used a tapeworm or two.

I couldn't eat raw cookie dough either. As children, our mothers told us we'd get worms. My professors taught us we'd get Salmonella or E. coli. Companies worked to reduce the risk of eating raw cookie dough, but I still couldn't eat it. However, I had no problem with chocolate-almond ice cream and ordered it for dessert. At my age, I ate what I wanted without guilt. It was time to throw caution to the wind. Everyone else placed their steak order, and we got back to the problem on the table.

"Before we try to identify an assassin, we should first ascertain a motive. Why would someone want me dead?" I began. "My guess is a disgruntled client. Do you all remember Mr. Phelps, who worked for the post office? He was upset because I was involved in the euthanasia of his dog that bit a little neighbor girl. The animal control officer collected his dog from his property and took it to the shelter, where they quarantined it for rabies."

"In my opinion, anytime a dog bites a kid, it needs to go," Rhonda interrupted.

"They followed the proper procedure, but this was the

third time they'd quarantined this dog for a bite incident. The local judge ordered euthanasia. The owner failed to respond, prompting the shelter to request that I put the dog down. Mr. Phelps was inconsolable, flat-out angry, threatening me, the judge, and the shelter. We were all a little on edge for a time. He had a gun collection and was known to be a good shot."

Rhonda jumped in, "Most people in Hays are good shots. The shooting range is more popular than the bowling alley."

Good point.

"Maybe the cameras over your front door will shed some light on his identity. Did they run the video?"

I shook my head. "The cameras were not rolling during the crime. They are never rolling. They're fake," I whispered so the world didn't hear.

"Are you kidding me?" Rhonda asked. "After all the episodes of 'See All Evil,' how is it that the clinic still doesn't have a working camera? Oh my gosh, I can't believe you!"

"Take that up with Pets Buy, Rhonda," I said, sharper than I meant to.

I might have neglected to inform Pets Buy about the fake cameras thinking it might have decreased the selling price.

I made the decision to overcome my misplaced loyalty to CEZID and be frank about the fact that my life might be in danger due to the uniqueness of my immune system. This information opened a whole new line of investigation for the girls. They were ecstatic.

Me, not so much.

Chapter 10

Just in case of an imminent pandemic, Kit headed back to her pharmacy to stock up on meds and inventory her prepping supplies.

The rest of us came to attention as we witnessed the two suits entering the restaurant. Emily whispered to Rhonda, our unofficial security detail, “Stick with Dakota. If they try to take her, stall them. I’ve got a plan,” as she headed for the door.

The Blues Brothers sat at the bar, wildly unsuccessful in their attempt to keep a low profile. After ten minutes of pretending we weren't watching them while they pretended they weren't watching us, Rhonda and I made the first move.

Oh, great. Here we go again.

As we invaded their personal space, I didn’t bother with pleasantries. “Where’s the plane? I thought you guys went back to your underground lab.”

No answer.

“Are you here to take me to Manhattan?”

No answer.

They stood out in Hickok’s like a sore dewclaw on a German Shorthair. How did these guys keep a straight face? I started laughing hysterically, my abs cramping. Yes,

I had abs, but they'd lost their six-pack arrangement. I sucked in air between fits of laughter. Tears rolled down my cheeks.

What did I know that these guys didn't? I knew my employees, and I knew my friends. There was no way they'd let these two city yahoos take me. Rhonda was armed and dangerous.

"May we step outside where we can talk?" one agent asked. Though it wasn't really a question.

"I'd prefer to stay inside where I have witnesses."

Both agents stood and grabbed me under my armpits. They lifted me off the ground so that my feet dangled in the air. Hard to get traction in that position. They whisked me to the parking lot.

I heard Harley's Harley come up the alley beside the restaurant. I saw Rhonda locked and loaded out of the corner of my eye. Uh-oh. Was this going to be a gunfight at the OK Corral?

"Rhonda, stand down. I'll be fine. I've dealt with these suits before," I said brusquely, although inside I was terrified.

I heard an ambulance speed northbound on Vine Street as every car pulled over. Hays people respected ambulances. The ambulance slid into Hickok's parking lot and came to a stop within inches of us. Emily was at the wheel and managed to block the black Chevy Suburban against the restaurant's Old West barbed wire railing.

Harley skidded to a stop, yelling, "Get on behind me… now!" I hesitated. Of course, I'd often ridden with Harley on her motorcycle, but this was a shootout on a bike. Couldn't I have ridden in the ambulance? I guessed Emily didn't want bullet holes in that vehicle. Harley, however, would have seen them as a badge of honor. "Emily alerted me to your situation. I gotcha, Doc!" Harley grasped my hand and pulled me on behind her.

We escaped with no shots fired. I was sure the G-men

were in shock. I assumed they'd never seen an ambulance skid sideways into a parking lot like that. Nor had they witnessed a crazy young lady on a motorcycle execute an extraction. Harley took the convoluted paranoid route—side streets, back alleys, two illegal U-turns—before we arrived at Rhonda's 'safe house.' Rhonda and Emily showed up minutes later.

After we high-fived each other for ditching the agents, we all engaged in a spirited two-hour debate about the motives for the incidents or a common thread between them. Harley left to secure her own trailer. Emily had another glass of wine. I went to bed and slept like a baby, knowing Rennie was on guard. No one would breach Rhonda's house.

We all woke up early. Emily and I had patients to attend to. Rhonda had prepared a breakfast of coffee, toast, and homemade sandhill plum jam. I thanked everyone for having my back last night. The three of us disagreed over whether Kit would be disappointed or relieved that she'd missed all the action.

"You should stay with me for a few more nights until we get some results from the police," Rhonda insisted.

"Nope. I'm not going to let this shooter uproot my life. I want to sleep in my own bed tonight."

"Okay, but I'm going with you to clear the clinic before I let you go in. Have you seen that cute Officer Wassinger again?"

"Who?" I said with my best poker face. This week was shaping up to rival that old dime novel—crime, intrigue, and romance included.

It had been a blessedly uneventful Sunday. Oh, I did attend church in the morning. Not so uneventful. Every time I showed my face, I felt like the pastor was calling me out for some sin, either from my college days or from my current life. How did he do that? Of course, I had a lot of options for him to choose from.

A bit creepy, though, if you asked me.

The congregation was friendly enough. Some of them were my clients, which made things a bit tricky at times. Did anyone really want to see their vet down on her knees at the altar, blubbering and asking God for forgiveness? They'd probably assume I'd removed the wrong kidney or overcharged someone for a nail trim. Personally, I wouldn't have wanted to see my M.D. up there crying her eyes out.

God only knew what *she* was confessing.

After beating the Baptists to Golden Corral for lunch, I decided to stop by Brock's business. He was, like me, always on the premises. The meeting with the Belladonnas had me thinking. Perhaps Brock had some insight into my blood donation under duress. After all, immunology, vaccine development, and antibody production were his specialties, his bread and butter. I called him when I arrived at the S.I.C. back door. Who knew what he was doing in there all by himself? He was a bit of a weirdo, so I didn't want to surprise him.

"Survivor Immunity Challenge Vaccine Company," Brock answered. Brock was obsessed with the TV show "Survivor," and renamed the company after his dad's passing. "How may I help you?" I was surprised he didn't have a programmed recording for after hours.

"Hey, Brock. It's Doctor Dakota. What's going on? I'm at your back door." He buzzed me in.

"Just catching up on some monoclonal antibody research. A company recently developed a new monoclonal antibody to treat parvovirus in dogs. My company should have been the first one to develop it. My father was a pioneer in the development of the parvovirus vaccine, and I'm his heir. It's not fair. They stole my research."

As Harley often said, "He sounds like the wheel is turning, but the hamster is gone."

But this was different. He was desperate.

I tried to cheer him up. "Hey, Brock. What do

radiologists' dogs do with bones? They barium."

No response.

I tried again. "What does a Labrador retriever's food go through before it can be sold in stores? It goes to the Lab for testing."

Nothing.

I moved on. "Brock, I've got some immunology questions for you."

Owl-like, he rotated his head toward me. "Go on."

"Did you hear about my kidnapping? It happened before the shooting."

"No, I am not aware."

I recounted the details about the agents and the lab at CEZID. I could see the hamster wheel turning in his head.

"You say you suffered a kidnapping because you may have increased antibodies to diseases? An alteration in your DNA that increases your immunity? I'm intrigued. Scientists might call that super-immunity. That means you have astronomically high levels of antibodies coursing through your system. Would you allow me to draw a sample of your blood?"

I paused to consider this request for a moment. Brock's father had outfitted his lab with the most expensive and accurate equipment available at the time. I supposed Brock had upgraded over the years. Perhaps he could shed some light on why my blood was so valuable to CEZID.

"Sure, have at it. I've replenished my blood supply since the kidnapping."

He looked like a twelve-year-old who had just been given permission to drive the family car. He gathered more than a handful of assorted test tubes and a tourniquet, a flashback to my CEZID visit. I began to regret my rapid acquiescence. He released the tourniquet after what seemed like a gallon of blood flowed into God knew how many tubes. My arm was an odd shade of blue, and my fingers were numb. I stood up and abruptly fell back into my chair.

"Whew. Are you sure you didn't inject something into me?" I asked.

Brock laughed. "No, I just extracted the maximum amount of blood an average person can afford to lose."

Funny.

"Brock, I'm not average." I was four-foot-ten and should have weighed one hundred pounds. I didn't think my extra fat should factor into the calculation. "You took too much blood for my size."

An eerie smile crossed his face. "Oops. Let me get you some orange juice."

Nope. Wouldn't drink anything offered by this wackadoodle. I was out of there. I wobbled out the back door, jumped into my Land Rover, and headed home.

Chapter 11

Monday morning, I was up bright and early. A commotion at the front counter had drawn my attention. The men in black were back.

"We need to speak to Dr. Dakota, please," they flashed their badges at London. They didn't need to. After all, no one would have mistaken them for locals.

"I'll have to see if she's in," London replied.

I loved this young lady.

I motioned her into the surgery room.

"London, tell them I'm doing brain surgery on a Chihuahua and can't be bothered."

London smiled, "Doc, you'll have to deal with them eventually. They know you're here. Oh, and you know there's no point in doing brain surgery on a Chihuahua."

She laughed as she walked off, as if going down a designer catwalk. How did she do that?

Here came the anxiety again. I thought of five red objects: an apple, a stoplight, a stop sign, blood, and a rash. I continued the downward spiral but pushed through with my behavior modification techniques. I thought of five blue objects as my breathing normalized: the ocean, the sky, Officer Wassinger's eyes, the blue top on a blood coagulation collection tube, and a patient who needed oxygen.

Ruby, you're warped, I thought.

"Dr. Dakota. Dr. Dakota!" I opened my eyes and blinked twice.

Great. The agents from the bar were in my lab.

"Good morning, guys. Did you have a good night? Missing anyone? Did you get your vehicle out of the parking lot?" I rambled when I was nervous.

"Dr. Dakota, you have it all wrong. We escorted you out of the bar Saturday night to protect you. We noticed a suspicious character eyeing you from a table near your booth."

"Wait. You were protecting me? I refused your surveillance. Why were you even in the area?" I asked incredulously.

"We are everywhere, Doctor. We stepped in as a precaution."

A suspicious character? I thought back to the bar patrons. Who was there last night? The Belladonnas were so intent on the case that we did not even consider that someone might try to knock me off there. It was Hickok's. Everyone knew everyone. A new person would have stood out like a cat at a dog park.

"I am so sorry. My friends can be a little overprotective at times," I apologized. "Hope we didn't cause you trouble with the Agency. I mean, a group of little old ladies and a vet tech outsmarted you guys. That couldn't have looked good to your bosses."

The agents scowled but offered no answer.

"So, should I be worried these guys are still around?" I asked.

One agent crinkled his eyebrows as if he thought I was an idiot. "Dr. Dakota, you are in extreme danger and high demand for reasons we can't reveal."

They left the clinic for parts unknown without offering any further information.

I guessed they wanted to know if I was still alive. I was, so far. Should I have altered my daily habits? How could I have altered my pattern when I rarely left the clinic? Should I have made a will? Chui and Lola would have gotten everything. Could a stuffed dog toy even be an heir? My entire estate consisted of my old Land Rover, a smattering of furniture that fit into one room, an old Kirby vacuum sweeper, my scrubs, a bottle of flea shampoo, and one dress with the tag still attached. Chui wouldn't have been able to use any of it except for the shampoo. Where would the two of them have lived? Who would have opened the bags of dog food?

Slow down, Ruby. You are still alive, so far.

I told Officer Wassinger I'd be at the station to give a statement. I had a full surgery schedule to knock out before I left: two dog spays and two tomcat neuters, plus whatever might show up as an emergency. I needed to tell London I had to go to the police station, but I was still a little gun-shy over traipsing through the reception area.

Gertrude was busy with her assembly-line grooming. She'd gotten an early start. The radio was on in her room, and a matted cocker spaniel was dangling in the grooming sling. I'd always gotten a kick out of the confused look on a dog's face when they realized they had no traction whatsoever to escape. The dog was at her mercy. Gertrude was as kind and gentle as a groomer could be. Clients often insisted that she keep the coat long, even though it had been months since they'd run a brush over the poor thing. Gertrude talked them into a shave-down for the pet's sake whenever possible. Imagine combing through a set of dreadlocks on a human…

The neighboring insurance agency had occupied my clinic before I took over the space and remodeled it. I had to knock down some walls and pour cement runs for the kennel. I installed an old cast-iron bathtub for grooming and dental use. Since I'd moved in, this had also become my personal shower. I rigged up some PVC pipe to hold a shower curtain. It already had a showerhead installed. No luxurious bathing in this tub. I was afraid I'd get ringworm or a bladder infection if I sat down.

The clinic still retained its cold, insurance-office layout: a long central hallway painted mint green, with rooms branching off on both sides. The front desk was across from Gertrude's room. London often stepped in to help groom after she completed all the intakes. Today, she walked a golden retriever named Hunter toward the grooming tub in the back. As she passed the office, the phone rang. Ramos squawked, "I'll get it," which London ignored. She stretched over the desk and answered the phone.

Unbeknownst to her, Hunter had his eye on Ramos. Suddenly, Hunter lunged for the parrot. After all, he was a bird dog. Ramos screamed as the dog shook the one-thousand-dollar bird back and forth on the floor like a chew toy. London screamed at the dog and into the phone, deafening the unsuspecting caller. At the same time, she yanked on the leash. Feathers flew everywhere. Gertrude ran over and beat the dog with her brush, trying to get it to let go of poor Ramos. Good thing it was a retriever, not a destroyer. He had a soft mouth and understood the command "Drop it!" which I yelled when I reached the front desk.

Poor Ramos rolled out of his mouth, covered in drool. He looked pale for a parrot.

After treating Ramos for shock, I placed him in the infant incubator given to me by a hospital that was upgrading its NICU. Birds were fragile but often bounced back if you could warm their environment. Of course, you had to be careful with the temperature, or you could roast them.

As I headed back toward the surgery room—thank goodness I had just finished the last neuter before the ruckus—my hands were shaking, my chest aching.

Oh, no. Here it came again.

The uproar must have triggered my anxiety. I realized I was reliving the shooting. I looked around the surgery room for an object that began with A. A was for anesthetic. B was for the balls I just removed from Tom Foolery. C was for the cone used to administer gas. D was for drugs in the cabinet, which I could have used right then. This took my mind off my anxiety and occupied it with an inane ritual that worked. Holding Chui in my arms often helped. After all, he was my emotional support dog. I retrieved him from his luxury dog run, and we snuggled for a few minutes until my heart rate returned to normal.

The rest of the morning was much calmer. When Hunter's owner arrived to pick up her dog, we gave her an abbreviated version of the parrot retrieval. Of course, we left out the part about Gertrude beating him with the brush. It turned out the owner was a florist. She was very apologetic. Ramos received a beautiful get-well bouquet from her every day for a week.

I glanced at my watch and suddenly remembered I was supposed to show up at the police station after lunch to give a statement.

Oops.

I'd been a little busy with the bird emergency, a puppy with its head stuck in a plastic bottle, and a couple of calls from clients who insisted they speak only to me.

I informed London that I'd be away from the clinic for an hour. She was holding Chui on her lap underneath the desk. London was Chui's second favorite person. She also had a box of dog treats in her bottom cabinet.

Chapter 12

"Is anybody home?" I shouted as I opened the door to the police station. "The dog whisperer is about to enter. Come out with your hands up."

I found this much funnier than the officer on the desk.

"Ah, Dr. Dakota. You could get yourself shot doing that." I recognized him as one of the responding officers after the shooting. He looked much thinner without his SWAT gear, but he was still not as attractive as Officer Wassinger.

"Yes, sir, I'm here to give a statement about the shooting at my clinic. Is Officer Wassinger here? I'll only recount the story to him. He was the first one on the scene, so I trust him," I lied.

I did trust him, but that wasn't why I asked for him. I just wanted to feel my stomach leap in my abdomen or whatever body part it was that he triggered.

"Yes, ma'am, he's on duty today."

I felt ornery, so I corrected him.

"It's Doctor, not ma'am. The word 'ma'am' comes from the French for 'my lady' and then translates as 'madam' in English. It makes me feel like I run a brothel, officer. That's not what you meant, right?"

"No, ma'am, madam, I mean Doctor. No disrespect

intended," he added, properly chastened. "Follow me. I'll take you to his office. He just made Detective. Since you're so concerned with titles, address him properly. He's Detective Wassinger now."

He chuckled as he pointed to a door down the hallway.

Detective Wassinger sat at a clutter-free desk—clearly a new detective's workspace. I knew from experience that in a few short weeks, files would cover that desk until there'd be no space for even a coffee mug.

Oh. I was thinking about *my* desk.

"Come in, Dr. Dakota. I was worried you wouldn't show up today. Weren't we scheduled for right after lunch?"

Oh, brother, a timekeeper.

"Yes, Deeetecteeeve Wassinger," I saluted him. "Congrats on the promotion. I was late because I was busy rescuing my parrot from a bird dog."

He raised his eyebrows but only asked, "Would you like anything to drink? Coffee? Water?"

"No thanks, Detective."

Did I just bat my eyes at him? Good grief.

"Okay, let's start with your full name."

Oh, no. I didn't want this guy to know my full name. I reluctantly answered, "It's Ruby Anne, but the last person who called me Ruby is still limping."

As long as we were hating on things, I wasn't too fond of the current usage of a person's first name after their title. This had come from my childhood when we addressed teachers as Mr., Mrs., or Miss. Dr. Ruby? Nope, not happening. Pastor Dave? Officer Randy? Ugh. It was so demeaning and detracted from the years one had spent in the pursuit of that title. I wasn't on a first-name basis with you; you were not my best friend. You were a colleague, a client, a pastor, a criminal, whatever.

However, Detective Wassinger could call me anything, anytime he liked.

"Take me back to Friday morning, Doc, from the

beginning." He took a yellow legal pad and recorded my response in perfect, legible handwriting. I didn't know whether he was computer-illiterate or whether a law required an officer to write in longhand.

My handwriting was completely illegible. I blamed it on the years of taking notes from rapid-fire professors in veterinary school. However, penmanship was the only class in elementary school in which I'd received an unsatisfactory grade.

Detective Wassinger gently led me through the terrifying moments without triggering any anxiety whatsoever. What was happening here? Had my attraction hormones canceled out my anxiety hormones? I needed to review my endocrinology notes. Was he feeling this electricity?

Probably not.

I tried to focus on my statement as I revealed every detail I could recall.

"I think that's all, Dr. Dakota. I'll let you know if I have any more questions."

What? Were we done already? "You can call me Ruby if you like," I responded like a silly teenager. Did I actually say that?

"Let's keep this formal, Doc. Okay?"

Awkward.

Back at the clinic, I worried about what Brock was doing with my sample. I gave him a call. "Brock, what have you found out about my blood?"

"Oh, Dr. Dakota, I was just about to call you. Your blood is magnificent."

I smiled. "I like to think so."

"Serology tests show you have an abnormal number of B-cells and memory antibodies. This is fantastic. It explains your broad immunity and could lead to the development of new treatments." He sounded like a kid with a new Oculus. "My lab is already gearing up to multiply the antibody-producing cells. This explains why CEZID was so interested in you and perhaps why someone took a potshot at you. This may be the breakthrough we've been looking for."

"Brock, I still don't understand. I'll stop by later this week, and you can fill me in on the details."

The donuts I'd brought in yesterday were getting stale, and I needed a break from this madhouse. I grabbed some cream-filled ones and wandered over to the Home and Barn Insurance Agency next door. The wind whipped through my parking lot, stirring up mini tornadoes of dust. The name Kansas came from the Sioux word for "south wind people" or "people of the wind." They'd gotten that right. The wind in Kansas never stopped blowing, as there were few trees to slow it down.

The agency's owners were friends from church. Darryl was busy on his computer. He was always on his computer. He grabbed a donut and returned to his screen. His wife, Glenda, was manning the front desk.

"Hey, how's the insurance business? Any new hailstorms, crop damage, or earthquakes?" I asked. All of those were bad for business. We had earthquakes in Hays, tiny ones. I sometimes felt them late at night when I was at the clinic. It sounded like a drunk had gently rolled his car into the side of my building.

One time, it *was* a drunk rolling his car into the side of my building.

"Nope. Pretty slow summer," Glenda said with a smile. I suspected she was the driving force behind this operation. "We're focusing on finding new clients."

Darryl and Glenda were some of the few insurance salespeople who'd maintained their membership in our church for years. Many agents had signed up on the rolls and approached every congregation member to sell policies. When they ran out of names, it was on to the next church, the next hunting ground.

Smart business practice. Poor church practice, I thought.

Had Brock been spreading the news about my blood, I wondered? I knew Brock visited them as often as he visited us. Darryl stared at his screen. I suspected he was playing Spider Solitaire, not researching anything.

"Have you guys seen Brock lately? Is he working on a new project?" I asked, probing for information.

Darryl mumbled through a mouth full of donut. "He mentioned something about a breakthrough. He's pretty secretive about his work, though."

Brock was constantly developing new preventatives and vaccines. None of them had ever panned out. "Better get back to the asylum. I've got an emergency coming in, a tomcat who can't pee."

I saw Darryl cringe.

I bid them goodbye and headed back to the clinic. As I plodded off, I contemplated that both female cats and women have shorter, less constricted urethras for urine flow. That's one thing we had over men.

Oh, yay. Let's celebrate.

This was a weird fun fact, but veterinarians were a warped breed. I enjoyed comparing the maladies of pets to those of humans.

Didn't seem weird at all to me.

Chapter 13

Dr. Morgan, my personal anxiety generator, pulled into the parking lot as I walked toward the clinic. He drove a Tesla truck, an angular, stainless-steel beast. It fit him. As he dismounted, he shook his head.

"Dr. Dakota, you should spend more time inside the clinic improving your revenue figures. Can't earn money visiting the neighbors." He said this through that sarcastic smile that looked benevolent to others but meant doom to me.

"I was checking to see if Glenda had seen Brock Benton lately." I tried to act nonchalant, but my stomach twisted into a volvulus, a condition seen in dogs in which the stomach rotates on its axis. It could be life-threatening.

I was sure it *was* in my case.

He followed me inside. I tried to walk like a sane person but wasn't feeling it. Why did I dissolve into a pool of despair at the sound of this guy's voice? I was a fully trained, licensed veterinarian who'd built a good practice independently. I shouldn't need his approval, but I did for some deep, dark reason.

"Let's look at your sales for the past month," he said.

In my sarcastic inner voice, I silently replied, "Let's look at your expense account records for the past year." He padded them. He wrote off vacations to exotic lands as research trips and claimed meals at the most expensive restaurants as business lunches he never invited me to. For some reason, my inner sarcasm never became audible around him, which was sad.

He missed a lot of my humor.

"I'll let London go over those with you," I replied audibly.

I knew he'd enjoy sitting next to her young, beautiful self. She could handle him. She was much more candid with him than I was. Brave girl. Of course, it wasn't *her* livelihood that was on the line.

"Oh, London, do you have a few minutes to help Dr. Morgan?" I knew she didn't, but she was a team player and understood the adverse effect he had on me.

"Sure, Dr. Dakota. I'd be glad to. Just let me finish the intake on this cat."

As I read the history of Copurrnicus, I laughed out loud. An astronomy professor at Fort Hays State University owned Copurrrnicus. This black cat was so dark it would disappear in an unlit room. He was in obvious distress. He let out a yowl when I palpated his abdomen. It was tense and painful. It felt like he had a grapefruit lodged in there. It was his bladder.

Male cats often developed "sand" in their bladder, which could plug their urethra. This plug prevented urine from flowing. I couldn't imagine how painful this condition was. Judging from Darryl's cringe reaction earlier, men *could* relate. I didn't know that much about men's urethras, but I did know that in cats, if the blockage wasn't relieved, it would end in death.

I explained the situation to the owner and asked when Copurrnicus had last eaten. Thankfully, his condition had taken away his appetite. He'd have to undergo anesthesia immediately to correct the problem. Harley prepped him and administered the drugs that would allow me to pass a catheter. Even though the cat was unconscious, I'd always imagined a sigh of relief from them when the blockage opened. I reminded Harley to keep her mouth closed. Male cat pee is a taste one never forgets.

After inserting the catheter, urine squirted out everywhere like water from an unkinked garden hose. I sutured a urethral catheter to the surrounding skin to keep urine flowing. Copurrnicus would sleep at the clinic for a couple of days until urine flowed freely.

Something gnawed at my already frayed mind. It wasn't Dr. Morgan. That was another feeling entirely. London kept him busy in the office. God bless her. Perhaps she could make my sales record look better than it was.

I couldn't explain why, but I had to check on Brock at his facility. It wasn't like he was my best friend. He was just annoying. It was actually Darryl who didn't like Brock. I once heard Darryl threaten to strangle him if he showed up again during hail season. Darryl was often in a bad mood during hail season. Everyone and his dog wanted their roof repaired and paid for immediately. I never took anything Darryl said seriously. He had a bit of attention deficit disorder, but he was lovable in a quirky sort of way.

I waited until Dr. Morgan left for lunch. "Harley, I'll be gone for 30 minutes. Cover for me. Check on Copurrnicus as he starts to wake up."

I snuck out the back door and crawled into my old 2012 Land Rover Sport. The smaller version allowed my short legs and chubby body to jump in, with handholds to assist. My parents had driven a much larger Land Rover in Africa. I was still fond of those 4WD vehicles, known for their ability to travel over rough terrain, not that I ever traveled over rough terrain these days.

I pulled into the Survivor Immunity Challenge Vaccine Company, S.I.C., parking lot. Brock had parked his car in his designated spot, the only vehicle in the entire lot. What was going on? This company worked around the clock, especially when Brock was on a hot lead for a vaccine. He didn't have many employees, but the ones he had were loyal. He didn't want any of his secrets divulged.

Something was amiss. The back door stood ajar. Brock never left this door unlocked. Never. His security rivaled Fort Knox: cameras, steel doors, and white tile walls that bounced sound like a gym. I called out his name. "Brock?" My voice echoed back, unanswered.

Too quiet. The hair stood up on the back of my neck like a Rhodesian ridgeback.

"Brock, are you in here?" I moved to his office midway down the hall. The door was open enough for me to see Brock's body lying on the floor beside his black steel desk.

There was a bullet hole in his forehead.

It looked like Brock had interrupted somebody who didn't appreciate the intrusion. File drawers hung open, papers everywhere. Some of them were soaking up the blood pooled around his head. Chairs tipped over, his awards and manuals knocked off the shelves. Somebody had been looking for something, and Brock got in the way. At least he tried to defend his puny little self. I began to weep, which surprised me.

Death no longer bothered me, after Africa. Brock wasn't even one of my favorite people, but I'd spent some time with him—more time recently after my CEZID forced bloodletting episode. If anyone could unravel the mystery of super-immunity, it was Brock. He seemed extremely excited about the prospect of a new treatment using my blood. I'd told him I wouldn't consent to share any more of my lifeblood with him until I spoke to the weird lab guy in Manhattan, which I hadn't taken the time to do. It wasn't on my priority list.

Still wondering why I was the only person in the place, I glanced up at a banner in the hallway just outside the door that announced a day off for all employees in honor of Brock's deceased father's birthday. I didn't think Brock even liked his father. Perhaps he sought an opportunity to be alone with his research.

Who knew? I'd rather vacation in Fiji if I wanted to be alone.

Call 911, Ruby. Call 911. An inner voice brought me back to reality. I punched in the numbers.

"This is 911. What's your emergency?" the operator asked in a monotone voice.

"This is Dr. Dakota, the owner of the Pediatrician to Pets Veterinary Clinic. I'm at Survivor Immunity Challenge Vaccine Company. I'm calling to report a murder." I also used my monotone voice. Perhaps I was callous. I asked the 911 operator, "Would you see if Detective Wassinger could come to the scene? He was so helpful the last time I called 911." I wanted more time with Detective Wassinger.

"How often do you call 911, ma'am?"

I had an incoming call. "Sorry, 911 operator, I have to hang up. My clinic is calling. I'll call you back." I switched to the incoming call. It was Harley.

"Hey, Doc. Did you get held up somewhere? We need you to sign some health certificates for two dogs traveling to Sweden. It's time sensitive. They need your signature today."

Boy, I knew what a pain in the behind those certificates could be. With numerous regulations, tight deadlines, and frequently changing state and national bureaucracies, navigating these challenges can be daunting. It was hard to keep up. I had Harley and London trained in most of the paperwork. They were on a first-name basis with the USDA lady in Topeka, but I still had to put my signature on them.

"Could you bring the certificates to me at the vaccine company? It seems that Brock Benton managed to get himself murdered. I may be here for a few hours."

Hopefully with a certain detective, I thought.

"Wait! Brock's dead? What happened to him? Are the police there? Are you okay?" Harley fired off questions faster than I could answer.

"I can't talk. Just bring the forms over, and I'll fill you in." I directed her.

"I'll be over as soon as I get a break," she fired back.

Harley was a dependable employee, but I suspected she wanted to see the body. I didn't dare call the Belladonnas. They would have shown up here like they did right after my shooting.

We Belladonnas all had detective instincts from our professions. Emily and I hunted down the causes of disease and pain every day. Rhonda, of course, detected at the station. Kit was also a detective. Once, she tried to hunt down a doctor who had sent in a prescription that interacted with the patient's other medications. Another time, she tracked down a doctor who signed too many opioid prescriptions for a questionable-looking pharmacy customer. We all loved a good mystery.

My phone rang again. It was the 911 operator. She was a little peeved. "Ma'am, you don't hang up on a 911 operator, especially when you're reporting a murder." I paced around Brock's office with the operator on the line.

"Are you alone?" she read from her script.

"Yes." I was always alone. I had no life.

"Is the victim breathing?" she asked.

"Not with a hole in his head," I answered.

"Is there blood?"

I rolled my eyes. "What do you think?"

"Have you administered CPR? Do you want me to walk you through it?"

"There's no need to do CPR on a corpse. I know dead. I am a doctor after all."

"Stay on the line with me, ma'am."

There she went with the dreaded ma'am, despite my having identified myself as a doctor. I never got any respect. I worked my behind off to obtain the right to be called Doctor. Veterinary medicine was one of the toughest doctorates available: mentally, physically, and emotionally demanding, with daily physical danger thrown in. We learned all the standard values for a healthy patient, as well as the disease conditions for not just one, but multiple species. A horse differed from a ruminant; a dog did not resemble a lizard in any way, shape, or form. I restrained myself and instead answered, "Lady, I know when a person is dead."

"Help is on the way," she responded. "Stay on the line with me."

I hung up again.

Chapter 14

I could hear the sirens approaching. Please let it be Detective Wassinger; please let it be Detective Wassinger. Was I shallow, or what? Here I was standing next to a dead body, thinking about my love life.

I opened the door. An officer who looked to be around 12 years old greeted me.

Seriously, was child labor still legal?

I began to wonder why my perception of age had changed as I got older. I liked to think it was because I'd gained wisdom, realizing that a 21-year-old lacked the experience, emotional maturity, and decision-making skills that I had at 62.

"Good afternoon, officer. I'm Dr. Dakota. I own the Pediatrician to Pets Veterinary Clinic. I found the body. His name is Brock Benton."

"Yes, ma'am. Is there anyone else in the building, ma'am?" Ugh. Again, with the ma'am.

"Not that I know of. They were all given the day off in honor of the founder's birthday, which I'm sure he appreciates from the grave."

Was that too catty?

"Does this guy live in town?" the officer asked.

"No, he doesn't live anywhere. He's dead."

I didn't think this kid got my sense of humor.

More officers showed up. The CSIs busied themselves with photographs and fingerprints. The local coroner, Dr. DeCamp, better known to me as Dr. Decomp, dragged in with a cigarette butt hanging out of his mouth. He was not a trained medical examiner. He was a doctor who moonlighted for the city. He was also a heart attack waiting to happen. I loved him, but I wondered how many murders went unsolved around here because he lacked proper training. He checked for a pulse, which had long since quit pulsing, and jabbed a meat thermometer into Brock's liver. He wrote something on a form and then gave the okay for the ambulance to take the body to the local funeral home. I knew the owner there. He was a funny guy for a mortician. I assumed they would perform the autopsy in his morgue.

Harley skidded in on her bike as the ambulance solemnly pulled away with no lights or sirens. "Hey, Doc! You get all the fun. Did I miss the body?"

I was glad there were no grieving employees or family members here. Harley could be a touch insensitive.

"Yes, Harley, they took Brock's body away. Did you bring the travel documents?"

Signing travel papers while a crime scene investigation was underway seemed a little heartless.

"Hey, Doc. Dr. Morgan left you a message. He said he needs to discuss your performance during his next visit. His veins were sticking out on his neck like he gets when he sees a dust bunny in the corner."

Harley was well acquainted with Dr. Morgan's idiosyncrasies.

"What's the worst he could do to me? Fire me? Make me retire?" I asked.

"Why don't you tell him to go to hell, Doc?"

Theologically, that might be exactly where he was going. As a Christian, I might have an obligation to intervene in that outcome.

Oh, like that was gonna happen.

Of course, I would love to retire, buy a place in Costa Rica, and spend time reading and relaxing in a hammock. Although I'd already sold my clinic, it didn't provide me with a permanent retirement income. It only paid off my debts, both business and personal.

"Gee, thanks for the advice, Harley. For one thing, I'm terrified of the man. He's twice my size, with serious mental issues. Who knows what he'd do? He gives me an anxiety attack every time he hits the door. Second, I can't afford to lose this job. Who's going to hire a 62-year-old, outdated, opinionated mini-person? I love my patients. I love my clients. I love my clinic."

I still called it mine, although it wasn't.

"Welp, can't help you there, Doc. I'm just saying bullies often back down when confronted. I've got your back."

That gave me some comfort. Harley was tough. I preferred that Rennie had my back, though. He was able to inflict more pain. I thought of the possibilities…

"Now that the fun is over, may I return to my clinic?" I asked the young officer.

"No, ma'am. You must accompany me to the police station to answer a few questions," he replied.

"Can't you just photocopy the notes from my last visit? Everything is the same except for the victim. I didn't see either perp. This one was long gone when I got here."

"No, ma'am, we can't. New crime. New interview."

And a new chance to see Hayes. Now I was calling him Hayes. He didn't give me permission to do that. Why was I such a girl all of a sudden?

I started to climb into the front seat of the police cruiser.

"I'm sorry, ma'am, you'll have to ride in the back."

What did that mean? Did they think I killed Brock? Did I look like a deranged killer? Maybe. I hadn't combed my hair all day, which wasn't unusual. I had blood on my scrubs from God knew what. And male cat pee.

Okay, perhaps I did look a little unhinged.

I climbed into the back seat. The smell of a drunk's vomit competed with my Eau de Clinic. Enclosed in a cage, I started to panic when a horrific thought hit me. Did I want former Officer, now Detective, Wassinger to see me like this?

When had I ever cared about my appearance, at least in the past 20 years? There was a time when I had been hot. That look only got me into trouble. I had this charisma that drew guys in. I was also, as they say, well-endowed. My eyes were turquoise, thanks to contacts, and they could make any male do just about anything I wanted. Never understood it, but I often used it. Even more manipulative, I could exude pheromones at will. My pheromones were probably no longer in production. If any remained, they must be outdated by now. Perhaps males no longer responded to my old model of pheromone.

Good chance.

I timidly asked the driver, "Is Detective Wassinger in the office today?"

"No, ma'am, he's on vacation for a week."

Whew. No danger of his getting a whiff of me today. He was probably in the Bahamas with a girlfriend half his age. This sounded like jealousy. I was the one who always made others jealous. Now I feared I was just old. I shut up for the rest of the ride. The same officer was at the desk when we entered the station.

"Oh, it's the veterinarian with the dangerous sense of humor."

At least he recognized me.

This interview wasn't as entertaining as the last one. This detective was all business. Detective Wassinger was all business, too, but I imagined there was a spark between us at times.

Probably just me.

The interview only lasted 15 minutes. I was relieved.

I needed to get back to my full-time job. Seemed like tragedy was cutting into my productive hours. Dr. Morgan wouldn't be thrilled since my bottom line wasn't as lucrative as he needed it to be. What if he did fire me? I would be jobless, homeless, and broke. Where would Chui and I live? When I adopted Chui from the animal shelter, I'd promised to take good care of him.

Deep breaths. Four-square breathing.

The young officer dropped me back at S.I.C. He opened the cruiser door for me. Chances were, I smelled even worse than before from the nervous sweat that soaked my armpits. Anxiety stalked me as I was concerned about the upcoming performance evaluation with Dr. Morgan. However, there were more pressing issues in my life, such as an assassin trying to kill me and a rogue virus destroying the world.

Chapter 15

I still hadn't heard from the CEZID people. Perhaps they weren't obligated to share inside information with me, but I *was* a veterinarian and a graduate of Kansas State University, where the facility was located. Some of the people in authority there were my former vet school classmates, and it was *my* blood they were manipulating. For what reason, I wasn't sure. Was there really a cure in my bloodstream? Could they use my antibodies to make a vaccine? Could my DNA explain why my family and I were protected from the deadly viruses found in East Africa? Should I report this lab event to the media? Should I have Chui's coat shaved down?

All pressing questions that would have to wait until I showered.

It was approaching closing time at the clinic, when owners picked up their groomed and hospitalized dogs. It was busy. Showering in the tub I shared with the groomer was problematic, especially during clinic hours. But I reeked. I snuck in the back door and tiptoed down the hall to the kennel room where the tub was located. The boarders, patients, and Chui were the only ones in the room. I shucked off my scrubs and stepped up on the stepstool, carefully throwing my leg over the tub's edge.

Good grief. The last grooming client left a cigar. Not a real cigar. A turd.

I scowled and went through some pointless blame-shifting. I should have spotted the little brown log before I took off my clothes.

My first tactical option was to pick up this small gift, get out of the tub, and dispose of it in a trash can. However, I was not parading around the kennel naked. Oh, I wasn't shy, but I still possessed some modesty. Plus, I couldn't imagine how freaked out a client would be if they saw me in my natural state. My second option was to co-exist with this piece of poop while I showered, praying it didn't dissolve around my feet.

Ick.

I chose the second option and tried not to gag as the poop did indeed dissolve in the warm water, releasing a pungent odor.

In burst London. "Oops. Sorry. What's that smell? Did a pack of wild dogs unload yesterday's roadkill dinner in our kennel? It's causing our clients to evacuate."

London was so dramatic, whereas Harley probably didn't even notice a change in the atmosphere. A bout with COVID-19 had damaged Harley's sense of smell.

What a blessing.

I clutched the see-through shower curtain to my body. Probably should have purchased an opaque one, but London seeing my naked body was not important at this point.

"I was just trying to clean up before my next client. Sorry. Gertrude left a stool sample in the tub. Well, not Gertrude herself, but one of her grooming dogs. I thought it might just go quietly down the drain. My bad."

Once I was decent again, I headed for my lab. Well, maybe not decent, but at least I didn't smell worse than the clinic. Harley was waiting to debrief the day… more like unloading on me. Hospitalized patients were improving, including a Pekingese hit by a car that had resulted in proptosis. In other words, the car hit him so hard that his eyeball popped out of its socket, still attached, just bugging out. Of course, after surgery to pop that sucker back in, the eye looked normal.

I provided treatment instructions for inpatients and reviewed the lab work that came back after lunch. Some clinics had sophisticated machines that tested blood values onsite, but I wasn't that desperate for speed in reporting. Pets Buy promised a blood analyzer in the future. For now, I sent our samples off to the local human clinical pathology lab. They picked up samples daily. Some normal ranges for humans differed from those of pets, but I learned to make the necessary adjustments. I could recite normal values for dogs, cats, and humans in my sleep.

When I needed a laugh, I sent the med techs at the lab some bird blood from Ramos and labeled it with my name. Ramos didn't mind. He loved a good laugh, too. Plus, he got a treat.

Bird red blood cells were weird little things, elliptical, nucleated, and quite spectacular under a microscope. Nothing like the round, nucleus-free cells of mammals. I couldn't wait to get the call from the new guy at the lab.

"Dr. Dakota. The sample sent in on your blood work is unusual. The cells are larger, and there's what appears to be a nucleus in them. They look like a thousand eyes peering back at me through the microscope. I've contacted your primary care provider, but I wanted to give you a heads-up."

I messed with his head. "What do you think I should do? Go to the emergency room? The blood transfusion center? Area 51? The zoo?"

It finally clicked that the joke was on him. He'd heard the rumors of the weird things I sent to the pathology lab. I loved to prank these guys. I considered myself the bright spot in their lives. They didn't have nearly as much fun as we did at the clinic.

"Oh, good one, Doc. What weird animal is this blood taken from?"

"This time, it's a parrot. Watch out for next time. You never know what's going to be in those tubes."

"Thanks, Doc, for keeping me on my toes."

"No problem," I responded. "Just trying to liven it up over there."

In contrast, the next day was so full of procedures that I had no time to reflect on the whirlwind stirring my personal life. Thoroughly exhausted and clutching a Biggie Bag from the nearby Wendy's, I turned out the lights and headed to my room in the back. I was never nervous about staying alone at the clinic. I usually had Chui. He was no Rennie, but his hearing was acute. That hairy little sausage could hear me open a bag of Cheetos from Harley's trailer next door.

Harley sometimes invited Chui to her place for sleepovers. Chui always took Lola with him. He was with Harley tonight. They got each other. They both resented the establishment. Harley even refused to get the REAL-ID star on her driver's license. Not that she ever flew anywhere. She thought the government would use it to track her location. Chui kept losing his rabies tag. I suspected it was on purpose. He didn't want to be tracked, either.

I hadn't broken it to him yet, but he had a microchip under his skin.

Chapter 16

Alone at the clinic, I kept hearing noises up front but was too afraid to go look. My loaded Smith & Wesson M&P 9mm EZ lay on my nightstand. Some nights, the euthanized dogs in the freezer visited my dreams, but this time I was awake.

It's possible that coming close to death intensified my PTSD symptoms. On top of that, I found Brock dead. Either of those would give a normal person the jitters. It sounded selfish, but I could worry about the rest of the world tomorrow. I had super-immunity. I finally manned up and tiptoed down the hall.

London had draped the night cover over Ramos's cage. I assumed he was sleeping under there. He made no sound at night. All the kennel dogs were quiet. I imagined they were listening, too. Why did I let Chui go with Harley tonight of all nights? As I headed into the lab, I noticed two surgery packs wrapped but not autoclaved, the sterilization indicator tape not yet activated. I'd need those packs in the morning, so I carried them to the autoclave. The door was slightly ajar. As I bent over to open it, in the darkness, I saw two eyes peering out at me. A low, demonic yowl emanated from the sterilizer. A paw with claws bared struck out at my face. I nearly jumped out of my skin and slammed the autoclave shut.

What in the crap?

Earlier that morning, a farmer in faded overalls and mud-caked boots lumbered into the clinic. He presented London with an oversized pillowcase tied shut with a rope and filled with undulating, caterwauling lumps; an undetermined number of feral cats he wanted neutered. He had trapped them the night before and somehow transferred them into this pillowcase. "I need these here cats cut and returned today. They're takin' over the barn. They're good mousers, though."

London kept her composure. She knew better than to ask when the cats last ate. Naively, London opened the bag, and cats spewed everywhere. These were wild barn cats whose only interaction with humans was to be trapped, thrown into a bag, and carted to the clinic in the back of a pickup truck. We fanned out through the clinic to capture the escapees. Ramos added to the mayhem as he squawked, "Here, kitty, kitty. Awk! Here, kitty, kitty."

He's fortunate the cats didn't eat him.

After an hour of hide-and-seek, with no help from the farmer, we managed to wrangle the fugitives into pet carriers and placed them in the surgery room. We then mass-neutered and spayed them all. At the end of the day, London handed them back to the farmer in the same (but washed) pillowcase.

We must have missed one, though. I cautiously opened the door again. This time, the cat from hell leaped halfway out of the autoclave, caught my arm with his claws, and retreated into his stainless-steel tomb. It would have been a real tomb if I had started the autoclave without looking deep inside.

Would I have even noticed the smell of a sterilized cat in the middle of the night? This cat was not about to let me cradle it in my arms and put it in a cage. I retrieved the injectable syringe pole, filled the syringe with an anesthetic combo, and jabbed the cat through the crack of the open door. He soon relaxed, and I took him to surgery to remove his manhood.

I enjoyed that. Then back to bed for a half-night's sleep.

Early the next morning, Harley brought Chui to the clinic. Chui held his little stuffed Lola in his mouth but dropped her when he saw me. I was still his favorite.

"Oh, Chui. I've missed you! I'm so glad to see you, you little ragamuffin!"

Chui's hair looked like he had placed his paws on a Van der Graaf generator, the one from high school physics lab that made your hair stand on end due to static electricity. Chui smelled like Irish Spring bar soap. Harley must have put him in the shower with her.

Was it weird that I thought this was normal?

"Hey, Doc. How was your night?" Harley was in a good mood. Chui had that effect on people.

"It was rather eventful, thank you for asking. Remember the cats-in-the-bag from yesterday? Well, we missed one. I almost ran him through the autoclave cycle." A thought crossed my mind. We might have missed more than one. I was keeping Chui with me tonight. "We should keep our eyes out for feral cat scat."

That made me feel like a big game hunter.

The phone rang. Ramos squawked, "I'll get it."

London outshouted him. "Doctor Dakota, you have a call on line one."

London sounded so professional. We only had one line. I took the call in my office so I could multitask. I looked over the morning surgeries and afternoon appointments.

"This is Dr. Dakota. Go ahead, caller. You're on the air."

I liked messing with people. It caught the caller off guard. The last thing this person wanted was to be on the air.

"Uh, did you say this is Dr. Dakota? I have some

confidential news. I'm not on the air, am I?"

Some people had no sense of humor; I mean, zilch.

"Who is this?" I asked, although I feared I knew the caller. It was the guy from CEZID.

"This is Dr. Leakey. We've received some rather distressing news. The FBI reports several deaths recently in multiple countries. The common link is time spent working with your parents in East Africa during the Ebola epidemic. An assassin has taken out five people so far. All had the same M.O. I'm calling to warn you."

"It's a little late for that," I replied. "Someone *already* tried to take me out."

I slowly lowered myself into my office chair.

"I'd rather not talk about this on the phone, Dr. Dakota. When can you get to Manhattan?" the nerdy doctor asked.

"I'm not taking the bus again. How about that sleek jet? Is it available?"

"It is not, Doctor, but we want to keep you safe. You'll soon notice a couple of agents shadowing you," he added.

"Also, too late," I responded. "They're already shadowing me, but my friends and I know how to lose them."

Maybe I should have quit ditching them whenever I got the chance. I often took things into my own hands. It was a rebellious trait I'd worked on since my mind-blowing, life-altering collision with Jesus. My spiritual GPS had been off course for many years, taking me down some dubious life-choice roads. I wasn't overly religious, but there was no other way to explain my supernatural experience that wintry day.

Early one morning, while driving on I-70 north of town in below-freezing temperatures, I encountered an icy exit ramp. My car began to spin out of control when a voice from over my right shoulder urged me to "turn into the spin"—contrary to what instinct would have suggested. The vehicle stopped spinning and came to a halt just short of the guardrail. There was nobody in the back seat. In that instant, I understood that it was the voice of God.

I was still a work in progress. There were many broken parts that needed fixing. You just couldn't rush some things.

"Are you saying the attempt on my life wasn't an isolated case?" I asked Dr. Leakey.

"I can't disclose any more information. I've probably already said too much. There will be no debate about this, Doctor. Your importance to your country on a scale of 1 to 10 is a 20."

Hmm. Maybe this guy did have a spine. I thought he was more of a jellyfish. "Look, Urkel, I don't have time to travel to the deadly virus incubator you call your workplace. Nor do I want to lose any more blood to you vampires. You'll need to provide some more intelligence before I allow two weirdos in black suits to stalk me."

"Oh, Dr. Dakota, these guys won't be in black suits. They're undercover. They could be anyone: a client, your physician, your waiter, your boyfriend."

"Whoa, hold on there, pardner," I interrupted, trying to sound Old Western. "You mean I won't know who is responsible for securing my safety? I have to trust you?"

I should have had Dr. Leakey call Detective Wassinger to compare notes on what they had on the shootings. There I went again, manipulating contacts for personal gratification.

Dr. Leakey finished the conversation by saying, "I will arrange the best time for your visit. That's all."

Still not going.

Chapter 17

A meeting of the Belladonnas was long overdue. I'd experienced anxiety attacks nearly every day. They used to happen only about once a week. The fear of suffering a heart attack wore on me. Vet school gave me just enough about cardiology to make me a danger and a nuisance to my cardiologist, who was on speed dial. I'd talked him into giving me a Holter monitor many times, with no abnormalities ever found. But when it happened, it was real. The Belladonnas stabilized me. They were my ballast, though none of them wanted to be called that. We all knew we carried a little extra weight around our hips.

I gave Emily a call. She picked up right away. "Emily, whatcha doing tonight? Wanna get the ladies together for a session?"

Emily, Kit, Rhonda, and I met at our regular watering hole. As we entered Hickok's, I saw the familiar faces of clients, bar regulars, and guys from the shooting range. One of these guys shouted, "Well, if it isn't the pair-a-docs."

Emily and I laughed but kept moving forward. We settled into our usual back corner booth, farthest from the bar. We sat there for two reasons. First, we didn't want undercover or out-in-the-open barflies to overhear us, and second, one of us was a little hard of hearing. I wouldn't mention any names, but the hearing loss was probably due to too much time at the shooting range. We didn't dare call it a disability.

Rhonda would deck us.

As we tore into our hearty steak dinners, the presence of my best friends comforted my soul. God had blessed me with loyal co-conspirators with whom I could share secrets. Something like warmth welled up inside my body.

Red wine used to do that.

"I'm grateful you all showed up. I was in a bad place and needed to clear my mind for a few minutes."

"Hey, Doc, any time you're feelin' low, we're always available for a steak dinner. You're paying, aren't you?" Kit asked.

"Not a chance," I retorted. "This has always been Dutch treat. You already get free pet care," I reminded her.

The next morning, I arrived at the clinic refreshed. I remembered my daily devotions, which I'd missed for a few days. In my defense, my mornings had been unpredictable and chaotic. Today God led me to open the "Jesus Lives" devotional. God often tailored my need of the day to a particular reading. This one was written as if Jesus were talking directly to me: "I live in you… Don't worry about whether or not you are a fit home for Me. I am well accustomed to living in unfit houses."

Whew! Talk about unfit houses. Mine hadn't been cleaned in years.

Jesus continued, "I joyfully move into these humble homes and start renovating them." Several remodeling TV shows came to mind: "Fixer Upper," "Home Makeover: Extreme Edition," "Tiny Homes," and my favorite, "This Old House."

I needed a major overhaul.

I wanted to check on the autopsy and crime scene results from Brock's murder. Of course, that meant I'd have to go to the police station, which opened the possibility of seeing

Detective Wassinger. He'd been relatively silent lately. Maybe he was ghosting me. What was I saying? We had nothing to ghost, no friendship, no relationship at all. I jumped into my Land Rover and headed downtown.

At the station, I saw him getting into his detective car, no longer driving a cruiser. "Hey, Wassinger. Nice station wagon, er, minivan. Are you thinking of starting a family of little perps?"

"Funny, Doc. No, I'm using this vehicle because I may soon be a handler for a sniffer dog who needs air conditioning and space for his large carrier. I know a minivan is not as intimidating a ride as yours."

My Land Rover needed air conditioning. It went out ages ago, and the heater fan blew constantly. How was that fair? The sniffer dogs received better treatment than I did.

"Where are you headed?" I asked pathetically. "Do you need someone to ride shotgun?"

Detective Wassinger looked at me like he was considering how to get out of this, but instead answered, "Sure, hop in. I'm headed for the morgue."

Oh, goody. I loved the smell of formaldehyde.

I crawled into the van, pulling myself up by the overhead handle, which was never in the right spot for leverage for short people. Randy Newman's song "Short People" came to mind:

"*They got little baby legs*
And they stand so low
You got to pick 'em up
Just to say hello."

Not my favorite song.

There was an uncomfortable silence between us. Small talk was not my strong suit. I wasn't even sure if I had a strong suit.

"Did you get any information back on Brock's murder?" Like he was going to tell me.

"That's what I am tracking down today. You know how

the coroner is around here. A little slipshod at times," he commented.

I did know. The coroner, Dr. Decomp, owned a beagle named Indiana Bones. He called him Dr. Bones because "he had his Dogtorate."

The coroner was not funny. He was desperate—desperate for a cigarette, a drink, and recognition. He never brought Dr. Bones in for his appointments; his wife did, and they were always six months overdue. I was excited to see him in his morgue or mortuary or wherever the detective was taking me.

Unfortunately, the ride was not long. No place was far away in Hays. I sat up straight in my seat to dispel the appearance of a hunched-over old lady. One phenomenon that often occurs in women as they age is a tendency to lean forward from the waist, both when walking and sitting. It is not a good look. Head down, butt out. But how would *you* walk if you had two grapefruits attached to your upper chest, which increased in size as you gained weight?

This raised my irritation with the concept of BMI (Body Mass Index). Shouldn't the BMI people acknowledge the fact that large-chested women are carrying around five pounds more weight on their chest than someone prancing around with a perky B-cup?

Should we be punished for our DNA?

It was getting hot in this air-conditioned van, at least on my side. Detective Wassinger seemed unaffected, although I caught him side-eyeing me occasionally. He probably wondered why I was so anxious to go with him. Who wanted to go to a morgue? I did, especially with him. We pulled into the parking lot of the Peaceful Rest Funeral Home. I referred to it as the Dust-to-Dust Mortuary. Dr. Decomp was not a licensed clinical pathologist, but he was authorized to perform autopsies. I knew he hadn't attended many meetings on current forensic autopsy methods.

That was no problem, in this case. Brock had died from

wounds inflicted by a bullet.

Detective Wassinger came around to my side and opened the door for me. What the heck? Was this some morbid dating ritual? Usually, I jumped out of the car the moment the wheels quit rolling, but for some reason, I hesitated. “Thanks. I might have hurt myself pulling open my own door handle.”

In days past, I was a force to be reckoned with. When questioned about my tiny size, I’d been known to challenge a client or two to an arm-wrestling match. This, however, was different. I appreciated the gentlemanly gesture.

Was I slipping… slipping into a crush on a detective?

We took the elevator to the basement, where the autopsy suite was located. I braced for the sharp, sour smell of formaldehyde. In the veterinary school’s anatomy lab, we dissected animals embalmed in formaldehyde: cats, dogs, cows, and horses. The smell clung to us all day. I’d never forget it. The anatomy professor was drenched in formaldehyde daily for years. He still looked good, with no wrinkles up to the ripe old age of 93. Food for thought.

The detective did not have to introduce himself. He’d been here many times. The receptionist pointed to Dr. Decomp’s office. The room reeked of cigarette smoke and tacos.

“Hey, Doc and dick,” Decomp greeted us, referring to Detective Wassinger’s new promotion. “How’re you all doing? Taken any wooden nickels lately?”

I told you he wasn’t funny. Back in his day, telling someone not to take any wooden nickels was a way of warning country folk not to let con men dupe them in the big city.

“Nope, can’t say I have,” Detective Wassinger humored him. “We’re here to get some insight into Brock’s death. Can you tell me what you found?”

“The victim died as a result of a gunshot wound to the head. 9mm bullet. Dead for approximately 12 hours. Ruled a homicide. No way was it a suicide due to the location and penetration angle of the bullet. I understand there was no weapon found at the scene. Brock was an odd duck, but no one deserved to die like that. They say the good die young... which would explain why I'm still here at 75."

He let out a laugh that nearly caused him to cough up a lung. This, in turn, prompted him to light up another cigarette. You'd think someone who'd spent his career looking at the tar-filled lungs of deceased cancer patients would stop smoking. But addiction was addiction. No logic would quell the urge.

"Hey, Detective, isn't that the same caliber as the shell casings found at my clinic?"

I was quick like that.

"Yep," he replied.

"Brock and I had the same big game hunter after us, like being on a safari, only we were the prey, not the hunter."

I knew what a safari was.

Dr. Decomp asked, "Do you guys want to see the body?"

"Nope, I don't think that's necessary. Could you tell if the gun was fired at close range?" the Detective asked.

Before Dr. Decomp could answer, another coughing fit began. He pulled a flask out of his lab coat pocket and took a swig. "Cough medicine," he said with a wink. "Down the hatch."

The detective asked again, "Was he shot at close range?"

Dr. Decomp responded, "Based on the lack of visible gunshot residue around the entry point, it was probably more than three feet away."

"Thanks, Doc. We gotta run." We made our polite goodbyes and exited before he could cough up a loogie at us.

"Anywhere else you need to go?" Detective Wassinger asked.

Yes, to the back seat, I fantasized.

"No, I'd better get back to the clinic. Who knows what fascinating infestations or encrustations might have walked in?" I sighed.

He looked a little disappointed. Probably my imagination. I used to be an expert at pushing guys away just to reel them back in again. That was the old days. Now I was just mush.

As he dropped me off at my Land Rover, his parting words were, "Perhaps we can get together again and brainstorm what's happening."

Be still, my beating AFib.

"Yes, I'd like that," I answered meekly.

As I slipped in through the clinic's back door, the ever-present Harley met me. "Where have you been, Doc?"

"Just visited the coroner to check on his findings. What's waiting for me on the surgery schedule?"

"There's only one cat neuter this morning. I've taken care of a nail trim, an anal gland expression, and a grass awn between some toes."

Oh, no. I missed a grass awn. Often, clients were unaware that these sharp, bristle-like seed heads could work their way into an animal's paw and cause irritation.

I loved pulling out grass awns. It was like a magic trick. Usually, the dog came in limping. The owner was unsure whether it was arthritis or an injury. Upon close examination, I would see that swollen mound of pink flesh between the toes. I'd deaden the area and retrieve my alligator forceps, which resembled scissors but have grasping jaws at the very end. These babies can enter the tiny hole in the wound, allow me to fish about, and pull out that offending grass awn without an incision. This always impressed the owner and satisfied my need to succeed in front of a client—and a patient.

Chapter 18

Not all my patients were animals. I occasionally performed some borderline illegal procedures on the kids of friends or for someone who couldn't afford a "real doctor." I could have gone to prison or lost my license, but it wasn't brain surgery, and I never charged them. Occasionally, parents simply wanted to find out if their child's finger was fractured before spending money on an emergency room visit. I had an antiquated X-ray machine from a retired M.D.'s clinic. It still did the trick. Pets Buy planned to purchase a new, safer one that would not scatter radiation all over the holder. Yes, the holder. There's no way a cat would stretch out and hold its breath while I jumped behind the lead shield.

Just before lunch, my friend Cheryl, who ran a daycare a couple of houses away, raced in with a child cradled in her arms. Cheryl seemed nonplussed. The child, not so much. "Dr. Dakota! Dr. Dakota! Huey just stuffed a raisin up his nose, and it won't come out! I've tried everything. I attempted to grab it, but his nose was too small to get my fingers up there. I clapped him on the back, but that just made him mad. I blew pepper in his face to make him sneeze. He just held his breath. He's a stubborn kid."

In the kid's defense, a woman four times his size just

tried to pick his nose, smacked him, and seasoned him. What do you expect after reading those fairy tales to kids?

I made Harley leave the room. No witnesses in case something went south. We put little Huey up on my cold stainless-steel surgery table under the high beam of my operating light. No Fear Free technique for humans. Cheryl tried to hold him down, but he fought valiantly.

To him, it probably looked like he was being prepared for surgery with no anesthesia. I could see his point. Cheryl tried to soothe him. As for me, I had limited experience with kids. However, my experience with dogs led me to give him a hot dog to chew on while I evaluated the situation.

Yep, high up in his nasal passage was a swollen brown raisin. It filled the whole cavity because, by now, it had time to suck up snot from its surroundings. Again, I reached for my secret weapon in the war against foreign bodies: alligator forceps. That instrument had paid for itself many times over. I gently inserted it into the little nostril and pulled out a plum—I mean a raisin. As I proudly held up the prize in front of Huey's face and began to lecture him on the dangers of sticking objects up his nose, little Huey promptly reached up, snagged the raisin out of the forceps, and ate it. Cheryl thanked me profusely and dragged Huey back to the daycare.

As I headed across the hall to retrieve day-old pizza from the refrigerator, which also served as a holding place for lab specimens and vaccines, I noticed a guy peeking in the front window.

What was he looking at? We didn't close for lunch. He could waltz right in the door. Was he a rookie plainclothes detective keeping an eye on me? Was this another attempt on my life? In my panic, I screamed for Harley, who was busying herself with washing the lab dishes. She ran in dripping water, and only God knew what else from her gloved hands.

"What's wrong, Doc? Calm down. Don't panic. Talk to me." She knew my attacks better than I did.

"I saw a guy peeking in the front glass," I gasped, clutching my chest.

"Oh, Doc, just chill. That's the man who replaced your front window. He brought the bill by."

There was good reason to be paranoid, but really, the window repair guy?

I might be paranoid, but it wasn't a time to stand around and let circumstances play out as they would. I immediately called my friend and classmate, Mary, at CEZID. "Hey, Hazbrook! What are you doin' up there? Planning some new biological warfare games?"

"This must be Ruby. Ruby Anne Dakota. How have you been? We haven't seen each other since our last class reunion. What can I do for you?" she asked, sounding like the professional in charge of the fate of the world, which she was.

"Someone's trying to kill me, and I need answers," I demanded.

"Ruby, I can't divulge sensitive information, but I'll check on it," Mary promised. "I know they are making progress in identifying the deadly Ebola-like virus. Hopefully, a vaccine will become available soon. My apologies for your involvement in this. Your super-immunity makes you valuable to many people, some of whom are good and others not. The lab wanted to keep you here for months, but I convinced them otherwise. Perhaps that was a mistake. Ruby, do you remember your time in East Africa?"

"Is that why I might be immune to this new disease? I thought immunity came with the territory in veterinary medicine. We face zoonotic diseases almost daily."

"That's true, but could you fill me in on what you remember about your time there?" Mary asked again.

"I do remember my parents worked alongside Doctors

Without Borders. There was an Ebola outbreak on the Kenya-Uganda border, and my parents worked to contain the virus. We screened travelers to help stop the spread. I wasn't doing medical work—just running errands and keeping baboons out of the kitchen. Nevertheless, I worked alongside suspected cases in the quarantine tent. Some of our workers fell sick, but the disease passed me over, even as I hauled and disposed of hazardous waste. My parents escaped it too."

"Perhaps it's a case of a novel immunity stimulant combination between your workplace and your Ebola experience," Mary suggested. "Your antibodies could save millions, Ruby. That makes you extremely valuable. We're racing to develop a treatment before the wrong people take you out. Please watch your back."

I was uncharacteristically quiet on the phone as my brain processed Mary's words.

"Ruby, are you still there?"

Until that moment, this had seemed like a game, a random series of events that didn't cause too much alarm. The Belladonnas were right. This was serious—a game played out on the world's chessboard. I could either be the pawn sacrificed or the king who saved the world.

"Yes, I'm still here," I responded. "What can I do to help?"

"Stay alive. You're not immune to death."

Chapter 19

I called an emergency meeting of the professionals. The Belladonnas were on their game tonight, and now I was all in too. After I filled the group in on my conversation with Mary Hazbrook from CEZID, Rhonda jumped in, "Let's nail these suckers. This isn't just about Dakota and Brock anymore; it's global. The Belladonnas are up for it."

"Where do we start?" asked Kit.

Rhonda replied, "Where one starts in any other investigation. Get phone records, credit card usage, and financial documents. My training taught me to follow the money. It's almost always about the money. Let's make a new list of suspects in light of Mary HAZMAT's—or whatever her name is—information."

Emily remained silent. "What? No suggestions, Emily? Cat got your tongue?" I asked. "Hey, wanna know where this saying may have originated? They used to cut the tongues out of liars' mouths in ancient Egypt and then feed them to the royal cats."

"Oh, gross, Dakota." Emily finally spoke a word. For a medical doctor, she had an incredibly low tolerance for disgusting things.

"Back to a list of suspects. Who stands to benefit by knocking me off?" I tried to stimulate suggestions.

"How about a former disgruntled client?" Emily suggested. "I have a few that would enjoy putting a bullet in me."

"Oh, surely not you, gentle Emily," Rhonda teased.

Emily continued. "I think if you have super-immunity, there would be some shadowy players bent on releasing viral weapons of mass destruction, threatened by your powers. Your cells might be able to fight off a pandemic."

"Now we're clicking," I jumped in. "I know who I'd like to take down over this: Jake Morgan. It would solve a lot of my problems."

Rhonda shook her head. "Jake is not the problem in your life, Doc. He activates it. He makes your anxiety worse and feeds into your insecurities, but he is not at the root of your problems. He's just a tick on the ear of a coonhound sucking you dry. It would help if you fixed yourself first. Get a hobby. Get a boyfriend. Get a therapist." Rhonda always cut right to the chase—no mincing words with this woman.

"You may be right," I agreed. "I'd still like to put him behind bars. Or at least neuter him."

Kit, the pharmacist, chimed in with her idea. "I can see how a vaccine-immunotherapy company would want to harvest your cells. Perhaps they could develop immunotherapies administered directly to treat the disease. This would reduce the need for vaccines."

"Great suggestion, Kit, but how does that get me killed?"

Kit paused for a minute. Her wheels were turning. "Well, for one thing, a big vaccine company would be threatened by any other company involved in this research. The first company to develop it will likely make millions. If the company already has millions of dollars invested in vaccine production, your cells' unique ability to fight off disease could reduce the need for its product. Thus, you and others with this super-immunity need to die to ensure the vaccine company's particular vaccine is the chosen solution for this disease."

"Thanks, Kit. That's great out-of-the-box thinking. Let's figure out how Brock's murder plays into this pharmaceutical conspiracy? Could a little vaccine manufacturer in Hays, Kansas, have ties to a much bigger picture? Brock did have my cells. Was he on the verge of a breakthrough in immunotherapy? He did seem overjoyed at the chance to get his hands on my blood. I just thought it was Brock being his weird self. I'll follow up again with Detective Wassinger on the city's progress with Brock's murder," I volunteered.

That ensured I would get to see my detective again. Did I sound like a stalker?

I began to hand out assignments. "Rhonda, you hack into whatever databases you can, in order to get some of Brock's financial information. Kit, take a look at the cutting-edge research of Big Pharma vaccine companies. What viruses are they looking at for vaccine development and thus big bucks? Emily, get us some research on treatments for viruses rather than mass vaccination. Consider monoclonal antibodies derived from animal or human cell lines. That should be a good start. We'll meet here in a few days to discuss our results. Now pass me the horseradish sauce for my steak."

The next morning, I got a call from Harley. Chui, Lola, and I were still asleep, our steak dinners heavy in our stomachs. My takeaway bag was always a doggie bag. Lola didn't eat. That was how she managed to stay so trim.

"Good morning. You just interrupted my dream where I was kissing Hayes," I mumbled groggily.

"What did you say? You kissed Hayes?" Harley caught my musing.

"No, I said 'missing in Hays,' as in Hays, Kansas." I was good at covering. "What time is it? I must have forgotten to set my alarm."

"This is a red alert! Red alert!" Harley yelled into the phone. That was our code for Dr. Jake Morgan's unannounced arrival.

"Really. Didn't he darken our doorstep a week ago?" I was fully awake now, my heart pounding.

"Nope, I figure it's been two weeks to the day, and he's already on a rampage," said Harley. "He chewed London's backside for covering for you, reamed me a new one for using too many exam gloves, and criticized Gertrude's grooming ability. Of course, she smirked and refused to answer, making him even angrier. The jugular veins on his neck were as big as Tootsie Rolls!" That mental image burned into my psyche. Jake had no idea what pressure I was under from *actual* assailants. He was just a bully.

After I pulled on some fresh scrubs and ran a brush through my hair, I trudged to the front, bracing myself for the onslaught. Dr. Morgan greeted me, "Aw, Dr. Dakota. Good of you to get out of bed to meet me. You know, I always say, time is money."

Time *was* money for big box stores. I focused on his throbbing neck veins, trying not to laugh at Harley's earlier comparison to Tootsie Rolls.

"According to the books, even with London covering for you, you are not meeting the dollars spent per client quota. Not even close," he criticized. "You may think this is funny, old lady, but I assure you the higher-ups will not."

He didn't just say "old lady," did he? I felt anger pushing aside my anxiety.

"Who are you calling an old lady? Over the last few weeks, this old lady has evaded kidnappers, dodged bullets, and discovered dead bodies. This old lady's mission is to save the world from the next pandemic. What do you do in your spare time, buddy?"

Jake did a double take. "What did you say about saving the world from the next pandemic? What are you talking about? You're no virologist or epidemiologist. You're just a broken-down hack who couldn't make her clinic profitable."

His spray-tanned bronze face flushed into a bright maroon. I must have hit a nerve. His anger seemed excessive.

"Dr. Dakota, your only job is to make this clinic profitable," he snapped. "Not to chase medical conspiracies outside of this clinic."

"Okay, you're right. Let's back off," I caved.

What a wimp. I was not fond of confrontation, but if my looks could kill... Speaking of kill, where was Rhonda's bite dog, Rennie, when I needed him? I was sure Jake would, in Rennie's brain, qualify as a threat. I didn't want to reveal any more information about the ongoing investigation, so I headed for the lab.

Jake fired a parting shot. "By the way, we need to talk. You can no longer live in this clinic for free."

Harley grabbed my elbow and dragged me into the lab before we both did something we wouldn't regret. Harley whispered, "I swear that man has Dr. Dakota Derangement Syndrome," which made me smile.

London overheard the ruckus and raced back to distract Dr. Morgan by asking him questions about the clinic's taxes. They disappeared into the back office.

God bless London for her sacrifice.

Chapter 20

At four p.m., I finished my last appointment and headed to the police station on 12th Street. Anticipation welled up in my soul or in some other body part. The desk officer recognized me and sent me back to the Detective's office. I was sure they buzzed him with their version of a Red Alert. He shifted the files on his desk as I darkened his doorway. I caught a smirk on his face as he acknowledged my presence.

"Ah, if it's not Ruby 'Annie Get Your Gun' Dakota. You do have a gun, don't you?" he asked.

"Yes, I have a gun. Do you want to see my license?" I responded.

Wanna frisk me? Why am I not offended? What's happening here?

"Do you have a Concealed Carry permit?" he asked.

Why did this sound sexy to me?

"Of course I do. In Hays, everyone and their grandmother has a CCP. Why do you ask?"

"Just want to make sure you're taking every precaution."

Aw, he cared.

"Don't worry about me, Detective. I have Chui, my guard dog."

"What? That little wiry-haired squeaky toy trapped in a

rat's body? The only danger to an intruder would be death by laughter."

"If you're done making fun of my family member, I just stopped by to see what's new in your investigation."

"Sorry I made fun of your relative. A Mary Hazlett from CEZID contacted us. She was concerned about your welfare and asked for increased protection around you. I volunteered."

Be still, my heart. He just volunteered to spend more time around me.

"I'm good with that," I answered too quickly again. "I mean if you feel it's your duty. Those undercover government guys are a bit useless."

"What undercover guys? Dr. Hazlett did not mention any other security measures in place." He was surprised.

"The FBI suits stepped in at the bar because they noticed a shady character watching me. Of course, that would be half the customers. But it was my friends who whisked me out of there."

"What bar? What friends? When was this?" he rapidly fired with incredulity.

"Hickok's, the Belladonnas, on Saturday night. I didn't think the police needed to be involved," answering each question.

"So, what makes you think you have the final decision on who needs to be involved? You're tangled up in a murder investigation. You don't get to make *any* decisions. You'll be on my radar from now on out. We can't have anything happen to our little pet doctor."

Oh, he was so sweet.

"I guess I'll need to put up with you dogging my every move," I conceded.

Did I really say that?

He scribbled on the back of his business card. "Here's my personal cell number. You need to check in with me whenever you are out of the clinic, take any trips, meet with your Belladonnas, and so on."

"What are you, my parole officer?" I snapped back. "What's next? An ankle monitor?"

"All trips, whether planned or unplanned." His gaze was penetrating, leaving no room for misinterpretation. "Ruby, you need to take this seriously. They've already tried to take you out once." That got my attention.

Oh, he just called me Ruby again. "If you're going to be my shadow, could I just drop the Detective title?"

"You want to call me Wassinger?"

"I was thinking more like Hayes."

He paused as if he was weighing something he wasn't ready to say out loud. "Hayes works."

Thank you, Jesus, we're now on a first-name basis!

"I came down here to find out more about Brock's case, though," I reminded him. Have you released his body yet? I know the employees at S.I.C. want to do a funeral for him. He didn't have any living relatives."

"No, not yet. It seems the feds want to bring in their pathologist. Okay by me. Anything to help solve the case. We do know the caliber of the bullet did match the caliber of the bullets in your attack, and they both probably came from a 9mm Glock, a handgun."

He paused and looked intensely into my eyes. "Ruby, I feel like I'm navigating this investigation with only half the information. What are you not telling me?"

Was it time to tell him about my life in Africa? I wasn't even sure I understood the connection myself. Plus, I'd promised not to disclose that information. But how could he protect me if he didn't have all the details? I relented.

"Okay, it's like this. When I lived overseas with my parents, I underwent exposure to several deadly diseases. I have a super-immune system, which kept me from contracting any of those diseases. Several people who were there at the same time and survived were recently assassinated. I don't know whether it was unique to that part of the world or to our immune systems. CEZID is trying to unravel the mystery of my immunity and protect the world from a deadly virus outbreak."

Whew! It was a relief to tell him the truth. Or maybe it just felt good to share a huge secret with him, something we now had in common. I also wanted him to know that my hitman might still be determined to finish the job.

"Wow. That's a pretty far-fetched story, Doc. You sure about that?"

"I am, Hayes. I feel safe in your hands, though."

That sounded pathetic, something a flirty teenager might say.

"Well, I'll do my best, pretty lady," he responded.

Where were we, the Old West? Yep, that was precisely where we were. Why was my face burning? Fever? Rash? Love? "Flattery will get you everywhere, Detective Wassinger," I managed, hoping my voice sounded steadier than I felt.

"Hey, I thought we were on a first-name basis now," Hayes smiled.

I slipped out of the station and approached my Land Rover. The Land Rover company's slogan is "Above and Beyond." That was exactly where they placed the grab handle that I needed to pull me up and into the vehicle. It was above and beyond my reach. There was always a bit of truth in slogans.

As I drove home, Jake Morgan and his rent-or-evict ultimatum sent fresh anxiety crawling through my body. So much for my previous Hayes-induced endorphin release. Pets Buy should be thankful they had a vet on call for emergencies and someone on the premises to reduce the threat of break-ins. Perhaps the Belladonnas should have checked on our ego-driven Dr. Morgan. There was no way he was squeaky clean in his business dealings. I remembered how suspicious I was of him as his associate vet. Our locked inventory of Demerol continued to decline.

Jake recorded it as meds used to treat colic in horses. Valid therapy, except we only saw about two horses a month. I was willing to bet there were some skeletons in Jake's closet.

Rhonda should be able to access his financial records. She was good at that. I wanted to take a peek at his investments. Where was his money going?

As I pulled up to the clinic, my foot hit the brake, but my brain did not.

Chapter 21

There were some advantages to living in the same place where I worked. For instance, my gasoline bill was negligible, even in a Defender 90 Land Rover, which was known to be a gas hog. The newer models achieved significantly better mileage, but they came with hybrid engines.

No thanks. No hybrid plug-in for me. Those were for lightweights.

Another advantage, home and bed were only a short walk down the hall. On the way, I collected Chui. Sometimes, a nap was necessary before I retired for the evening. I never got enough sleep.

I always tried to do my daily devotional reading in the morning, but my morning that day had other plans. I pulled out my Oswald Chambers and read, "We have no right to judge where we should be put, or to have preconceived notions as to what God is fitting us for. God engineers everything; wherever He puts us, our one great aim is to pour out a whole-hearted devotion to Him in that particular work. Whatever your hand finds to do, do it with all your might."

That settled it. I'll do it with all my might. This guy would face punishment for his attempt on my life and for taking Brock's. I was the only common thread here. It was my responsibility to ensure justice. My parents would have wanted me to do this. And now it looked like the Lord was on my side, too. Chui looked at me as if I were mad as a hatter.

Perhaps I was, but I slept better than I'd slept in weeks.

I plowed through the next morning's surgeries, mostly spays and neuters. As I headed for the front, Harley waylaid me. "Doc, it's an easy schedule this afternoon: new kitten exams and vaccinations." It was a relief that no challenging cases requiring research and drawn-out treatments were on the schedule. There was too much on my mind at the moment.

In veterinary school, our professors informed us that the most valuable lesson was not to memorize the information but rather to know where to look it up. We couldn't keep everything in our heads, even though they tested us on what we could memorize. There was no internet. It was tougher back then.

Clients were savvy. By the time I saw them at the clinic, many had already researched online and compiled a list of possible causes of their pet's distress. This always caused me feelings of inadequacy coupled with anxiety, especially when they wanted to discuss a disease that I would have never considered in my list of initial diagnoses. Here was where I questioned myself, which triggered my Imposter Syndrome.

Imposter Syndrome affects medical doctors and veterinarians alike. In practice, we often focus more on our failures than on our successes. It was easy for me to downplay all the accurate diagnoses, lives saved, and pets returned to their homes healthy again after treatment. Instead, the reel in my mind replayed the times the outcomes were not ideal. Clients who were "internet experts" contributed to this feeling. The battle between the mask I wore to convince others of my worthiness and my inner voice, which insisted I didn't measure up, was exhausting.

Medical doctors, in general, face the high expectations society places on them. Add to this their tendency to have low self-compassion. A study published in the *Journal of the American College of Surgeons* found that 90 percent of female surgeons and more than two-thirds of male surgeons experience Impostor Syndrome. Burnout, depression, and anxiety often accompany this syndrome.

Bingo. My point exactly. My life exactly.

I wished people had a little more compassion for their M.D. and their vet. We all struggled. I constantly reminded myself that I had four years of college, four years of veterinary school, and decades of experience.

As I entered the exam room, I came face to face with a cream-colored, matted, and mad Persian cat, the infamous Miss Pringle. She was not happy to see me. We'd met before, and it didn't go well. In human medicine, patients understood that doctors had their best interests at heart. However, Miss Pringle perceived me as the enemy. All this ball of fur understood was that this vet smelled like alcohol (the rubbing kind, not the drinking kind), blood, disinfectant, and an assortment of previous surgical patients who might pose a threat to her.

Mrs. Meier put her pride and joy on the cold table. Harley finally came in to assist. I swore Harley hid out in the back when she saw trouble coming. I tried to look at the situation through Miss Pringle's large, beautiful eyes as I fondled her abdomen, pulled her ears, pried open her mouth, and stuck a lubricated thermometer where no man had gone before. No wonder animal patients often turned on their vet.

When I came at her with a one-inch needle, it would be like a medical doctor coming at his patient with a foot-long needle, based on an average cat weight of 10 pounds versus an average human weight of 140 pounds.

Terrifying.

To make matters worse, her fur clung to her skin in mats. I didn't know where the fur stopped, and the muscle began. As I injected, a stream of vaccine poured down Miss Pringle's side and onto the table. I'd misjudged the thickness of that mat. This explained why she didn't flinch.

How embarrassing.

I had discussed the necessity of daily grooming with this owner numerous times. I gave Mrs. Meier the option of sedation—for the pet, not the owner—to shave off that two-pound furball that Miss Pringle carried around on her body. "Oh no, Doc, she must keep her lovely coat! I might enter her in the cat show next month. If you shave her down, her fur might not grow back."

Oh, brother. I'd seen all kinds of things growing under those mats. I drew up another injection and hoped this one would hit the target.

Up next, a black Lab scheduled for vaccinations. However, this owner was an "Oh, by the way, since I'm here, Noodle has a bump on her chest that I'd like you to look at" person—an opportunist. This saved him an exam fee and delayed my scheduled appointments. I ran my fingers over the bump and noticed a tiny hole in the middle. As I looked closely, I saw movement inside that lump.

I was ecstatic.

This was one of my favorite diagnoses. I asked for more history. "Has Noodle been drinking out of a pond lately?"

"Yes, Noodle always swims in our farm pond."

I pulled out my trusty alligator forceps and a pencil and carefully explored the opening. When a worm peeked out, I grabbed it with my forceps.

"What's the pencil for, Doc?"

"You'll see." I pulled the thin worm out of the hole, wrapped it gently around the pencil, and began to wind. The worm kept coming. When it was all over, there was about a foot of Dracunculus worm around that pencil. The owner was both dumbfounded and disgusted.

I loved it. Talk about job satisfaction.

Chapter 22

As the day wound down, London buzzed me on the intercom. "Dr. Dakota, you have a call on line one, unknown caller."

I answered, "Incontinence hotline. Please hold," trying to control my laughter.

Unknown callers usually meant scams. This response was funny to me because of my own urinary urge incontinence. I actually might have wet myself a little.

"Just playing with ya. Who's calling, and how may I help?"

An eerie voice came over the line. "You don't know what you are meddling with. You are in way over your head. There are forces at work that would be happy to see you dead."

No kidding.

The voice continued, "You and your over-the-hill spinsters need to back off, or something could happen to one of your loved ones."

Click. The call disconnected.

Seriously? Who used the word 'spinster' anymore? Was that what we were? This jerk should have known he couldn't use my loved ones as leverage.

I didn't have any.

"Harleeeey!" I yelled. "Come up front immediately!"

Harley slid into the lab as if she were on a skateboard.

"What do you need, Doc?"

"I just got a threatening phone call, and I'm headed for a panic attack."

"Calm down, Doc. I get creepy phone calls all the time. You haven't been on a dating site recently, have you?"

"NO, I haven't been on a dating site. Someone just threatened my life!"

Harley ignored me. "Sometimes I get calls from guys who want to strangle me, but I think that's something different. What did this guy say?"

"He said I should back off, or something might happen to my loved ones."

Harley went into a fit of laughter. "He doesn't know you very well, does he?"

"Okay, Harley. I'm not kidding. This is serious."

Really? Should I have been happy that I didn't have any loved ones to threaten? Now it sounded rather sad.

"Should I call someone? Report it to the police? Have the call traced?" I rapid-fired the questions at Harley.

"Doc, you never can trace these guys. They bury their identity through proxy servers and funnel communications across countries."

She sounded like she had tried this before, which was a bit concerning.

"I'm going to call Hayes. He'll know what to do."

Harley got that quirky smirk whenever she sensed I had ulterior motives.

"Harley. Please stop it. I'm terrified."

"Sure, Doc. You do you. It's six p.m., and I've got plans. I'm leaving for the day." She slid back down the hall.

Really? Was Harley that unconcerned about my welfare and her job security? I didn't understand this generation. Why didn't they suffer from anxiety over their future as we did at their age? I dialed the number on the back of Hayes' card. He picked up after only two rings.

"Hey, Dr. Dakota. Are you okay? Do you need help, or are you just checking in?" At least *he* was concerned about my welfare.

"Hey, Hayes. I just had a threatening phone call and wasn't sure what to do. Do I call AT&T, the FBI, or you? I'm a little shaken up."

Boy, was that an understatement.

"Did a name come up on the caller ID? What did they say?" Hayes asked.

"No name, just 'unknown caller.' He told me there were forces at work that would be happy to see me dead, and that the Belladonnas and I should stay out of it. Then he threatened my loved ones."

"That's not good. Do your loved ones live around here?" Hayes asked.

"No, they don't."

It was too painful to explain. The truth was that my parents were both killed overseas in a carjacking incident, making me an orphan in a matter of minutes. Everyone said I was blessed not to have been in the car with them. Not sure about that assessment.

"What do we do? Can you trace the number?" I pressed on.

"Perhaps. I'll check with my supervisor to see if we can get permission to access phone records. It still may not shed any light on the caller. Do you want me to come over after work? I get off at six-thirty," Hayes offered.

"I'd feel better with some company at the clinic tonight," I said, much too quickly… again. Especially if it meant spending time with Hayes. "Perhaps I could get some sleep."

Oh, that sounded far too much like an overnight invitation. I rephrased it. "You could calm my nerves so I can sleep after you leave."

Hayes hesitated a beat and then answered, “I’ll be there. Should I bring dinner?”

Dinner? Dinner? I should cook for him. I didn’t cook. I didn’t even have a stove. “That would be great. I eat anything,” Did that sound weird?

“I mean, I love all kinds of food. You choose.”

Chapter 23

It was already six p.m. Only thirty minutes remained to shower and tidy up my room. After checking for foreign material, like turds, I jumped into the grooming tub and took a five-minute shower. Then back to my room, where I put on a clean pair of scrubs and flip-flops. Should have thought ahead to get my annual pedicure. Since makeup wasn't part of my routine, that wasn't a problem. Maybe it should have been, but I wouldn't know where to start. In my opinion, applying makeup to old skin was like spackling over cracked plaster. A touch of blush and lip gloss will have to do.

Fait accompli.

Tidying up only emphasized the sadness of my one-room home: a double bed with no headboard, a recliner that no longer reclined, a 24-inch TV, and two TV trays doubling as nightstands. Guests weren't exactly lining up. I tossed my soiled scrubs into the hamper—tomorrow's problem.

Where would we eat? The surgery table was probably not an option. Ah, the TV trays would work. I cleared off my alarm clock and old used Kleenexes, put a bottle of Tylenol PM back in its box, and wiped the trays with an antibacterial hand wipe. I hoped the disinfectant smell didn't interfere with his appetite.

What was I saying? In this clinic, a disinfectant smell would be an improvement.

Hayes knocked timidly. I checked my appearance in the full-length mirror, decided the look was as good as it would get, and rushed to the back door. Hayes was out of his detective clothes. I'd never seen him like this. I had expected him to show up with a gun on his belt. His hair had recently been cut and styled, unlike mine, which was weirdly wavy in an old motion picture star sort of way. I refused to have a hairstyle that required more than minimal attention. When I emerged from the shower, my hair only got a quick scrunch with a towel. That was all the styling it would get.

He was wearing Armani again, and I was wearing eau de flea shampoo. What could he possibly see in me? Or did he always show up for protective duty looking like this? We shook hands as if this were a business transaction.

Oh, Lord, help me.

I took the bags of food he was carrying and ushered him to my room.

"I didn't believe you lived in your clinic when you gave us your home address at the station. You're a bit of a minimalist, aren't you?"

That was an understatement. A minimalist could have thrown out half his possessions and still own more than I did. "I like to travel light," I answered.

When was the last time I travelled anywhere?

"What did you bring for dinner? I'm starved."

Actually, I was well fed. Just making small talk. The takeout bag he held came from the only Chinese restaurant in town. Why was there always one Chinese restaurant in every small town in Kansas? Did the Chinese government look at a map of the U.S. and decide Hays would be a profitable location? It wasn't like we had many Chinese residents. I wasn't complaining. I loved Chinese food…

and Italian… and German… and Indian, the East kind, not the plains kind… and Ethiopian.

"Doc, I hope you like Chinese. I brought chopsticks and paper plates."

Maybe he thought I didn't have silverware. I didn't—only disposables from takeout. It never occurred to me that we'd need something to eat with or on.

"There's sweet and sour chicken, cashew chicken, and Mongolian beef. Hope you're not a vegetarian, Doc?"

I was in love. All my favorites. "Good choices, Hayes, but could you drop the 'Doc' and just call me Ruby? Only you and a chiweenie are allowed to do that."

"Okay, Miss Ruby. Let's eat."

Eating like a lady wasn't possible. For one thing, I wasn't adept at clicking those two wooden tongue depressors together. Second, hunger had taken over. My habit of wolfing down food like someone on their way to an emergency was hard to break, because often that's precisely what was happening. You never knew when the phone would ring or a tragedy would hit your front door.

Dainty, I was not.

"Whoa, Ruby, where's the fire? We have all evening to put this food away."

My face reddened. My pace slowed, but now it felt like I was eating in slow motion. He must have thought I was some hick from the sticks. Wrong assumption. I'd traveled all over the world and dined with kings, or at least presidents; both my parents were M.D.s, and I was fluent in a couple of languages. It wasn't like I grew up in Cowtown, USA. Hays wasn't even a cowtown.

That would be Dodge City. Kansas.

After we finished off the food, I asked Hayes, "Would you like to watch a movie or discuss the case?" He looked like he was waffling between the choices.

"A movie would be nice," he said.

Yay, the hunky man won over the detective man. That,

or he just didn't want me to know too much about the shooting. How would we ever agree on a movie choice?

"What about a good western?" he asked, solving the problem. "I brought *Butch Cassidy and the Sundance Kid*."

This guy didn't get out much either. He pulled a DVD out of his bag… obviously a premeditated move.

Bless his heart.

I did have a DVD player. I might even have a VCR crammed in behind the toilet, next to my dignity. Now, where would we sit? I offered him the recliner while I took the bed. I preferred to watch it side by side, but it was too soon.

We both sat there in silence, staring at the screen. I assumed he was as uncomfortable in this dining room/bedroom/movie theater as I was. My mind wasn't on the movie. It kept wandering down fantasy trails. What if he…? What if I…?

Stop it, Ruby. You are just a victim of a shooting to him. Not a femme fatale.

"Ruby, would you mind if I sat beside you on the bed? This non-reclining recliner is killing my back."

Yikes. Did he just ask that? If my answer was yes, was I too easy? What was *easy* these days? Were we so old that we no longer had time to play games? No way of knowing. I decided not to answer. He hoisted himself out of the chair as I scooched over to one side to give him room. That was my answer. He was careful to stay on his side of the bed. It reminded me of the old sitcoms where the director required the actors to always keep one foot on the floor in bedroom scenes. One foot on the floor wouldn't slow anyone down in the Netflix romantic scenes of today.

Hayes wore a cross necklace, not that I stared at his chest. That was a plus. His Armani was drifting my way. Do cologne manufacturers add pheromones to their recipes? That would explain the sensuality, the animal instinct boiling in me. My pheromones were in high production mode. I tried to remain as still as possible in this endocrine overdrive. He seemed comfortable just watching the movie. When Butch and Sundance went out in a blaze of glory, Hayes slowly got up off the bed. As he rose, he looked over his shoulder and winked at me.

I thought I was going to pass out! Was he playing with me?

"I'd better call it a night. Are you going to be OK here alone?"

I wanted to say, "No, please stay," but my mouth, apparently operating without my consent, said, "I enjoyed the evening. The phone call rattled me, but I'm much better now."

He gathered up the empty food containers, ejected his DVD, grabbed his bag, and headed for the door. I jumped up to see him out. Chui was yapping in the kennel. He hated to be left out of anything.

"Thanks for the food and the movie," I offered.

"Thanks for the companionship," he replied.

Companionship? That sounded better than, 'Thanks for the victim watch.'

"Next time, maybe we could meet at my place," he said as he headed out.

My breathing was amped up, but not from anxiety.

"I would enjoy that," I answered, as I gently shut the door, lingering a minute in the Hayes-induced endorphin release.

It had been too long.

Chui continued with his protests. I rescued him and Lola from their kennel apartment. All three of us would sleep well tonight, but then Lola always slept well.

Chapter 24

Saturday morning at the clinic was blessedly uneventful. After closing at noon, Chui and I drove to Frontier Historical Park to watch the bison and walk the swinging bridge trail. We both needed the fresh air and time to think. My brain, predictably, had other plans and spent the entire walk replaying every moment of the previous evening with Hayes. On the way home, I grabbed takeout from the Taco Shop for Chui and me. We both fell asleep watching Turner and Hootch, Chui's favorite.

Sunday morning, I dragged myself out of bed early, helped Harley with kennel duties, and headed to church smelling faintly of cat urine. I hit the women's restroom before entering the chapel. You could always tell a veterinarian in a public washroom. They're the ones who wash their hands *before* using the toilet.

Sometimes, clinic emergencies interfered with my church attendance. I could watch online, but that was no substitute. Being present mattered. God knew attending would improve my week, especially after a difficult one.

My mind wasn't really on the service. As I got into my Land Rover, I realized we had several loose ends. The Belladonnas had been actively researching, but we needed to compare notes. Perhaps Emily would offer her house for our meeting. I picked up my cell phone and called. "Hey, Emily. Have you found out anything about immunotherapy?"

"Yes, I was just about to call you. We all have a lot to mull over," Emily replied.

"Would you mind hosting us tonight? I asked. I don't need to eat another big steak dinner."

"Sure, let's all get together at my place at seven," Emily responded.

"Sounds good to me."

We gathered at Emily's sprawling white brick ranch on Thunderbird Drive. Her home never failed to impress. She'd worked hard for what she had. People often accuse doctors of making too much money, but they earn every penny through years of education, countless nights spent on call, and the emotional toll of life-or-death decisions.

Emily was a classy lady and an elegant host. She led us into her sitting room, where a small table was set with a fine china teapot and cups, a matching sugar bowl and creamer. The silver tray held an assortment of what the British call biscuits, but what we Americans call cookies.

"Wow, Emily, you went all out for our meeting!" Rhonda commented. "This beats Hickok's. No noise, no drunks. Better give me a mug. Those teacups look breakable."

Kit rearranged things on the table to suit her OCD. Emily poured tea for each of us. I took mine with milk and sugar, a holdover from my time in East Africa. I chose two Pepperidge Farm® Milano® cookies and two Sausalitos®, a fancy chocolate chunk cookie with macadamia nuts. I sank into the cushions of her sectional cloud couch, taking care not to spill my tea. I loved Emily's house. We all loved Emily's house.

"I don't know about you all, but I feel we need some extra help," I suggested. "Let's pray." We all bowed our heads, and I forged ahead.

"Dear Heavenly Father, we come before you tonight

knowing that we have no business hunting down killers. However, we keep finding ourselves in the middle of things. We need Your help figuring out who shot at me, who killed Brock, and why. We ask for Your protection and guidance as we dig into this mess. Lord, please help us solve this without any of us ending up in the emergency room. In Jesus' name we pray. Amen."

Emily, Kit, and Rhonda echoed in unison, "Amen."

"Ok, let's get this brainstorm going. Who wants to start?" I queried.

"Me. Pick me!" Rhonda hammed it up.

"Okay, Rhonda, what do you have?" I asked.

"I've been looking into Brock's financials. His profits have been marginal. S.I.C. recently purchased expensive equipment to produce something called monoclonal antibodies, but the money trail gets lost there. I couldn't find where he got the money for the equipment. Here's where it gets interesting, though. It seems his will left everything to Dr. Jake Morgan."

This group had seen plenty of shocking things in their careers, but this new information left us in complete silence.

Kit recovered first. "What's that all about? It makes no sense. He and Dr. Morgan were never friends."

"No, not friends, but Brock wanted his father's business to continue after he was gone. With no living heirs or family, perhaps he chose Jake, a savvy businessman he could count on to continue the work," Rhonda speculated.

"Maybe a savvy businessman, but a horrible human," I chipped in. "That puts Jake right up there at the top of the suspect list, assuming he knew about the inheritance. Did you find anything shady in Dr. Morgan's financial dealings?"

"Shady dealings, no, but interesting," Rhonda said. "Dr. Morgan invested heavily in Immunovax, a company that produces both animal and human vaccines."

"I'm familiar with Immunovax," I said. "I've purchased their vaccines before."

Rhonda continued. "Dr. Morgan has been a part-time pharmaceutical rep for Immunovax for years and receives stock as a perk. Over the past year, though, he purchased a large additional volume of stock, making him one of the company's top shareholders. I think Kit has some information on what this company is researching."

"Immunovax is heavily involved in vaccine production on the human side," Kit jumped in. "Of course, they make several vaccines for dogs and cats, but the human side is much more profitable. They can gear up vaccine production quickly in the face of a new disease. According to the research, they already appear to be developing a vaccine against a new disease. It's all very hush-hush, but I have my sources."

"Get this," Emily was anxious to add. "Brock's vaccine company was on the verge of discovering a way to harvest and then clone antibodies or use DNA sequencing to produce a treatment instead of a vaccine for viral diseases. It is very cutting-edge research that has far-reaching implications, not only for viral diseases but also for cancers."

"So that's why Brock was so anxious to get his hands on my blood. It's chock-full of antibodies. Animal viruses rarely infect humans directly; however, I've encountered many animal diseases throughout my life. It could be a gold mine for him."

"Imagine, a little vaccine company in Hays, Kansas, might be on track to save the world. But why would Jake knock off Brock before he finished the monoclonal antibody research?" Rhonda asked. "Wouldn't he make more money if he waited until the rollout? It might never come into being without Brock at the company's helm."

Rhonda was always thinking about the money.

"Good point. If he's working for Pets Buy and heavily

invested in Immunovax, would Jake even have time or expertise to oversee the development of such a complex project for S.I.C.?" I asked.

Emily expanded on her research into immunoglobulins, but most of our eyes glazed over. Too complex. Too much information. She finished by asking, "Dakota, it might help if you tell us the whole story about your time in Africa. You've never shared that with us, and we're your closest friends. We deserve to know what caused you to be in this predicament."

I really needed to share these details with my close friends. "You're right, Emily. An explanation is in order. After all, I might be putting you in danger just like Brock. I remember my time in Kenya and Uganda well, too well. My parents had great faith in God and prayed together daily. They believed they were "called by God" to minister to people overseas, and so was their daughter."

But was I ready to relive the trauma and pour out my heart to these friends?

I took a deep breath and continued, "Both my parents were physicians, and as such, they were invaluable resources to their team. I was one of those children whose parents yanked them out of their birth country and transported them onto foreign soil to improve the lives of people living in war-torn or poverty-stricken developing countries. We often became more fluent in the local language than our parents or diplomats, and at times, officials pressed us into service to translate sensitive conversations. We had a deep understanding of what was happening on the ground because we'd lived among and loved the local people."

I paused to take a drink of my tea. I had the Belladonnas' full attention.

"My parents were working on the border of Kenya and Uganda to help stop the spread of Ebola. I worked alongside them as their runner. This history and its overwhelming exposure to death at a young age left me with some mild PTSD, which manifests as panic attacks. Evidently, it has also left my immune system with elevated levels of killer antibodies. That's why I'm such a hot item right now."

"Oh, Ruby, you should have told us!" Emily reverted to using my first name. "It helps us understand why you are the way you are."

"Yeah, we just thought you were weird on your own, not because of some trauma in your youth." Again, Rhonda was brutally honest, speaking without a filter.

"Oh, this is all starting to make sense," Kit chimed in. "The pieces of the puzzle are falling into place." I knew missing jigsaw pieces in a puzzle drove Kit crazy. "I am so sorry, Ruby."

"Hey, all of a sudden, I'm Ruby to you guys now? Don't feel sorry for me. I've had an amazing life, met incredible people, and traveled to the most exotic places. If I must suffer a little anxiety, I still say it was all worth it. Dodging bullets wasn't exactly in the job description, though. Unexpected downside."

"Ruby, can you tell us how your parents died, or is that too personal?" Emily asked gently. She always tried to psychoanalyze me. I knew she meant well, but did I want to go down this road that would wash out in tears?

Nope. Not doing it.

"Someday, maybe we can discuss my parents, but I'd rather keep on task for now. Let's list the suspects again."

The women started chatting. "Do we have two different suspects? One for your shooting and one for Brock's?" Kit asked.

Rhonda put her two bits in. "The way I see it, the prime suspect is Dr. Morgan for both. First, he's a maniac. Second, he has financial reasons."

Emily disagreed. "My money is on the vaccine company already investing millions of dollars in a new vaccine. They stand to lose the most from Ruby's antibodies and Brock's breakthrough on the immunity horizon. They could have hired a hitman to take you out."

"I'm with Emily on this," Kit agreed.

Rhonda chimed in. "Dr. Morgan could have hired the hitman."

"I'm still mulling over the vet client who might go postal on me. There is no reason to believe these incidents are related. We could have two different criminals here. I think we should all go to Brock's funeral to see who shows up," I suggested.

"Not me. I do not do funerals," Emily protested. "It brings back memories of the many beloved patients who died while under my care. Funerals are gut-wrenching and not just for me alone. Many doctors refuse to attend funerals."

"I'll be there. Brock and I had a good business relationship. He often ordered medications used in his work from my pharmacy. He was a good customer. Always paid on time," Kit said.

We were all waiting for Rhonda to chip in. Her chin rested on her folded hands. "Brock rarely contacted the police department until recently, when there were a couple of disgruntled employee threats. Normally, he was laid-back, but lately, the only thing that mattered was completing the current research, even if it meant working 24-hour shifts. That didn't always sit well with employees. He received a few threats from people who thought they deserved a life outside of work. I agree, we should check out the attendees at the funeral. The murderer may show up to pay his respects."

"Respects? He murdered him, for God's sake!" Emily uncharacteristically raised her voice. "And what do you think he'll look like, a European guy with a mustache in a black trench coat?"

"Just sayin'. The perp often shows up to see the grief he

caused and to allay suspicion," Rhonda defended herself.

I added my two cents' worth. "Rhonda is right. There are several reasons to attend. As for me, I want to go out of respect for Brock. Sure, he was annoying, but he was also brilliant. He wasn't as ambitious as his dad, but he wanted to help people. It wasn't all about the money. There might only be a few attendees since he had no family."

Who would make the arrangements for *my* funeral? I was there for my parents, even though I was young. My eyes watered, and my nose dripped. I quickly changed the subject.

"Okay, who's up for more cookies?"

Chapter 25

The next morning started with the less glamorous side of veterinary medicine. I extracted a few teeth from a foul-mouthed poodle, then discovered maggots living under a matted fur clump on a sheepdog's head. Flies had set up housekeeping while the dog went months without grooming. With those appetizing procedures behind me, I told London I was taking an extended lunch break.

I stopped by Arby's for mozzarella cheese sticks and a Diet Dr Pepper. What was the point of drinking a zero-calorie soda when consuming almost 700 calories of fried cheese? I had saved 150 calories. That was the point.

Lunch was just an excuse to get out of the clinic. What I really wanted to do was check out Brock's office for any leads on the murder. It might still be a locked-down crime scene, but I had to try.

My Land Rover rolled to a halt in the parking lot. A Tesla truck filled Brock's reserved parking space, with a vanity plate beaming: "Viral Vet."

Jake's car. What was he doing here?

I leaned forward as my stomach began to cramp. Did I want to subject myself to his toxic tirade? I thought of Brock—kind, talented Brock who deserved justice.

Yes. I would do it for him.

The back door was locked. The security camera picked up my image, and the secretary, Lottie, buzzed me in.

"Good morning, Dr. Dakota. What may I do for you today?" Lottie's familiar, soothing voice put me at ease.

"My condolences on your loss," I said softly. "He was one of the good guys. I'm here to take a quick look at his office if the crime scene tape is down."

"It sure is, Doc. They took it off this morning. But you'll have some company in there. Dr. Morgan beat you to it. The office is still a mess. We haven't had the cleanup crew in yet."

"That's okay. Messes don't bother me. I don't know what I'm looking for. Just want to help catch whoever murdered him."

"We all do. You go for it, Doc. If there's anything we can do to help, just ask."

She seemed a bit too cheery for someone who might soon lose her job. I trudged down the hall as if going to an execution. No point in delaying the inevitable confrontation with Jake.

Or maybe there was. Instead, I wandered down the research lab wing.

The first open door revealed a college-age woman hunched over a microscope. She looked up, seeming happy for the interruption.

"Good afternoon, Doc," she said.

Did I know her? I'd visited this building many times, usually after hours to see Brock.

"Doc, it's me, Kendall. I'm Titer's mom."

Now I remembered—not her, but the cat. Titer was a male Bengal with leopard-like spots. I'd once joked he'd be a great companion for Chui, my own little leopard, except Chui despised cats. Lola didn't mind them, though.

"Oh, Kendall! How's Titer's tender tummy doing?"

Bengals were notorious for chewing on things they

shouldn't, especially houseplants.

"He's doing great since I replaced my plants with artificial ones. What may I help you with?" Kendall offered.

"I'm here to inquire about Brock's death," I said, trying to sound official. "I know employees weren't here that night, but perhaps you might have noticed someone or something unusual in the days before the murder."

"Nope. Both the police and the FBI asked the same thing. I've racked my brain, but nothing stands out. I spend ten to fifteen hours a day in this windowless lab. There's so much to do with the new research."

"That doesn't sound like much of a life for a beautiful young lady," I said.

It didn't sound like much of a life for an old lady, either.

"Tell me about the new research, Kendall. What's in development?"

Her expression locked down. "Sorry, Doc. I can't divulge research data. We're all sworn to secrecy about this project. Brock threatened to take our firstborn child if we talked." She gave a weak laugh. "I don't have kids, except for Titer, and they can have that expensive, dyspeptic cat. Why are you investigating anyway? If you want information, contact the police."

"Okay, sorry to bother you, Kendall. And sorry for your loss."

She was a cold fish. I supposed researchers were a different breed, but she didn't even like her own cat.

I continued down the hall. My heart rate picked up with each step—not from exertion, but from anticipation. It would be interesting to find out why Jake was here, not that he'd tell me the truth. He was a liar.

He'd always been a liar.

At least Brock's name was still on the door. The door stood open, but Brock would never walk through it again.

I peered inside and saw Jake's hulking frame rifling

through Brock's desk. The sight made my blood boil.

It felt like sacrilege.

"Dr. Morgan, I'm surprised to see you here," I said with false cheeriness.

Impeccably groomed as always… a light blue knit shirt complemented his eyes and featured the prominent polo player logo. His haircut was fresh, not a single stray hair on his neck. His once-athletic physique had shifted under the pull of gravity and excessive pizza consumption, but he still had a formidable presence. His cologne hit me like a wave, made me queasy, and brought back memories of past interactions from when I was a new graduate employed at his clinic.

A new wave of anxiety washed over me. I fought to keep my expression calm and steady. My hands trembled as I forced myself to breathe slowly, determined not to let Jake see any hint of weakness.

"Dr. Dakota." He flashed a predatory grin that never reached his cold eyes. "Are things slow at the clinic, or are you still gearing up for a new job as a private detective? I thought we talked about this."

I smiled back stiffly, thinking of all the unpredictable animals I'd encountered over the years, the ones you could never quite trust. There was no humor in his expression. He assumed he was talking to an idiot.

Maybe he was.

"No, Dr. Morgan, just looking around for a cold-blooded killer. Know any?"

The forced grin melted from his face.

"Dr. Dakota, you need to focus on your clinic job. You are treading on thin ice as it is."

I wanted to scream at him, tell him how much I hated him for belittling me in front of clients, for stealing my self-confidence, confidence that had never returned despite my years in practice. But I held it in.

"Dr. Morgan, I am here to review Brock's office

paperwork for any clues related to his murder. Do you have any thoughts?" I kept my voice neutral, hoping he'd let something slip.

"Why would I? I barely even knew the guy."

I made no mention of what Rhonda had told me about Brock's will. Let him hang himself with his own lies.

"Brock Benton was a squirrelly little nerd who had no idea how to run a profitable business. If I were at the helm, this company would make millions," Jake bragged.

"Not without his brains and creativity, you wouldn't," I shot back, surprising myself with my boldness. "He was a genius. Maybe he was slightly on the spectrum. What genius isn't? But he cared about people. That's something you know nothing about."

Those jugular veins in Jake's neck popped out again. I kept the Tootsie Roll visual at the forefront of my mind and breathed deeply.

"What do you know about running a business?" Jake scoffed. "You managed to fail at something this pathetic two-bit town needs, a small animal clinic. That takes talent."

"Maybe I can't run a profitable business," I said, my voice rising, "but you're the worst boss I've ever known. You lead by intimidation, fueled by your feelings of inadequacy. Plus, you're just a jerk. And Hays is not a pathetic, two-bit town!"

The words hung in the air.

Oh, that wasn't helpful. I was definitely fired now.

Jake jumped out of his chair. As he rushed toward me, I regretted baiting him. His eyes bulged like a pug's. I threw my arms over my head as he towered over me. Was he going to hit me, strangle me, or chest-bump me?

Probably not that.

He sputtered, "You aging, overweight Oompa Loompa."

Oh, that was hurtful. I remembered Sandra Bullock's self-defense advice from "Miss Congeniality": S.I.N.G. Hit them in the **S**olar plexus, **I**nstep, **N**ose, and **G**roin. I was too short for some of those moves, but I was at perfect eye-level with his groin.

"What's going on in here?" An elderly security guard poked his head cautiously around the corner. "I saw you two on the surveillance cameras. Looked like a fight between a Munchkin and the Wicked Wizard of the West. No offense, sir, but my money is on the Munchkin."

"Stay out of this. It doesn't concern you," Jake barked.

I improvised, "We're just having a little disagreement about lunch—Jersey Mike's or Subway."

The security guard fixed his gaze on me, clearly not buying it.

"Are you sure, Doc? Don't want this big guy to get hurt." He laughed as he attempted to diffuse the situation.

"Thanks, but I'm headed back to the clinic."

My hands still shook as I jumped into my Land Rover without using the handholds. It was remarkable how adrenaline could make even complex physical tasks easier. Jake could have hurt me, but at least I hadn't cowered. Instead, I'd fought back.

Why was I not panicking? Was this what developing a spine felt like?

Panic attacks caused a surge of adrenaline, too, but this reaction was entirely different.

Maybe, just maybe, I was making progress.

Chapter 26

They held Brock's funeral at New Beginnings Church on East 22nd Street. The local funeral home director was handling the formalities. He greeted all attendees at the door. Of course, he knew everybody. We were all his future customers.

The parking lot was full. I had no idea Brock would draw such a crowd. It was an odd assortment of humans from all walks of life: vaccine company executives in expensive suits and sedate ties, S.I.C. employees, and gamers in their best T-shirts and K-Swiss sneakers. I had forgotten that Brock played online games to wind down.

I guessed these guys were his real family.

Our vet clinic was well represented. We'd shut down for a few hours. London wore the appropriate little black dress. Harley showed up in black motorcycle leathers, and Gertrude came in her black grooming apron. No judgment here. I was in black scrubs. The other Belladonnas arrived together, minus Emily, hankies in hand. Except Rhonda wouldn't be caught dead carrying a hankie. The New Beginnings Church faithful were in attendance to provide the meal afterward.

God bless them.

I kept an eye out for Jake and Hayes. I knew police

officers often attended funerals to spot potential suspects. Hayes came in late and stood with arms folded at the back of the sanctuary. He looked so handsome in a detective-issue black suit. Jake was nowhere to be seen. What was up with that? You didn't attend your biggest benefactor's funeral?

Like I said. Jake was a jerk.

Pastor Wilson preached a killer sermon—poor choice of words. I was always amazed how this pastor could make a dearly departed stranger sound like an old friend. He knew things about Brock that I didn't. Of course, I knew things about Brock that he didn't, things which wouldn't be appropriate to bring up at a guy's funeral.

Like most people at funerals, I pondered what would be said at mine. I also considered where I would end up for eternity. I trusted that if I believed Jesus was the Son of God, that He died for our sins and rose again to rule with His Father, I would be with the in-crowd. Still, I worried that the road to heaven might be too narrow to accommodate my recent romantic thoughts.

Speaking of romance, I stopped to talk with Hayes as we filed out. "Nice service," he said.

I nodded. "I guess so if we base success on attendance. See anybody who resembles a murderer?" I asked. He smiled that cute, quirky smile.

"Ruby, I came to honor Brock, not to look for perps."

"Oh, sure, me too."

We walked out together. He headed for his car as he gave me a little wave. I had hoped he'd follow me to mine, but nope.

He was on duty.

All Pediatrician to Pets clinic employees returned at the same time. I unlocked the back door and disarmed the alarm. A choir of barks and meows greeted us, as did the odor of a dog left in the kennel too long. We tried to walk the boarders several times a day, but their evacuation schedules didn't always align with ours. Harley headed toward the kennel room to assess the damage.

I collected Chui from his bed. He was a pouter. If he didn't get to go places with everyone else, he'd withhold affection for approximately 20 seconds. Then he was all over my face, licking with glee that I'd returned. He wouldn't have enjoyed the funeral anyway. Lola seemed noncommittal today.

She was pretty noncommittal every day.

Chui and I headed to my room to change out of my formal scrubs and into my everyday scrubs.

Something was different.

My room was never tidy unless I'd invited company over, but it seemed messier than usual. Someone had rifled through my mail and jammed my personal papers back into my filing system—a blue plastic box. My laundry appeared untouched. No one wanted to dig through that pungent pile of unknown risks, not even me.

I left Chui to defend my domain and headed down the hall. I stopped at the kennel, the grooming room, and the reception desk to ask whether anyone had been in my personal space. All denied having any motive or the guts to venture into my room.

I believed them.

It must have happened while we were all at the funeral. The only person who could breach the alarm system was Jake the Snake Morgan. What would he be looking for? He was furious yesterday, and he'd avoided the funeral today.

I was more than slightly unnerved, but duty called. The delayed appointments began to fill the waiting room. We weren't a fancy clinic with separate entries and waiting rooms for cats and dogs. Clients and patients mingled as they exchanged friendly greetings or growlings. We tried to usher them into an exam room as quickly as possible.

I waded into this mayhem and helped Harley sort it out. A sketchy-looking Dalmatian was harassing a Maltese, although the Maltese held her own. London jumped in and helped drag the Dalmatian into the first exam room. As the dog sniffed around, I noticed his coat appeared patchy and dull. His chart reflected a slight weight gain since the last visit.

"How's Blaze today?" I asked. Blaze's owner was a firefighter with the Hays Fire Department.

"Well, Doc, Blaze doesn't seem to have his usual get-up-and-go. Whenever the alarm sounds, he usually rushes to jump into my truck. Lately, he just wants to stay cuddled up in his bed, not like him at all."

I performed a thorough exam, collected a skin scraping to rule out mites, and drew blood for lab testing. Based on his coat condition, breed, and history, I suspected hypothyroidism. He was lethargic, sought out warm places in the station, exhibited hair loss, and weight gain. If the blood work confirmed my diagnosis, treatment would be a simple, inexpensive medication.

"I'll call you when we get the results back. We'll know better what's going on with Blaze and how to treat his condition." I bent over and hugged the Dalmatian. "We're going to help you with that hair loss, buddy. Nobody wants to go bald, especially when you're trying to impress the lady dogs."

The rest of the day went smoother than usual until Darryl showed up, plastic Home and Barn coffee cup in hand. He headed back to the lab without checking with London, which always irritated her. She liked proper procedures to be followed, but Darryl never followed protocol.

"Hey, Doc! What's shakin'?" he asked.

I shot right back, "Oh, the flab on my arms, my butt, you know, most body parts these days."

Darryl and I had an ongoing competition to see who could get in the first jab. "Where's Glenda?" I asked. I hoped she was right behind him. Glenda kept Darryl in check.

Somebody had to.

“She’s busy filing claims,” he answered.

“So, what do you hear about Brock’s death?” Insurance agents often had the inside scoop on local events. “Should the population of Hays be worried about a serial killer on the loose?”

“I don’t know. You should ask the Hays Police Department about that,” he replied. “From what I hear, you may have an ‘in’ with a certain eligible detective.”

I blushed and fumbled for an answer. “Uh, Hayes is just a friend, a friend without benefits,” I clarified.

“Sure, Doc. I’ve never seen you blush in all the years I’ve known you. I can spot a budding romance when I see it.”

“Darryl, I’ve got a few more patients to see. Greet Glenda for me on your way out.”

That was my polite way of saying, go back to work and your wife.

Chapter 27

Between clients, I followed Darryl's advice and rang Hayes for updates. He answered right away, a promising sign. I tended to look at the bright side when it came to my new love interest.

"Hey, Ruby. Any new kidnappings, shootings, or dead bodies? You're pretty much a full-time job for a new Hays detective," Hayes teased.

"Yeah, you're so funny. None of that was my fault. I was just an innocent bystander."

Well, maybe not so innocent.

"Have you received any new DNA results in Brock's shooting? The Belladonnas have uncovered some interesting information about Jake Morgan. I could fill you in after work if you have time."

Please have time. Please have time.

"Speaking of Jake," Hayes replied. "I have an interview planned with him tomorrow. Could you give me some pointers on what to ask?"

Was he asking me for help? Be still, my heart.

"Sure." As always, I answered too quickly.

"Great. I'll pick you up at 7 p.m. if that works for you. We could talk over dinner."

7 p.m., 7 a.m. I didn't care. Anytime was good for me.

There I went again, making something out of nothing. He probably just wanted a reason to write off dinner on his expense account.

Still, new energy, or estrogen, coursed through my veins. I was suddenly in a fantastic mood. I breezed through the last two clients. They were vaccinations that Harley could handle, though I always liked to check in. They weren't only clients and patients; they were also friends.

I wandered down the hallway to my room and scooped up Chui. London had already walked him, so he settled comfortably into my bed. "Chui, what should I wear tonight? Black scrubs or civilian clothes?"

Black always made me look thinner.

After a quick shower, I settled on an olive-colored Walmart T-shirt. It was longer in the back to cover my derriere. That was kind of you, Walmart.

"Chui, I look good in olive, don't I? It's my color."

Thirty years earlier, an Amway rep had done my color palette and determined I was an autumn. I'd tucked that advice away like Esther in the Bible, "for such a time as this." Chui didn't answer, but I imagined he nodded in agreement.

At seven p.m., a rat-a-tat-tat on my back door activated Chui's bark mode. "He's here, Chui. He's here!" Chui looked unimpressed as I moved him aside with my foot to open the door.

Ooh-wee! Hayes got better looking each time he graced my doorway. He wore jeans and a soft, oversized Kansas City Chiefs jersey I desperately wanted to touch. I didn't, of course.

That would be weird.

We walked Chui back to his pup palace, but he didn't settle in. Instead, he shot Hayes that walleyed look of skepticism, the same one he gave me when I told him his vaccination would be "just a little pinch."

Hayes opened the car door for me. After he settled into the driver's seat, I asked, "What do you have planned for tonight?" I immediately regretted it. This wasn't a date. It was a debriefing, or a briefing on my part.

"I thought we might head out to that little limestone restaurant in Victoria. They have great German food. Do you like bierocks?"

"They are one of my favorites."

I didn't know if that was true, but it *could* be. I wanted him to like me.

"Great, we can discuss the case on the way over."

As we pulled out of my parking lot, Hayes was all business. "Ruby, you said earlier that you and your Belladonnas had some information on a few people involved in this mess. This medical stuff is way over my head. The more I know, the less I understand. Can you fill me in?"

I loved it when he used my name, even if it *was* Ruby. The gentle way he said it sent nervous signals up and down my legs, causing piloerection. That sounded bad, but it only meant that the hair on my legs stood up.

Oh, no! I forgot to shave my legs.

"The Belladonnas have valuable skill sets," I began. "I can't tell you where the information comes from, but I can give you a heads up on where to look for motives."

"I'll take it," he fired back.

"Okay, one of us discovered that the pharmaceutical company, Immunovax, has been developing a vaccine against the new Ebola-like strain that killed two lab workers in Manhattan. They've already invested heavily in production."

"Okay, but how does that help me?" Hayes asked.

"Just be patient, Hayes. There's a lot to unpack here. I'll help sort it out for you when I'm done."

It sounded like I knew what I was talking about.

I continued, "Another bit of information came in about

immunotherapy research, treatments for viruses rather than vaccines that prevent them. There's some cutting-edge research in this field, and we think Brock was on the verge of a huge discovery."

"Wow, Ruby. Still not getting it," Hayes said.

"Well, we don't necessarily have all the pieces, but through someone who shall remain nameless, we know Jake is involved financially with Immunovax, and for reasons unknown, Brock left S.I.C. to him in his will."

"He did what?! That could explain why he wanted Brock dead. Ruby, what part do you play in all of this?"

Hayes asked things I didn't know the answers to. Still, I spoke up, reluctant to color his investigation, but unable to stay silent.

"The Belladonnas think Jake looks like the culprit, or he hired someone to get rid of Brock. I know he doesn't like me, but I can't imagine him trying to knock me off."

We pulled into the restaurant parking lot. I'd never been here before. Dark wood paneling and dim lighting gave the place a cozy tavern feel. German beer taps projected from the wall behind the bar.

It smelled like cooked cabbage and bratwurst. Upbeat polka music filled the room. I half expected guys in lederhosen playing accordions to jump out at any minute.

Hayes chose a table so he could sit with his back to the wall, a law-enforcement tactic. Our cute blonde waitress, dressed in a traditional red dirndl skirt with a frilly white blouse, spoke in a German accent, chopping her words as she rattled off the specials. Her ancestors were undoubtedly from the old country. She left with our order, and Hayes returned to the topic.

"Again, what does all of this have to do with you, Ruby?"

Unsure about disclosing my connection, I hesitated. The researchers at CEZID and the Belladonnas already knew, and that alone might have put them at risk. Did I want to do that to Hayes?

I forged ahead, "Hayes, I've decided to trust you with some confidential information. Please be careful who you share this with."

I hoped he, too, liked the sound of his name as it flowed gently, almost lovingly, from my mouth. I told him of my time in Africa and my exposure to multiple diseases without ever contracting them. He listened intently; his eyes filled with sadness. Was that sympathy? I didn't need that.

Just as I finished, the waitress delivered our bierocks to the table. "Ruby, do you mind if I pray before we eat?"

I liked this guy more and more.

"No, that would be nice, Hayes." He bowed his head, as did I, and in the gentlest voice, addressed the Lord.

"Dear Heavenly Father, thank you for this meal and our time together. I ask that you help us both through this investigation and keep us safe. Bless the hands that prepared these delicious bierocks. In Jesus' name, Amen. Let's eat."

Short and sweet, like me.

"Most delicious cabbage and hamburger roll I've ever eaten!" I exclaimed. Hayes nodded, his mouth full. We exchanged pleasantries about the restaurant, the clientele, and the bartender. I wanted to order a beer. What else did you drink in a German pub?

But I didn't.

One might lead to two, and so on. Hayes might have been on duty. In college, tabletop dancing had been my specialty after a few beers. Normal enough then, but not something Hayes needed to witness tonight.

Hayes seemed to be holding back, as though he had something he wanted to tell me.

"Ruby, I had an enlightening call from the FBI today. They gave me some information on the company Immunovax, the same one you mentioned earlier."

Good, he was going to trust me.

"A woman who works as a secretary at Immunovax contacted an agent. She sits in on board meetings and records the minutes on her computer. However, this meeting was different. They said things that made her uncomfortable. When the CEO asked her to keep the conversation off the record, she secretly put her phone on record." Hayes paused as if he didn't want to continue. "That recording was chilling, Ruby. They spoke about a person in Hays, Kansas, who has super-immunity. I have the written transcript on my phone. Do you want me to read it? I think they were discussing you."

"Of course. Read it if this is my life they're talking about."

Hayes opened a file on his phone and read from the transcript:

"Executive meeting between CEO Samuel Jacobson and COO Charles Thomas."

CEO Jacobson: "How can we stop her and her rare immunity from affecting the vaccine marketing?"

COO Thomas: "What do you mean by stop her?"

CEO Jacobson: "Whatever it takes."

COO Thomas: "I'll take care of it. We've got a person on retainer who has helped us handle these sensitive situations in the past."'

CEO Jacobson: "I don't want to know details. Just handle it."

Hayes continued. "You hear the CEO direct the secretary to delete this conversation from the minutes, but she continued to record it with her phone. The FBI did a background check on Jacobson. He didn't rise to CEO without leaving a few bodies in his wake. People who get in his way often mysteriously disappear."

"Yikes! They *are* talking about me, aren't they? Perhaps Jacobson was behind the threatening call I received. That explains a lot."

Hayes's voice took a worried tone. "Yes, it does, Ruby. When the secretary heard about the death of the owner of a competing vaccine company, she contacted the FBI and turned over the recording. They're looking for the person who handles their 'sensitive situations.' It wasn't a random break-in or shooting. Assume you're still a target."

"What about Jake's involvement?" I asked. "Was he the shooter or just an investor?"

"I'll know more tomorrow after the interview," Hayes answered. "Now that I have your information on him, we can focus on his possible involvement."

"I don't know whether to feel relieved or panic at the idea that there's still a killer out there."

"Are you ready to head out?" Hayes asked.

No, never. I wanted to stay there with him forever. Instead, I answered, "Okay with me." That was unconvincing.

We stepped outside. For once, the relentless Kansas wind had surrendered.

"Don't know if we're any farther along, but I appreciate your input into the investigation," Hayes offered as we loaded into his car.

"I hope you come up with something before I have to dodge another bullet." A knot tightened slowly in my gut.

"We'll get them, Ruby. I'm expecting a call from the FBI tomorrow. Watch your back and put me on speed dial."

We pulled up to the clinic. Like a good detective, he cleared the building before I entered. We exchanged awkward goodbyes at the door. He leaned over and hugged me. I wanted to hang on a little longer, but he pulled away. I tucked my head, so my dilated pupils didn't give away what was happening in my body.

"Night, Hayes. Thanks for the dinner," I said to my shoes.

"Goodnight, little Ruby. Stay safe."

Little Ruby? Really? That was an endearing term, right?

Chui barked to remind me he was still in the kennel room. I opened the gate, and he ran to my room with Lola in his mouth. Guess we'd be three in bed. Not what I'd dreamt about. God was still working on me.

Chapter 28

It looked like today was cat day: spays, neuters, and dentals. All cats.

Cats aren't quite as easy to handle as dogs. Cats squirm. Some can twist within their skin while simultaneously nailing you with a back claw. However, Harley was a no-nonsense immobilizer. I knew we weren't supposed to 'scruff' cats anymore, but it had a calming, almost paralyzing effect on them. It was reminiscent of how a momma cat carried her kittens. A momma cat was a no-nonsense restrainer. When she needed to move her little ones to protect them, she grabbed them by the scruff of the neck and took off. She wanted no squirming or backtalk.

Neither did I.

The morning went smoothly. Emily dropped by to share lunch, carrying two Biggie Bags™ from Wendy's. I loved Biggie Bags™—practically everything I could want, all in one bag for $5.00. Now that was a bargain. The price didn't matter, though. Emily always bought. I loved her.

"I'm curious. What's going on with the case? Did anybody else turn up dead?" she asked.

I shuddered. "No, not yet, but the day's young. Hayes took me out for dinner Friday night, and I brought him up to speed on our findings. He shared a few of his."

"Like what?"

I didn't answer her. Would it be a betrayal of Hayes's confidence?

"Dakota, you can't keep that information from the Belladonnas. Share and share alike, right?" Emily had a point.

"Okay, but this is not to go anywhere else. Just to the Belladonnas." I filled her in on Hayes's conversation with the FBI.

"Perhaps Rhonda can get you some body armor," Emily suggested.

"I'm not wearing anything that makes me look fat," I shot back.

"Do you want to look fat, or do you want to have a hole through your heart? That's the choice."

We finished eating, and Emily headed back to her clinic.

Hayes called right after lunch to fill me in on Jake's interview. He was pretty loose with information these days. I took that to mean he trusted me.

He probably shouldn't, since I shared almost everything with the Belladonnas.

"Ruby, the interview with Jake was very enlightening. It seems he loaned Brock the money to purchase his new equipment. Jake took out an insurance policy for half a million dollars to protect his investment. He knew that without Brock at the helm, the research might not continue, and he wanted to be able to recoup his money." Hayes took a breath while I processed this information.

"So, does that give Jake more of a motive or rule him out?" I asked.

"I'm not sure yet. My intuition tells me that Jake had nothing to do with your shooting. Nor do I think he'd kill Brock after investing so much money in his company."

"Oh, rats. Hoped I'd see him behind bars. Wait, if you interviewed him in town, that means he's on his way to the clinic." I hung up on Hayes.

Great! It's time to panic. I issued a red alert to my crew: pick up every piece of lint on the counters, vacuum the front doormat, put refills in the plug-in Air Wick® air fresheners, and dust the toilet paper holder in the clients' bathroom. It was a lot of work to keep up with Jake's OCD, but it ensured a dust-free, almost odor-free environment and, thus, a less confrontational one.

The day wound down without any sign of Jake. That wasn't like him to miss a chance to belittle me. I called his phone.

No answer.

It was time for London to lock up the clinic and for Harley to walk the dogs out back. Harley's terrified screams for help echoed down the clinic hallway. London and I raced to the back door, which was wide open. The Kansas wind howled in like a coonhound on a hot trail as fur bunnies swirled about.

My first thought was to yell at Harley for leaving the door open. An animal could escape; thieves could breach my nonexistent security. My second thought was to ask her which dog had slipped its leash. If a dog got loose in our parking lot, it was a straight shot onto Vine Street. When that happened, we all dropped everything. I usually hit the ground and prayed while London and Harley fanned out like heat-seeking missiles.

But Harley's screams for help were more gut-wrenching than either of those scenarios. I rushed around the corner to find Harley pounding on the side of Jake's Tesla, unable to open his truck door. She cursed in frustration.

"Where in the crap are the door handles on this freaking cyborg?" She called Jake's name, but there was no answer. I could barely see his hulking frame through the tinted glass.

"London, call 911. Tell them to send an ambulance and police."

For once, Hayes didn't cross my mind as I rushed to Harley's side. I'd ridden in Jake's Cybertruck before. At the time, there was no bullet hole in the window. Praying that Jake had hit the unlock button inside, my hand found the panel to the right of the window. The door responded, opening a few inches. Harley yanked it wide.

Jake's body slumped sideways onto the console. Bright crimson blood splashed across the tactical gray interior. His perfectly ironed Ralph Lauren shirt now had a few blood-stained wrinkles from a bullet.

"Jake, Jake, what happened?" I could see a bullet hole in his shoulder. He was semiconscious but unable to speak. I circled to the truck's opposite side.

Looked like Jake should have ordered the Tesla aftermarket bulletproof package.

Harley reclined the seat as much as possible.

It never occurred to me that there might still be an active shooter lurking somewhere. Nor did I have a PTSD flashback to my earlier shooting. Emergencies always demanded a response, whether the victim had four legs or two.

When the passenger door swung open, I spotted a bullet hole in the interior door panel. The bullet hadn't exited the tough stainless-steel exterior. The police should be able to retrieve the bullet. I saw one hole in Jake's left shoulder. Blood was pooling beneath his feet. The exit wound must be underneath him. Jake took shallow breaths.

"Jake, it's Dr. Dakota. I'm going to check you out. The ambulance is on the way."

He moaned.

"Jake, can you hear me? Don't move. We need to try to stop the bleeding." He dipped his head slightly.

I placed both hands on the wound and pressed carefully until the bleeding slowed. There was possibly a fracture beneath the wound. No time or need for gloving up. I assumed his body weight was putting pressure on the exit wound.

"London, get some pressure bandages and the blanket off my bed. He's shocky."

The sirens were already blaring in the distance. The Ellis County Emergency Management building was just a few blocks south of my clinic. Another great reason to live in a small town. Help was always near.

London returned with the requested items. Harley continued to apply pressure to the entry wound while I cut off Jake's expensive shirt.

I was gonna owe him one for that.

There was no space for a tourniquet above the wound. London brought elastic gauze decorated with cartoon dogs, which we applied over the bandage as we waited for the ambulance. Jake was too bulky for us to move.

Harley arranged the blanket to cover the lower part of Jake's body. It began to wick the blood on the floorboard. "London, direct the ambulance back here," I ordered. "Don't let them go in through the front door. They need to pull into the back parking lot."

She did as she was told. A minute later, the ambulance squealed in. Two capable young men jumped out, carrying bags and an oxygen tank. Relief washed over me as I didn't want to be responsible for anything that happened to Jake.

People knew we didn't get along.

With help from his colleague, the EMT rolled Jake up to observe the exit wound and applied another pressure bandage. The other EMT established an IV line and administered normal saline.

A minute later, Hayes's white van pulled in, sliding to a stop, followed by a black-and-white unit.

Oh, brother, these guys and their slides. Too much "Live PD."

All the same, my heart rate jumped, and my stomach lurched. It wasn't actually my stomach, but there was no better way to describe the sudden movement inside my abdomen. My respiratory rate had already increased from the bandaging effort, though it wasn't all about the emergency. Hayes raced towards me, gripped my shoulders, and stared into my eyes.

"Are you okay, Ruby? Who got shot? I heard the alert over the radio. I thought the shooter might have succeeded this time."

There was real fear in his voice.

"It's Jake Morgan. He has a through-and-through bullet hole in his left shoulder. I bet there's a slug in the passenger door. From the looks of his poor parking job, someone shot him as he turned into our lot." After I assured Hayes I wasn't the victim but the first responder, he returned to detective mode and rushed to the truck to examine the crime scene.

"Hey, guys. Whatcha' got here?" he addressed the EMTs.

"Got a shooting, sir, Jake Morgan. Looks like the bullet passed through his left shoulder and came out the front below his collarbone. It could have been much worse. He's lost quite a bit of blood, but I think he'll make it, thanks to Dr. Dakota and her crew."

Harley told them the exact time I had applied the bandage. Hayes helped the EMTs remove Jake from his truck, placed him on a gurney, and then loaded him into the ambulance. The ambulance sped off with sirens blaring.

Hayes approached with a measured, deliberate stride to where London, Harley, and I were huddled. "Since Jake is in shock, he's unable to tell us what happened. Do you ladies have any ideas? Were there any witnesses?"

We gave a communal shrug.

Harley began, "It was six p.m., and I just led the first two dogs outside for their evening walk. As I rounded the corner, Dr. Morgan's truck sat at a weird angle in our lot. There was a hole in his window, with blood splattered all over. His body was slumped over the console. I tried but couldn't get that freakin' door open. Have you ever seen a door handle anywhere on those monstrosities? What's up with that? Do first responders have to take special training in door opening?"

She was on one of her frustrated rants.

I jumped in to keep us from staying an extra two hours while she went off on new vehicles. "I helped Harley open the door and assessed Jake's condition. He was bleeding heavily. We applied bandages to control the bleeding and waited for the ambulance. Jake was never fully conscious. Remember, you told me he was in town, so I assumed he'd stop by to assess the clinic's condition. We were all waiting for his surprise visit. Boy, was this a surprise."

Hayes informed me I'd need to stop by the station tomorrow for a formal interview. He then headed back to the truck to consult with the other detectives now on the scene.

No goodbye. No see you later. Duty called.

Chapter 29

London and I helped Harley wrap up the evening dog-walking routine. I put Chui in my room and locked up the clinic. We climbed into my Land Rover and headed for Hays Medical Center. A quick speed-dial alerted the Belladonnas. No sign of Rhonda's car in the hospital parking lot, and she should have beaten us there. She must be on duty.

Harley, London, and I walked through the emergency entrance as if we belonged there. After all, it *was* Hays. We knew half the people on duty.

They directed us to Jake's room. There was no one there. The charge nurse, Irma Schneider, was at the nurses' station.

"Hey, Irma. How's Cat Scan's feline acne?"

"It looks much better, Doc. Thanks for the advice," she replied.

"Good to hear. It's hard for a cat to get a date with a chin covered with zits," I quipped.

"Oh, Doc. You are probably looking for Dr. Morgan. He's in surgery. You can wait in his room. I'll pop in and keep you informed of his progress."

"Thanks, Irma. You're a jewel."

All three of us flopped gratefully onto the couch in

Jake's room.

"Doc, why do you think he lost consciousness? What are the chances he'll wake up and talk?" Harley asked.

I began to answer her questions when Kit and Emily appeared at the door.

"We got here as fast as we could," Emily explained. "Rhonda pulled a double shift today at the station. Thanks for the call, Dakota. You know we don't like to be left out. What happened at your clinic?"

"We had a little surprise at closing. We found Jake Morgan outside the clinic, in his truck. He'd been shot. Looks like a hit job. Sound familiar?"

"Is he alive?" Emily asked.

"The EMTs think he'll pull through. He was still unconscious when he arrived at the hospital and is in surgery now," I replied.

"Hmm, probably lost consciousness due to blood loss. If you caught him early enough, the odds are that he will recover." Emily answered the question we had on our minds.

We all wanted Jake to ID the perpetrator. I hoped his memory was sharper than mine. We dozed for a while on the couch. London leaned on Harley, who leaned on me. Kit and Emily went to the cafeteria to pass the time and eat pie.

Irma glided silently into the room and gently shook my shoulder. "Doc, the surgeon just sent word that Jake is out of surgery and awake. It went well. They'll bring him to the room soon."

I texted Emily and Kit. It was only a few minutes before the attendants wheeled the gurney in, gently transferred Jake onto the bed, and hooked up his monitors. It was good to hear his heartbeat. His chest was swathed in white gauze, and his left arm rested limply at his side. He wouldn't be talking anytime soon. He couldn't even acknowledge our presence. Emily reassured the nurses that we wouldn't overstay our welcome. We bid our goodbyes to the monitor, which beeped back indifferently.

We would return in the morning. My brain—running on fumes and Diet Dr Pepper—sensed something lacking, though.

"Shouldn't he have some security tonight?' I asked Kit and Emily. "What if the hitman decides to finish off the job?"

Was that *concern* coming out of my mouth?

"You're right. You should call Hayes," Kit agreed.

I speed-dialed him. "Hey, Hayes. How are the CSIs doing? Find any bullets? The Belladonnas and I had an idea. Shouldn't Jake have some protection in the hospital? After all, the guy with poor aim will probably try again. Why are these assassins such bad shots? I'm not complaining, you understand."

I talked too much, and Hayes sounded tired. Three shootings had already stretched the capacity of this small police unit. "Already on it," he said. "There should be an officer there now. I understand Jake has just come out of surgery. We'll talk tomorrow." Hayes hung up.

Upon arriving at the elevator, the door opened, and a young officer in a neatly pressed light blue uniform stepped out. We steered him towards Jake's room. "I'll be here all night," he informed us.

"Anybody up for fried chicken?" I asked, and we were off to the new Al's Chickenette, the best fried chicken in the county.

We could relax now.

Chapter 30

Funny how a rebound from an emergency increased one's appetite. After eating our fill of fried chicken, we detoured off Vine Street and headed back toward the clinic. We were all curious, plus Hayes was still there. Yellow crime scene tape cordoned off the parking lot. Not much left to see. London and Kit decided to go home while Harley went to her trailer. Emily joined Darryl and Glenda, who stood near Hayes as if for protection from the evil that had just landed. They seemed to be in shock themselves. I rarely saw Darryl speechless. It must terrify them to think someone shot a man right next to their insurance agency.

What was I thinking? He was shot next door to my business, too.

"Hey, guys," I greeted them. "Too close to home, huh? I guess Hayes already asked if you saw anything."

Glenda offered, "Darryl surveyed crop damage in the country all day while I held down the fort. I spent most of my time organizing the back room. I didn't hear a thing. How about you all?"

"Nope, we were in preparation to fend off a stealth attack by Jake. Sorry, no disrespect, since he's languishing in the hospital," I replied.

"Were you able to talk to him?" Hayes asked. "What did

the doctor say?"

"No, and nothing," I answered. "He was still out of it when they wheeled him into his room."

"Now, what do we do with you, Ruby?" Hayes asked with a wrinkled brow.

"Me? What do you mean?"

"I know you act tough, Ruby, but you must be worried. Not only is Brock dead, but someone took shots at both you and Jake—in your own backyard. How many bodies must drop before you accept protection?"

I'd refused any further security details. The FBI might still be around. Who knew? They were invisible. They'd missed the guy shooting at Jake, though, so how good could they be?

Hayes's question went unanswered, but it caused a black chasm to open in my psyche. Who was I fooling? I didn't want to die. Hadn't done anything of significance since leaving Africa. What would my legacy be, a spot in the all-time fastest cat spayers hall of fame? Hardly tombstone material. Brock was dead. Jake wounded. Was this all my fault? The question landed like a physical thing. I couldn't breathe. I was still standing, which felt like a minor miracle, but my body had clearly stopped consulting me. *Dear God. I'm not a fainter. I refuse to be a fainter. Help me...*

"Dakota, Dakota, wake up." I heard Emily's gentle voice calling me and tried to focus.

"Where am I? Did I have an Al's Chickenette grease overload? Do I need triple bypass surgery?" The fog started to clear from my brain.

"You're in the hospital, Dakota," Emily answered me. "You passed out, and we couldn't wake you. With Hayes's help, I took the liberty of admitting you for observation. You're a lot easier to convince when you're unconscious."

I couldn't argue with that.

"Pets Buy has procured a relief vet for as long as

needed. Dakota, listen to me." Emily was in doctor mode. "You're exhausted. Your body shut down for its own protection. You've been going along like you don't have a care in the world when everyone around you sees a traumatized, overworked, unhealthy, shot-at, stressed-out human being. Dakota, you need rest, protection from yourself and others… and a better diet. There's a guy from the FBI outside your door. Jake's down the hall. You're in good hands. Now get some rest."

Tears slid down my cheeks. Nobody had cared for me like this since my parents died. Maybe I was just a little tired after doing everything on my own for so long. Still had to protest this move, though, to save face. Learned that lesson in Africa, where transparency and accountability took a backseat to saving face. Don't call out a politician for corruption. It might embarrass him. For my part, I had to appear strong.

"Emily, what are you thinking? You know me. I can handle anything: biting patients, angry clients, unruly staff, and inaccurate assassins. On top of that, toss in a murder. Thanks, but I don't need your pity or time off."

I wondered if Hayes helped dress me in this open-backed gown?

I continued to sob between words. My blubbering might be more from the thought that Hayes saw my backside in white cotton granny panties than from my pathetic life.

"Dakota, Hayes is outside," Emily said. "He's here as a friend, not a detective. Do you want to speak to him?"

I hesitated for about 20 seconds, which felt like a long time to me.

"I don't think I'm ready yet," I answered. "Could you have him come back tomorrow? I don't want him to see me like this."

Few people had seen me cry. Nobody knew how often I sobbed on the inside, though. I asked Emily to leave with Hayes.

As soon as they departed, I yearned for them to return. The darkness rolled in again. I didn't want to be alone in a room with an overweight, broken-down, 62-year-old, washed-up vet—alone with myself. It was terrifying.

I had nothing, no home, no savings for retirement. After selling my clinic to Pets Buy, I thought I could afford to retire and travel. Wrong. Most of the proceeds from the sale went toward paying off credit cards and business loans. I had no life, no husband, no children.

I was alone.

The heart monitor beeps amped up.

Perhaps I was also suffering from some compassion fatigue, an occupational hazard of veterinarians. I couldn't fix them all. Not 'fix,' like neuter, but 'fix' as in repair. Sometimes, there was just no treatment, no answer but euthanasia. I hated that part of my job. I couldn't make everyone happy. Heck, I couldn't even make myself happy.

Now, one of my friends was dead, and I couldn't undo that either. Did I cause Brock's murder? Someone tried to take my life. Jake narrowly escaped death. Why were they punishing my friends? Who were they? Was my immunity up for sale to the highest bidder? Who wanted me dead?

I wanted me dead.

This monologue droned on in my head as I continued to spiral.

The nurse found me uncovered in bed, curled up in a fetal position, unable to stop weeping. She had orders for a sedative as needed.

It was needed.

Wait, did Emily say relief vet? How did I miss that? Nobody could take my place! I built that clinic from the ground up. Clients came to the clinic because they trusted me, not some new graduate or an out-of-date old guy trying to supplement his income by subbing. I needed to get out of here.

Oops. Not steady enough to walk. My knees buckled. I

grabbed the bedrails and fell back into bed.

"To die, to sleep—perchance to dream."

Chapter 31

Nurse Ratched awakened me at six a.m. Really? No one got any rest in a hospital.

Where was I when I lost consciousness last night? Oh, yeah, trapped in an unsettling documentary of my life playing repeatedly in my head, a video soon to be released on the boring Weather Channel.

At least I hadn't died.

My breakfast consisted of oatmeal, dry toast, and cranberry juice. Just shoot me now.

Thank goodness I heard Rhonda's voice in the hall. Here was someone who *could* put me out of my misery. There was a commotion surrounding her arrival. She cautiously stuck her head in the door.

"Get those hands in the air, lady," Rhonda shouted. "Delivery comin' through, via German shepherd." In trotted Rennie with a McDonald's bag in his mouth. I accepted it and looked through its contents: Sausage Egg McMuffin®, hash browns, a coffee with sugar, and two creamers. I made a mental note to put Rennie in my will.

"Thanks, Rennie, and thanks to you, too, Rhonda." I was sure Rhonda had put Rennie in the driver's seat when she pulled up to the pay window. Rhonda loved to pull stunts on people. She also knew good food.

"How'd you sleep, Doc? Sorry, I couldn't get in on the fun yesterday. One of those young dispatchers neglected to show up for duty. Not that I minded, I picked up some overtime. Sounds like a close call for Dr. Morgan. When I heard the 911 call and location come in, I was afraid it was another attempt on your life. Better him than you."

"I don't know about that, Rhonda. I think it should have been me. It would be a smaller loss."

That was pathetic.

"What are you saying, Doc? You give 100 percent of yourself to others all day, every day. You worry about your patients as if they were your family. I've seen you stay up all night with a surgery patient to make sure they pull through. Then you're back at it in the morning without a wink of sleep. You're one of the most dedicated women I know."

"Thanks, Rhonda. I appreciate it." I was unable to absorb her words, though. There was a border wall between how I saw myself and how others saw me. It would take more than flattery and breathing into a bag to bring me out of this one. I gently petted Rennie's head as his tongue lolled out of his mouth.

His breath smelled like an Egg McMuffin®.

"Rhonda, you know you're not supposed to feed Rennie greasy food. His pancreas won't tolerate it."

Rhonda replied, "Okay, Doc, you tell him that when you're the one ordering with his face leaning over your shoulder. A bite dog can be pretty persuasive."

I understood what she was saying.

"Remember that night I kept Rennie at the clinic when I made some ramen noodles? He had his dog food right there, but he insisted on pushing the microwave button. Did you teach him that? When the food came out, he huddled over me like a Kansas City Chief center over the football as I waited for it to cool."

"What can I do to cheer you up, Doc?" Rhonda asked. "I

hear you might be out of commission for a while. Harley told me she's preparing for the new relief vet to show up. Guess that will be hard on everyone."

I sighed but didn't respond.

"Seems to me you owe Dr. Morgan an apology," Rhonda said. "We all do. Don't think he shot himself, do you?"

I still said nothing.

"He was your pick because he's caused you so much grief over the last few years. I also thought it was Jake from the financials I uncovered," Rhonda added.

I kept quiet, focusing on Rennie instead. It's interesting how dogs can steady someone, even when that someone feels completely out of control.

Rhonda continued, "Well, I'm no psychiatrist, Doc, but it seems to me that reaching out to those who have made your life miserable might be a way back to happiness. Not meddlin'. Just sayin'."

Could she possibly be right? I blamed Jake for so many of my failures. He could have been the father figure I needed, but instead, he was a villain.

"Thanks for the analysis, Rhonda, but I don't think you have any idea of what happiness looks like to me." I slid down in the bed. "Could you and Rennie head out now? I'm tired."

Rhonda shrugged. So did Rennie. He followed her out the door.

I was alone with myself again. I scanned the TV channels, which included 50 news channels, boring documentaries, mind-numbing game shows, and pharmaceutical commercials for diseases even a veterinarian had never heard of.

Nothing of interest.

Maybe Rhonda was right. The retirement was forced. The pity party was optional. I had to do something.

Should I visit Jake?

What did Emily—or even worse, Hayes—do with my clothes? I couldn't face Jake in this practical joke of a gown. Seriously, who designed these one-size-does-not-fit-all wearable bedsheets with a flapping back door? I suspected they were meant to keep one insecure and in bed.

There had to be a set of scrubs around here somewhere. God must have heard my request because the laundry guy was just outside my door. Perhaps the duty nurse and the laundry guy had something going on between them. She was giggling like a spotted hyena.

I reached into the basket and pulled out a scrub top, only to shove it back when I saw the brown, unidentifiable goo that clung to the fabric. Not squeamish, just unwilling to expose Jake to hazardous material. I tried again. This time up came a pair of oversized scrub pants and a mismatched top with a cartoon syringe print.

Really? Did doctors think this instilled confidence?

The scrub pants were so huge that I could have pulled them up around my neck and skipped the top altogether. Arm access would have been impossible, though, so I cinched the drawstring around my waist as tight as it would go. The excess drawstrings dangled to my knees like two spaghetti strands. I rolled up the pant legs 12 inches. What a respectable spectacle of a doctor I made. I reached into the shirt pocket and pulled out a bloody 4x4 gauze.

Oh, Lord!

Now, what room was Jake in? Could he still be in the ICU? There was no way to breach that unit in this absurd get-up. There was a doctor's coat on the back of a chair in the nurse's station. With confidence, I strolled behind the counter and donned the coat as if I belonged there.

Clyde Miller, M.D. at your service.

No one even looked up. I hightailed it down to the ICU.

I hit the button on the wall, and the two automatic doors flew open like I owned the place. No questions asked. Jake lay in a bed halfway down the row. He looked at me and started guffawing—deep, rolling laughter that must have disturbed his wounds. I waddled towards him, pant legs unrolling, trying not to face-plant before I reached his bed.

In my previous encounters with Jake, I would have been angry at his laughter because I knew it was meant to torment me. Today, I caught a glimpse of myself in a glass divider and joined him, convulsing in hysterics. My pants dropped to my knees in the process, which only brought on more howling from both of us.

If laughter healed, then we were both on the mend.

Once we both caught our breath, I started the conversation. "Jake, I'm glad you're still alive but ashamed I might not have been so thrilled a week ago."

"We've had our disagreements, haven't we?" he said. "I know I can be aggressive when managing employees. That's just how I'm wired."

"It's more than just disagreements, Jake. I rarely challenge your decisions. You are an effective clinic manager. It's just that your management style alienates people. Because of my past relationship with my father, I sometimes fear confrontation with those in authority. And you feed on that."

My body was trembling. I was still afraid of him. He still held my future in his hands. Don't let me start crying. Breathe, Ruby, breathe.

"Jake, let me explain. This issue dates back to when I was a young veterinarian in your clinic. You questioned every diagnosis, even in front of staff and clients. That humiliated me and made me doubt my ability to do the work. I felt like an impostor in a lab coat, neither worthy nor intelligent enough. Thirty years later, when I couldn't keep the business afloat and had to sell to Pets Buy, that was just one more confirmation. And to my dismay, when you showed up as the corporate manager, terror washed over me again."

Jake remained silent. Was he still breathing? Maybe a

blood clot had entered his brain. He pushed the button to raise his upper body. He winced and then began to speak.

"Ruby." He never called me Ruby. Weird. Must've been the anesthesia talking. "This experience has made me reevaluate my priorities. I'm financially set for life. My investments have paid off well, but I miss practice. I miss the hunt for answers. Sure, I can order people around. I'm the size of a bull."

An angry, snorting bull, I told myself. No talent there. Just management by fear and intimidation.

"I'm set to take over Brock's S.I.C., but do I want to? I'm no researcher. Don't want to be trapped in a lab with mice for company. My wife is quite tolerant, but we have no kids or real friends. Perhaps what is missing is a life outside of my job."

Uh-oh, this sounded familiar. Did we have more in common than I knew?

"Jake, it's not that I dislike you." Was that my voice? "You just scare me when you get that look. You know, the look."

"Ruby, I need to admit something. I'm harder on you because I'm afraid of you, too."

"Afraid of me? I'm four-feet-ten on a good day!" I laughed.

"No, seriously, when you were just a young vet, my clients started to ask for you, not me. That hurt. I prided myself on my relationship with my clients."

You meant your relationship with your *female* clients. Jake always made sure his secretary assigned him the young, beautiful suburban housewives with their whatever-doodle dogs. I was sure the doctor-client-patient relationship extended far beyond clinic hours. He even had a bedroom in the clinic for "overnight emergencies." Oh, sure. I guess lust could be considered an emergency.

"Jake, I'm shocked. I never tried to steal your clients."

"No, not consciously, you didn't. They just gravitated

toward your genuine love of their animals. My goal was to belittle you wherever I could. I was relieved when you finally moved on from my clinic. My next hire was less compassionate," he admitted.

A nurse in animated stethoscope-covered scrubs interrupted us. I missed the days of crisp, white dresses and matching pleated cardboard hats.

Much more respectable than scrubs with cartoons.

"Excuse me, Doctor Miller," she said, holding back a smile as she read the embroidered name on my coat. "Or whoever you really are." Her gaze swept over my baggy scrubs and flip-flops. She clearly did not buy my disguise. "You'll have to leave. It's time for a blood draw."

Don't have to tell me twice. I was outta there. No way did I want this to become a weep-on-each-other's-shoulder session.

"Good talk, Jake. See ya later."

He couldn't wave, but he nodded.

Did we settle anything? I thought so. I felt a burden lifting from my chest.

Or maybe that was just from not wearing a bra.

Chapter 32

I smelled the lunch cart in the hall. Despite my complaints about breakfast, I looked forward to lunch. That must have been a good sign. I needed to beat the lunch cart back to my room. Call me crazy, but I loved hospital food. What they saved on breakfast, they poured into lunch and dinner: mashed potatoes, green beans, and a tiny slab of meat. There was always brown gravy if the slab was beef, and white cream gravy if it was chicken. Jell-O for dessert.

No nurses were at the station. They must have been on break. I ditched the Dr. Miller coat and reluctantly put the peek-a-boo peignoir back on. I crawled into bed just in time for my tray.

Yep. Called it. Beef.

After devouring every morsel, I lay back and patted my stomach. Hospital stays had always left me ravenous, not that I'd spent that much time there. Just the occasional wounds inflicted by ungrateful patients. Fairly sure that some of those meds stimulated my appetite. Whatever. I loved to eat.

What just happened in Jake's ICU cubicle? Were my many years of suffering from wounds inflicted by Jake Morgan over?

Nope. Other than food, I wasn't much improved.

I fell back on my pillow and silently recited my favorite scripture, Psalm 91. "…No harm shall come near you. No disaster will come near your tent. He shall command His angels concerning you. They will guard you in all you do and lift you up lest you dash your foot against a stone."

I slept through the evening meal and beyond. Nurse Torture startled me with an early morning wake-up call. At least they'd let me sleep all night. Not exactly joyous this morning, but not ready to leave this earth quite yet.

So many questions. If Jake didn't shoot at me or kill Brock, then who did? Same person, or two separate nightmares?

Perhaps my classmate at CEZID had some answers. I picked up my phone from the bedside tray and called Mary.

"Good morning. K-State Center for Emerging and Zoonotic Infectious Diseases. May I help you?" The receptionist's cheery demeanor was at odds with the weighty nature of that place. It was like closing a conversation with the National Nuclear Security Administration by saying "Have a nice day," when they knew there might be no tomorrow.

"May I speak to Dr. Hazlett, please? This is Dr. Ruby Dakota calling."

"Please hold," she replied. Her voice suggested Mary would not take my call.

Little did she know.

"Hey, Ruby! You've been on my mind these past few weeks. I assume you're still alive," Hazlett quipped.

I forced a laugh. "Yep, just dodging bullets out here in western Kansas. How are things in your doomsday dugout?"

"Oh, about the same. You know, just protecting the world from a gruesome demise."

"Mary, I need answers. If you can't talk on the phone, I'll come to Manhattan. I'm on leave from my practice right now."

"What? You, on leave?" she asked. "Now that's a first! The Ruby Dakota I know would never let her clients and patients down, not even long enough to take a vacation."

"Seems I suffered a bit of a breakdown. You know, the forced flight to Manhattan with the FBI Blues Brothers, my head nearly aerated by a bullet, my friend murdered, and my boss wounded—more than even I could handle. I didn't desert my post, though. Corporate brought in a relief vet."

"What can I do?" Mary asked, although she already knew the answer.

"You could stop all this craziness around me. What in the Sam Hill are you working on up there? Why are my friends and I such hot commodities right now? I am tired of all the secrecy. That very secrecy threatens my life. I need answers!"

Near tears again, my voice quivered. Mary must have heard it.

"Ruby, I can't tell you everything on the phone, but I can clear up a few things. Part of our mandate here is to develop vaccines for zoonotic diseases. There was a lab incident, as you know, where a new Ebola-related virus infected and killed two of our lab assistants. When it hit the news, we feared this lab leak could escalate into something much worse. If the virus fell into the wrong hands…" She paused. "Several registered vaccine companies have legally obtained the virus from us and continue researching vaccines for profit. Immunovax and, most recently, S.I.C. have ongoing projects. The competition is brisk, and who knows what other bad players might be in the game?" She took a breath.

"But why am I at risk?" I asked.

"Ruby, your DNA and T-cells might be the key to a rapid treatment. Your super-immunity could cut research time by years and might negate the need to produce large volumes of vaccines. Our lab continues to manipulate your blood cells to find the genetic answer. I suspect Brock at S.I.C. was on the same path using your cells. Does this ease your mind a little?"

"Ease my mind? Are you kidding? The fate of the entire world might rest on my blood! Aren't there other super-immune people in the world you can put at risk?" I asked.

"That's a good question. Three other aid workers were on site in Uganda with your parents. We have no way of knowing whether they were super-immune individuals, but evidently, someone took them out just in case. There seems to be a connection between your exposure to the Ebola virus and your specific immune system. That's all I can tell you right now.

Stay safe, Ruby."

Click.

Why did everyone hang up on me? Was everyone so caught up in their own lives that they forgot to say goodbye?

I called her back.

"Mary, I think we accidentally got disconnected. I can't help but think that some of my mental puzzles would come together if I had that one final piece, the one about my parents' passing. My parents were researching a group of female Kenyan sex workers with natural HIV immunity despite constant exposure."

"I have some of the story from your parents' research papers. Fill me in on what you knew as a young veterinary student," Mary urged.

How much should I tell her? My parents' involvement in research was a constant in my life. When they called to inform me that they were relocating to Nairobi to work with the U.S. government, it struck me that once again, their work would take precedence over my needs, my wants. They loved the challenge of dangerous research and would jump at the chance to study immunity at a moment's notice.

But did they not think about me? They never visited on parents' weekends or football game days. They didn't help me move in or out of the dorm. Of course, I understood it was impossible for them since they were so far away, but it still hurt. It never occurred to me that anything bad could happen to them.

I decided to relate the backstory to Mary. "In Kenya, I assumed my parents were in the development process for a vaccine against HIV. A company known as LifeShield competed with the U.S. government for the rights to produce it. Although they rarely spoke to me about it, they must have been under tremendous pressure. Huge profits were probably at stake, government bureaucrats bidding against pharmaceutical execs, each claiming to own whatever vaccine the researchers discovered."

"That story is still being played out in the industry today," Mary added.

"As I remember talking to them about their work, they told me that HIV was elusive. It could mutate faster than any vaccine could keep up with. Then, a few months after my parents died, LifeShield's research showed that HIV replicated and mutated so rapidly that any vaccine was seen as ineffective. Project abandoned. Funding cut."

A wave of nostalgia hit me. Just before I graduated from vet school, my parents surprised me with a plane ticket to Kenya to celebrate their 25th wedding anniversary. I jumped at the chance to visit my beloved Africa and could still see my mother and father hunkered over microscopes in the research facility, hunting down the key to this unique HIV immunity.

I continued. "My parents knew that they, like the HIV-positive women, had some super-immunity. I don't remember them ever being ill. They never missed work due to illness, viral or bacterial. They used to discuss this trait, calling themselves "bulletproof" right in front of me. Mary, do you think they knew that their super-immunity might pass on to their daughter in a mega dose?"

"I suspect they had some inkling that this could happen, but DNA research has come a long way since then, Ruby. What else do you remember?" Mary probed.

"Before I left that summer, they asked me to donate blood for their research. I think my parents saw a different path forward. When the vaccine failed, they turned to the freak living with them—me. Not only were they scientists, but they were also treasure hunters."

Was I the map as well as the gold?

"Do you want to hear the story of my parents' death?"

Mary was slow to answer. "Sure, if it isn't too painful for you. It might be relevant."

Yes, it was too painful, but I continued anyway.

"All I was told about their death was that they returned home at night along their road in Runda, an upscale neighborhood in Nairobi. Their driver stopped the car at the gate of their compound. Typically, the compound guard immediately opened the gate to let them pass and then quickly closed it to prevent carjackings. This time, there was a delay. The gate remained motionless. Their driver leaned on the horn with no response. Two hooded, armed men jumped from their hideout in the bougainvillea bushes and approached the car from both sides. My parents were in the back seat. My dad jumped out, possibly to protect my mother. He was immediately shot, as were my mother and the driver. The two men disappeared into the darkness.

This account came from eyewitnesses at the duka, a little shop down the road. My parents' compound also had an alarm company that usually responded to the guard pressing his panic button. No alarm sounded that night."

"Ruby, I had no idea! This happened just before we graduated? You never said a word! I knew your parents had died, but not like this. I'm so sorry."

"Thanks, Mary. There was no explanation. No real investigation. It seemed that the U.S. Embassy was initially involved but quickly backed off. The media blamed the incident on local carjackers, although they didn't steal my parents' car. The government flew their bodies back to the U.S. Their funeral was a closed-casket ceremony. I never had any real closure."

"Ruby, any time you need to talk… just give me a call."

"I have to go, Mary. We'll talk again soon."

There was a slight commotion outside my hospital room door. Thank goodness that conversation with Mary was over. It had put me on the verge of another massive meltdown. Perhaps someone ordered extra protection for me. It was nice to be loved or considered valuable by someone.

I heard Kit threaten the sentry with a lethal injection. As a pharmacist, she wasn't bluffing. Moments later, she strolled into my room looking like the cat that just ate the canary.

As a vet, I should've felt sorry for the canary. I didn't. She approached my bedside.

"You are never going to believe what I just discovered!" Kit's words tumbled out at a high pitch. "Immunovax has been around a lot longer than we knew. It was previously known as LifeShield but changed its name in early 2000. It is now the same company we deal with today, Immunovax!"

My world suddenly tilted on its axis. My hospital sippy cup dropped to the floor. Liquid exploded as the lid popped off.

That's precisely how my brain felt.

"Immunovax was LifeShield?" I was stunned.

I lay back in the bed as the room began to spin with Kit's revelation.

"No," I whispered. "That's impossible." Even as I said it, another puzzle piece fell into place. My trembling hands gripped the hospital bed rails. "Could LifeShield have been involved with my parents' murder? Did LifeShield cover its tracks by rebranding its name?"

Kit reached for my hand. "Dakota, the Belladonnas will help uncover this plot."

My shock was already fading, anger rushing in behind it.

Kit continued, "Then we'll put our heads together. Get creative. That's what we do. We solve puzzles."

But this wasn't just another puzzle. This was war.

Chapter 33

Rhonda and Emily showed up, completing our quartet, and just in time for my institutional dinner. I'd already informed my easily intimidated door guard that I would be expecting additional visitors. He alerted the hospital kitchen, but they didn't care. Meatloaf night, Rhonda's favorite. For once, I wasn't hungry. With my blessing, she demolished that brick of meat, the mashed potatoes, and the peas, barely coming up for air.

"Okay, women. Listen up." I rallied the troops. "Kit has some new information on a company called LifeShield, a company that competed with the work my parents did back in Kenya."

"Wait. Your parents? I thought they died when you were in vet school," the ever-vigilant Emily asked.

"Yes, they did. They were doing HIV research back then. Even though they were ahead of their time in research models, they lacked the necessary technology. Even so, they must have been onto something. Their research information may somehow be related to my immunity. LifeShield was a private company that competed with the U.S. government and my parents. Kit discovered that this same company, under the new name Immunovax, is currently developing vaccines against emerging infectious diseases."

I watched my friends' faces as they digested this new information. Emily was the first to respond.

"Dakota, I am so sorry about your parents. Do you think LifeShield was involved in your parents' death because of their work? How are you processing this?" Emily always thought of others' feelings.

I quickly recounted the story of my parents' carjacking with all the unanswered questions.

Rhonda, the vigilante, butted in. "I say we arm ourselves, show up at the gates of Immunovax, and get some answers. A little firepower always gets better results than jawing across the table at lawyers."

Oh, brother. Good thing she was about to retire.

"Hold on. We don't even know for sure that they're involved," Kit reminded us. "Yes, big pharma is known to pay huge bribes and is probably culpable for a few deaths, but we don't have any evidence that they interfered with your parents' research."

"Kit, would you take notes on your tablet?" I asked. "I've kept some details to myself. The FBI provided Hayes with information about Immunovax's CEO. It seems there is a whistleblower who recounted a board meeting in which the members discussed getting rid of someone in Hays, Kansas, a person with super immunity. Hello, that's me!"

Emily exploded. "Why didn't you tell us? That's vital information, Dakota!"

"Please forgive me. I wasn't sure if I should share Hayes's inside information from the FBI. Hayes seems to trust me now, and I didn't want to ruin that."

Rhonda barged in again. "Okay, okay, we forgive you. We all understand confidentiality. Let's explore why Immunovax would want to target people in Hays, Kansas. Why Dakota? Why Brock? Why Jake?"

"I might be able to answer two of those questions," Kit volunteered. "Perhaps they targeted you because your DNA might hold a more effective solution to a pandemic than vaccination. That frightens them and their investors. The same goes for Brock. He was on the verge of identifying the genes that make you super immune."

"Okay, I buy that," said Emily, "but why Jake? He was just an investor and a rep for the company."

"That's a good observation," I added. "As much as I dislike him and am as happy as anyone to see him wounded, I can't justify an attempt on his life by a drug company. Let's leave that for now. A new train of thought: how do we uncover LifeShield's connection 40 years ago with Immunovax's suspected current involvement?"

"From a police perspective, a crime back in the eighties is a cold case—an ice-cold case on the other side of the world," Rhonda added.

"From my perspective, the Embassy was probably dealing with a developing country's often corrupt police force," I suggested. "Any attorney, police chief, coroner, or judge could have been bought off. Perhaps there's no way to prove interference in the case. The U.S. government is not always upfront with evidence."

"Jeez, Dakota. Can you come up with any positive suggestions?" Emily chided. "I've got an idea. Once, when we suspected Medicaid fraud at the nursing home where one of my patients resided, the government seemed uninterested in pursuing the nursing home administrator. My clinic set up a 'sting' operation to uncover what was happening there. One of my nurses applied for an office job and tracked the billing statements. She discovered and documented hundreds of thousands of dollars in double-billing by the doctor and the nursing home. She also documented falsifying the needs of patients, making them appear sicker than they were, and billing for a higher level of care than they received."

"How does that help us? Should we disguise ourselves as researchers at Immunovax?" Rhonda asked eagerly.

"No, you'd need an extensive resume to pull that off. However, one of us could volunteer to run errands around the office as a go-fer. That skillset is more manageable," I suggested.

Rhonda replied, "And what are we supposed to look for? I don't think they'll record a receipt for a hitman."

"I'm looking at the Immunovax website right now," Kit said. "Under Job Opportunities, they list janitorial services. Rhonda, since you have some days off, you might be able to get a job in that department."

"You want me to go there and clean toilets?" Rhonda protested.

Emily replied, "All we want is to get you in the building, so we have eyes and ears on the ground."

"Their headquarters are in Kansas City, and you'd blend in perfectly," I encouraged, though I doubted she could pull it off.

"You mean a Volga German cleaning lady with a distinct accent acquired from her non-English-speaking grandmother? I think I can manage it. I have a cousin who lives in Kansas City."

Rhonda had cousins everywhere, and she was always up for an adventure, especially if it was an undercover one.

"Let's do it then! Kit, would you create a fake LinkedIn account for Rhonda and complete an application on the Immunovax website? This will be fun," I said, though I questioned my enthusiasm. I wanted to support Rhonda's efforts. She might uncover a breakthrough in the case.

"So, what are my qualifications? Broom pusher, trash can unloader, toilet bowl attendant?" Rhonda asked.

"All of the above," I laughed. "Jack of all trades. Every company needs one of these specialists. Just make yourself look good, but not too good. I wouldn't mention your degree in Criminal Justice or your many years of service with the Hays sheriff's department."

"I'll do my best," Rhonda agreed.

"Okay, that's settled. What else do we need to explore? I don't want to put any of you in danger. Are the ballistics back on the bullet from Jake's car door?" I asked.

"Not yet," Rhonda responded. "I'll keep checking."

"Emily, would you be willing to review my parents' research notes from Kenya? Perhaps they mentioned a threat to their life. Please be careful, though. I wonder if those notes were what Brock's murderer was looking for when he ransacked his office. I gave Brock a copy shortly after he drew my blood in hopes he would glean information from their research for his current project."

"Doc, there was no mention of those notes found at the scene of Brock's murder. Do you still have the originals?" Rhonda asked.

"Yes, I put the original notes in my safety deposit box at the Sagebrush Savings and Loan, and a copy in my safe."

"I'd be happy to take a look at them," Emily volunteered. "I need a break from reading medical abstracts on weight-loss injections and bird flu pandemics."

"Look for any references to their super immunity and what they knew about LifeShield," I directed.

"What do you need *me* to do?" Kit asked.

"Dig deeper into LifeShield's connection to the U.S. government. If you can learn more about their research and why they squelched it, that would be helpful," I suggested. "As for me, I'll check out of this inhospitable hospital this afternoon and lay low. Whoever wanted me dead before must want me even more dead now that we're on their trail. I'll get in touch with Hayes to see how the case is coming along."

Emily winked at Rhonda, who made rude kissing sounds.

"All right, you guys. Rhonda, why can't you be more like Emily—polite, reserved, and non-judgmental?" I chided.

Emily bent over in a spasm of laughter. So much for

polite and reserved.

Kit uploaded Rhonda's profile to LinkedIn. I had to admit it was convincing. She wrote a stellar resume for a janitor, using some of us as references. Immunovax had two janitorial positions open.

Must have been a lot of dirt around there. I hoped Rhonda would find it.

Rhonda heard back from their HR manager almost immediately. Wow. The company must have been desperate. I guess there weren't many people looking for jobs working with biohazards.

After checking out of the hospital, I settled back into my clinic apartment. I can't really call it an apartment. It's only a room with a bed, a shower in the kennel, and a microwave in the lab, but it felt like home. I proceeded to finagle a way to put myself in Hayes' path without being obvious. It had been a while since we talked. Hoped he wasn't hurt by my refusal to see him at the hospital. Sometimes it was better not to be seen at all than to be seen on a bad hair day with an IV in your arm and a bedpan peeking out from under your bed.

I dialed Hayes's cell phone. Each ring took me a notch lower on the emotional ladder, from the high of expectancy to the low of rejection. I hung up after six rings. Didn't want to appear too desperate. I exhaled my disappointment.

Just as I ran out of breath, my phone rang.

Be still, my heart. It was Hayes.

"Hello, who's calling?" I quipped.

"No one who wants to talk to you," he snapped back.

"Well, why did you call me?" I asked, feigning annoyance.

"I didn't call you. You called me. I was in the shower. I don't take my phone in there with me," he defended himself.

My mind wandered to a picture of Hayes in the shower. Bombs were going off in the battlefield of my mind. I tried to make myself picture him wearing clothes. But really? I was old, not dead. This reformed Christian life was not without temptation. My hormones got the best of me.

"Need someone to towel you off?" I asked.

It sounded like his phone had banged on the floor.

Hayes recovered, stuttering. "Ruby, that doesn't sound like you. D-did you mean it?"

"I never say anything I don't mean," I teased.

"I'll be right over," he responded.

Chapter 34

"Got the job!" Rhonda said with excitement as she burst through the back door of the clinic. I shouldn't have unlocked it in anticipation of Hayes's arrival.

Not here. Not now. What bad timing, or was it God's way of protecting me from throwing myself at Hayes? God had a funny way of putting stumbling blocks in my pathway, especially when that pathway might lead straight to hell.

Good grief.

"Rhonda, that's great!" My facial expression was a mixture of glee and desperation. I was happy that she'd found a way into Immunovax, but I tried not to let my frustration with her ill-timed visit show. "When do you start work?"

"I start Monday, in two days. Don't know if I have the skills to pull this off, Doc."

"What? You don't think you can empty trash cans, shred documents, or mop a floor? Rhonda, you've worked with janitorial staff at the police station for years," I answered.

"Yeah, but they always worked at night when I was usually home. I don't even know where to start."

"They'll give you instructions on their system and

probably pair you up with a senior broom pusher," I added.

"Yes, but what happens when the job requires more technical know-how?" Rhonda asked.

This was a side of Rhonda I'd never seen. She was always so confident, so comfortable in her law enforcement duties. Talk about a job with unpredictability; she dealt with unpredictability every day before her semi-retirement. Perhaps the weight riding on her success in this undercover assignment was too much. It was probably illegal, too, but that never bothered Rhonda if it was for the public's good.

I tried not to be too abrupt with her, grateful she'd volunteered, but love took priority over chit-chat.

"Hey, Rhonda. I've got a patient coming in soon. It's a confidential situation. His dog swallowed his girlfriend's lipstick, and it's not his wife's shade. You understand."

I hated lying to her, but this was one of those rare situations where loyalty to a friend took a back seat to the exhilaration of a new boyfriend's touch.

"Let me walk you to your car." I opened her car door and shoved her in. "We'll talk tomorrow. Bye."

Just then, an unmarked car pulled in with Hayes at the wheel. Rhonda looked at him. He looked at me, and I looked down at the ground.

Busted.

Rhonda peeled out of my back parking lot with a big grin as she gave me a thumbs-up. I didn't know whether to be bold and approach Hayes or stand there looking foolish.

I didn't want to appear too forward or too desperate. Oh, God, you sure could get in the way of an old lady who wanted to feel loved again.

As soon as Rhonda was out of sight, Hayes bolted out of his car and rushed toward me. He grabbed me and held me tight. Was he afraid I might get away? I buried my face in his chest. My breathing rate amped up, and I was sweating profusely. My mother always told me ladies didn't sweat, they perspired. She'd clearly never met a hottie like Hayes, or else she'd forgotten what it was like when my father first held her. This was definitely sweating. Darn my natural deodorant. I'm going back to those aluminum-filled ones.

"Ruby. I thought we had our first fight," he whispered into the top of my head.

What was he talking about? We didn't even have a relationship to fight over.

"When you wouldn't see me at the hospital, I was convinced we were over."

Again, what was this "we" thing? It was true that men were hunters and responded to the loss of their prey by doubling down on their efforts. I'd known this since I was a teenager. If you wanted to attract a guy, act like you didn't even know he was in the room. Or refuse him access when you were in the hospital.

"Oh, Hayes. I wasn't angry with you. I just didn't want you to see me in such a weakened, post-panic attack condition," I spoke into his shirt pocket.

Most normal-sized people didn't know what it was like to be a foot shorter than their love interest. I once saw a newspaper picture of my high school boyfriend and me walking across a bridge. He was 6'2" to my 4'10." I mistakenly thought it was a father with his elementary school-age daughter.

Hayes was still squeezing me. I didn't want him to let up, even though my calves cramped from standing on my tiptoes. I relaxed in his arms and let out a tiny fart. Hope he didn't hear that. Better change location quickly! "Hayes. Hayes. Let's go into the clinic and continue this discussion."

Putting a godly face on this hopefully ungodly convergence, I locked the back door, ushered Hayes into my boudoir, and tucked Chui away in his kennel condo. He would have disapproved. Plus, I didn't want him to watch.

Chui made me nervous when he stared.

Upon my return, Hayes re-engaged with me, and my

heart raced. I was frightened—not of Hayes, but of what might come next. Where should I put my hands? I was just above eye level with his belt buckle. Stop that, Ruby. Let Hayes lead this dance.

If I stretched just a bit, I could kiss him on the neck. I did that gently. He lifted me off the ground, bringing me closer to his face. My legs dangled in the air, no traction, just attraction. Our kisses became more frenzied. I felt like a teenager who had suddenly found herself alone at home with her boyfriend for the first time, without supervision.

Whoopee!

"Doctor Dakota! Doctor Dakota! We have an emergency out here! Why isn't Chui with you?"

It was Harley. She had keys to the back door so she could walk the dogs on weekends. Hayes and I both froze.

Oh no. This couldn't be happening. This could be my last chance for love. Rhonda and Harley should start a club, the Untimely Intrusion Society.

"What do we do?" Hayes whispered. With all my heart and hormones, I wanted to tell him to keep quiet, but I didn't think either of us could manage that feat when in such close proximity to each other. I began to giggle. Yes, giggle, like a schoolgirl caught passing notes in class. Hayes's brow furrowed in confusion or unrequited desire, but then he let out a low chuckle as he set me back on solid ground.

"Oops. Am I interrupting anything? Is Hayes here, too?" Harley asked.

"Yes, he's here visiting. Let us get our clothes on first," I teased, immediately opening my door. As I opened the door, I saw that Harley's face was beet red. Hadn't seen her this flustered since…ever.

Harley didn't fluster.

"I, I, I'm so sorry. Maybe it isn't an emergency. It's just that Rennie is vomiting nonstop in between squirts of diarrhea." Harley's voice cracked.

"Wait. Why do you have Rennie?" I had lost my irritation for a moment. Rennie needed me.

"I was sad. I just broke up with my boyfriend, so I asked Rhonda if Rennie could stay with me for a few days," Harley whispered.

"What's he been eating in the last 24 hours?" I probed.

"You know, the usual." She squirmed, avoiding eye contact as she answered.

"You understand that Rennie has GI tract problems. Rhonda has cautioned you about his diet, Harley."

I was surprised how seamlessly my brain could move from arousal mode to diagnostic mode.

"You, of all people, should know Rennie has a sensitive digestive system. He is on a bland intestinal diet. No McDonald's, no Dairy Queen."

"What kind of life is that for a dog?" Harley asked.

"A life without diarrhea, vomiting, or intestinal pain. That's what kind of a life it would be, and you wouldn't be interrupting me at all hours of the day and night."

All right, that was harsh. I immediately regretted it when I saw her eyes glisten with tears.

"I'm sorry, Harley. That's not fair. Let's help Rennie."

I ushered her and Rennie away from the door, aiming them toward the surgery room. Hayes stuck his head out of my room like he was trying to avoid gunfire.

"Hayes, I'm so sorry." Boy, was I sorry. "I've taken an oath." I held up three fingers like a Girl Scout. "To prevent and relieve animal suffering. Their needs come before mine. Could we take up this, uh, discussion another time?"

Hayes nodded curtly. "I think we'll meet at my place next, if there's ever a next."

My heart dropped. What did he mean by that?

My compassion for animals and my staff always outweighed my personal needs. I watched Hayes stroll toward the door, not knowing if I would get another opportunity to be held by him.

I performed an examination on Rennie, who looked miserable. His head hung down, almost touching the table, and saliva dripped from his mouth. Every time I palpated his abdomen, he flinched.

"Harley, you know pancreatitis can be serious. It's excruciating for the dog and could lead to the destruction of the cells that secrete insulin. Too many attacks and Rennie could develop diabetes. You know what our clients go through as they attempt to regulate their pets' blood sugar levels. It's an emergency. You were right to bring him over. I'll have to inform Rhonda."

"I feel just terrible, Doc." Harley was almost in tears. "I would never have intruded on your private time, especially with Hayes. We all think you two are a match made in heaven. I didn't want to call the relief vet. Rennie doesn't know her, and he's, uh, you know, a bite dog. You're probably the only vet he's ever known. Rhonda says he trusts you."

I didn't know about a match made in heaven. It was a match made somewhere, though. Of that, I was sure. Why else would I spend my nights fantasizing about Hayes?

"No problem, Harley. I love Rennie, too, and don't want him to suffer. Let's give him some meds to help him get some relief. No food for 24 hours."

"Oh, Doc," Harley argued.

"No food, I said."

Now, for Rhonda. I called to give her the news about Rennie.

"How bad is he, Doc? Is it okay to leave him alone at the clinic?"

"He's not alone. Harley is with him. I gave him fluids and something for pain. He's gonna be okay. You guys must quit feeding him greasy junk food. Stick to his intestinal diet." I reminded her to meet us at Hickok's to brainstorm her next move at Immunovax.

She was going to need God's intervention.

Chapter 35

It was a rare, slow time at the bar. Only a couple of cowboys were shooting pool. The quiet was depressing. The place's age showed. The beer-infused atmosphere of a Friday night might disguise it, but in the fading afternoon light and with few patrons, the glittery façade paled. Emily, Kit, and I squeezed into our booth just as Rhonda walked in.

"Hey, Rhonda. Congrats on your second job. They don't realize what a great hire you are. If you steal info from them, though, they probably won't consider you for Employee of the Month," Kit popped off.

"Got that right. I just hope I don't end up in the county jail where I'm the dispatcher. That'd be a kick in the head, wouldn't it?" Rhonda commented.

"We're praying that doesn't happen, but it will take a miracle to position you in the right place at the right time. Did you get a uniform and ID badge yet?" I asked.

"Nope, I'll pick them up Monday. I start cleaning in the mail room."

Emily had an idea. "Dakota, I was thinking. Remember the virology intern who spoke with you at SIC?"

"You mean Titer's mother…uh, Kendall." I was surprised I remembered her name.

"Perhaps she could help us. She might know someone in her field who works at Immunovax. It's worth checking it out. And what about the whistleblower from the Immunovax meeting? What happened to her? Is she still in Kansas City?" Emily asked.

"Good idea, Emily!" I agreed. "I'll head over to S.I.C. Monday morning. I'm still on sick leave, not that it matters to some people."

"What do you mean?" Rhonda asked.

"Ugh, it's just Harley and her timing," I replied.

Rhonda was satisfied with that answer. Did she know about Hayes? Did Harley tell her? Did Harley have to feed that dog a double cheeseburger?

We had much more to discuss, but the Belladonnas finished off our pitcher of 'Nojitos,' a virgin version of a mojito, and left for our respective homes. As I headed for the clinic, I realized that the hospital might release Jake tomorrow. His wife, Melanie, would probably care for him at home, although I'd rarely seen her. How he figured into this plot was still a mystery to me. Maybe I should pay him another visit.

I parked near the entrance of Hays Medical Center and made my way to Jake's room. He was watching *Enjoying Everyday Life*, a TV show hosted by Joyce Meyer, a Bible teacher.

What was up with that?

He startled when I stepped into his room. "Uh, hey, Ruby. Come on in and sit down. I'm glad to see you," he said.

Who stole my boss? In the old days, he'd never been glad to see me, except when he was preparing to leave his clinic in my hands while he went on a three-day weekend. Guess he figured I couldn't wreck his business in three days.

"Jake, I thought I'd pay you a visit before they kick you out tomorrow. How's your shoulder feeling?" Now that he'd admitted that jealousy drove his animosity toward me, I had more compassion for him; not weepy, but at least humane.

"Oh, I'm healing fine. They say there's no nerve damage, for which I'm grateful. I'll be back at work in no time."

Oh, great. Just what I wanted to hear. Not feeling quite so compassionate about that news.

"Jake, I have a couple of questions for you. First, we all noticed you didn't attend Brock's funeral. What kept you away?"

It took him a while to answer. "Ruby, I was going to tell you. I was inspecting your room at the clinic for health or housing code violations. After the fight at S.I.C., I wanted an excuse to kick you out. I am so sorry for invading your privacy."

"You could have at least put things back where you found them. Second question, did you see anyone lurking around my clinic the day of your shooting? Someone on a rooftop, anything?" The roof of any business across the street offered a clean shot and a clean exit.

"That part of my day is a bit fuzzy. It was unmanly of me to pass out. Sorry you all had to see that. I recall pulling into your parking lot, but then my memory goes blank until I arrived at the ER. It bothers me that I can't remember details."

Jake seemed genuinely concerned that he had no recall of the incident. Not surprising.

"That's okay. Don't stress about it, Jake. The Belladonnas and I are investigating these shootings. There's got to be a common thread. There may even be a link to the death of my parents many years ago."

Why was I sharing this with him? He'd never asked about my family. For all I knew, he could be in on everything.

"Your parents are both dead?" he asked. "I'm sorry to

hear that, Ruby."

What? He was still calling me Ruby. It was *always* Dr. Dakota, although it sounded like he was mocking me when he said it. I often called him Jake the Snake outside the clinic. That was me being disrespectful to him.

"Thanks. It was a long time ago. Any word on who will take over Brock's business?" I asked.

"Nope. Don't think it will be me. I'm making a change. Work is no longer my primary focus. I'm not taking on any new responsibilities. I need to spend more time with my wife."

Under my breath, I added, "Instead of other men's wives."

He knew I knew about his clandestine meetings in the extra bedroom at his old clinic. The staff always used to joke about those young suburban housewives who came into the clinic for a pet vax and a personal 'booster.' He even tried to entice me back there once, but I had standards. Low ones, but still… My rule: avoid personal relationships with your boss.

I would have been more likely to neuter him if given the opportunity.

"That sounds like a good plan, Jake," I said, not believing he could change. "When do you think you'll be back at my clinic? There's no rush. Corporate sent a relief vet to fill in for me until I'm ready to return. There's no point in checking on her sales. She's temporary." I hoped that was true. "I need to shove off now. God be with you, Jake."

What was I saying? He was about as far from God as a man could be. However, God often used tragedy to give us a grip on what was essential in life.

And no one was beyond the saving grace of God.

Chapter 36

The next morning, my phone jangled on my nightstand. It was Rhonda. "Hey, Doc. How's my Rennie doing?"

"I checked on him last night at bedtime. He was sleeping," I answered. "Harley texted me this morning that he's doing fine, practically a new dog. She'll probably put him back in my room later where he can rest on my bed."

"That's good to hear. Off to the big city now. I'm all set to move in with my cousin. Kansas City, here I come!"

I worried more about the city than I did about Rhonda. She could take care of herself, and I prayed she'd uncover something to help us end this fiasco.

"That's great, Rhonda. We'll miss you around these parts. Keep the Belladonnas posted and be careful."

We signed off, but I had an uneasy feeling about this. It was like watching a Chihuahua snatch food from a Great Dane's bowl. I suspected it might not end well.

Time to check in up front to assess the damage caused by the *locum tenens* veterinarian. This was a mistake, but I couldn't help myself. They were all probably at each other's throats. Clients must be fleeing by the hundreds. They came to my clinic because of me. After all, it was me Harley trusted with her sick dog, not the relief vet.

I cautiously stepped out of my room and headed for the front. Chui saw me but ignored me as I passed by the kennel. I stood outside an exam room and listened.

"Yes, Mrs. Younger, I know Dr. Dakota has been your vet for years, but she needed a break. Could you give me a chance to diagnose why Pixie is limping on her back leg?"

The relief vet, whose name I didn't know, was trying to soothe a lady who'd lied to me for years with a dog that had never shown a replicable symptom. Pixie was a parti poodle with a low pain tolerance. This would be a good one for Dr. Newbie to figure out. It took me years to understand her… and her dog.

"Well, I guess it couldn't hurt. Just don't do anything that will make it worse. How long have you been out of vet school?" Mrs. Younger, a former nurse, was on her game today.

I assumed Dr. Newbie ignored that question while she reviewed Pixie's history, which could fill a large filing cabinet. Yes, we still used paper files in the exam room. I was more comfortable with that than entering information on a tablet. I didn't want patient histories to disappear into a cloud. With corporate ownership, though, that would change soon.

"Pixie has been limping for days. She barely touches her back leg down. When she does, she screams. She is in constant pain. I can't sleep because of her whining. Doctor, I'm overwhelmed. Please help us," Mrs. Younger pleaded.

Because of the silence, I assumed Dr. Newbie examined Pixie without eliciting so much as a whimper. I waited for her verdict.

"Mrs. Younger, I've reviewed Pixie's history and completed the exam. Physically, she appears to be in good health. I am unable to elicit any pain whatsoever from either back leg. There's just nothing there."

Mrs. Younger's voice trembled. "But Doctor, at home, she won't put any weight on it. I don't understand why she's fine here."

Dr. Newbie made a shocking suggestion. "Mrs. Younger, I cannot prescribe pain medication in good conscience at this time. Perhaps we could set up a house call so that I can observe Pixie's behavior in her home environment."

What the heck did she just prescribe? Did she offer to go to a client's home? NO, NO, NO! Just give Pixie the anti-inflammatories and pain meds and send them happily on their way. They'd return soon enough with no improvement—a frustrating cycle of treat and repeat.

"Oh, Doctor," Mrs. Younger replied. "You don't have to do that. I didn't know your clinic made house calls. My house is too messy to have someone visit."

"Mrs. Younger, I just want to get to the bottom of Pixie's lameness. If you are in such distress, I can arrange an appointment with a counselor who specializes in working with pets and their owners during challenging times. We want to help Pixie, but we also care about your well-being."

Oh, no. You've done it now, Dr. Newbie! I knew Mrs. Younger was about to unleash a torrent of rage.

"How dare you! Are you telling me I'm crazy? I am not imagining this. You are a poor excuse for a vet. I need to see Dr. Dakota. She understands. Pixie and I visited many vet clinics before I found this one. None of those other vets found anything, but Dr. Dakota always finds out what's wrong."

I cringed behind the door.

Maybe catering to the client's whims wasn't always the best thing to do. That was my people-pleasing behavior at work. Perhaps I should have suggested mental health care for both of them. It was just so much easier to diagnose something, issue meds, and escort her out of the exam room.

"I'm taking my business elsewhere, young lady!" Mrs.

Younger continued her tirade. “Perhaps you need to go back to vet school.”

She let out a humph, picked up an embarrassed Pixie the parti poodle, and stormed out without paying.

I was livid. My blood hit a rolling boil, and everything shrank down to one target: Dr. Newbie. She'd just lost us a good customer, faker or not. I shut the exam room door hard enough to make a point before I barked at the new vet.

“Doctor, I don’t know what kind of medicine they’re teaching in vet school these days, but that was the worst doctor-client interaction I’ve ever eavesdropped on. Not only did you suggest she needed counseling, but by offering to go to her home, you implied that you did not believe her. Doctor, you lost the clinic a client, a good-paying one.”

My eyes stared daggers at this young vet. When her eyes started to fill with tears, I was brought up short. What was I doing? I was turning into Jake the Snake! Between Harley and this impressionable young doctor, I’d managed to inflict emotional pain on two young women that could last a lifetime. It felt like all the air had been sucked out of the room and out of me under the weight of what I’d just done.

How could I have been so cruel?

“Doctor, uh,” I paused. “I’m sorry. I don’t know your name.”

“It’s Dr. Simpson, Valerie,” she whimpered as she wiped her nose on the sleeve of her exam coat.

“I apologize for my aggressive behavior,” I began. “Yes, your approach to Mrs. Younger differed from mine, but I believe you were interested in both her and Pixie’s welfare. Over the years, this clinic has tolerated and placated her but never addressed the real issues in her life. You called her bluff, gave her two options, and stood your ground. I admire that.”

“Dr. Dakota, I’m sorry about losing a client. These days, they teach us to address not only the patient but also the owner. Owning a pet is stressful at best. It is helpful to offer psychological options for the client even though they may refuse."

Oh, great. She was about to school me. Now I really felt terrible.

"From the repeating history and your humorous remarks in the notes, I explored the possibility that Mrs. Younger suffers from Munchausen syndrome, the name used when you were in school. This condition has been renamed Factitious Disorder Imposed on Another—FDIA, for short. Not an easy one to deal with. Usually, the client is a woman with some medical background and appears to be well-informed on her pet's condition. She may even injure the pet at home to elicit the presenting complaint. Her incentive may be to get the attention she craves from the veterinarian and the staff. Another possible motivation may be to obtain drugs. Mrs. Younger seems to fall into that rare category of attention-seeking. I think you'll get another chance at her. After all, she was angry with me, not you."

I slunk back to my room, chastened. This young doctor knew what she was talking about. She was more holistic than I ever was. Not only had I rudely challenged her diagnosis and treatment plan, but I'd also been shortchanging my client. Still, all this psychiatry stuff for vet medicine sounded like a lot of blah, blah, blah to me.

Maybe I *was* too old to be in practice. Should my diploma have come with an expiration date, like milk?

CHAPTER 37

Back in my room, marinating in my misery, my phone rang. It was Hayes. My heart rate ramped up to hummingbird level. I let it ring a few times, then picked up. "Hello, this is Dr. Dakota."

"I know this is Dr. Dakota," Hayes snapped back. "I called you, for heaven's sake. Ruby, I have some news on the bullet they dug out of Jake's door. It's not a match to the ones from your clinic attack or Brock's shooting. Those were both fired from the same handgun. This one appears to have come from a sniper rifle, a .308 Winchester.

"Does that mean two shooters? Another motive? That complicates things," I observed.

"Not necessarily. He could have used the sniper rifle just because he was farther away from the target. Who would want Jake dead?" Hayes asked.

"Over the years… let me think. For Jake, that would be about a hundred women and their husbands. Oh, and Jake's wife, Melanie, and me."

Oops, that was a mistake. "It wasn't me, just so you know."

"Everyone is back on the suspect list again. Where's Rhonda been the last few days?" Hayes asked.

No mention of the other night. Did he have dementia?

Didn't he feel what I did? This man was so frustrating.

"She took a week off to visit her cousin in Kansas City," I fibbed. I could have dementia, too. So there. "She might do a little research while she's there."

"Research? Isn't the headquarters for Immunovax in Kansas City?" he asked. "She isn't doing anything stupid up there, is she?"

How could I answer that? If I told him the truth, Rhonda could be in big trouble. If I lied, I could be in big trouble.

No question, I lied.

"She needed a break from dispatch. It's been busy lately, with the full moon and all."

All the Belladonnas complained about full moon crazies: Kit at the pharmacy, Rhonda at the sheriff's department, and Emily and me at our practices.

"I understand," agreed Hayes. He saw his share of crazies nearly every day. "Hope Rhonda gets some much-needed rest. I've got to get back to work. Talk to ya later."

Was that it? Business, no pleasure? All I could think about was that night and what might have happened if Harley hadn't interrupted us. Maddening, but I knew Hayes was dedicated to his job. He didn't mix it with his personal life. Maybe police guidelines didn't allow him to become involved with a victim.

On Monday morning, I stopped by S.I.C. to talk to Kendall. As usual, Lottie, the secretary, buzzed me in and asked what she could do for me.

"Is it okay if I step into the lab and talk to Kendall?"

"Oh, Kendall? She's taken a new job at Immunovax in Kansas City. It was a step up for her, and with all the uncertainty about S.I.C.'s future, it was good timing."

"Thanks, Lottie. I'm happy for her. Next time I'm in Kansas City, I'll look her up," I replied, heading out the door.

I wondered if she would take Brock's research with her. Surely, Brock required her to sign a nondisclosure clause.

I pulled up to the clinic's back door, unlocked it, and fully intended to get some rest. I headed for Chui's chain-link apartment, but he was not there. I heard London up front as she locked up for the day and covered up the parrot cage. When she spotted me, her face lit up as if she had just seen Taylor Swift.

"Doc, it's so good to see you. I missed your sneak attack visit on the new doc."

She laughed when she saw my nose crinkle up. "Don't worry. She's gone for the day."

We hugged like old friends. "How are you feeling?" she asked.

"I'm doing great, but where is Chui? I miss him like crazy."

"He's with Harley. She took him home after work. Rennie's been there, too, because Rhonda's visiting a cousin in Kansas City. Rennie and Chui are now best buds. Rennie has quit carrying him around in his mouth like a stuffed toy."

That must have been humiliating for Chui.

"Harley said she'll bring him to work in the morning."

"That doesn't work for me. I need to see him now." I headed for Harley's trailer.

I hoped Chui still wanted to come home with me. Harley tended to spoil him with treats. She answered the door with a raised eyebrow and a smirk.

"Ah, just in time. Chui was about to sign adoption papers with me."

"I may not be his birth mom, but he's still my baby,' I joked. "Heard you're fostering Rennie, too. You're a jewel. Don't know what Rhonda and I'd do without you. Thanks for loving on him."

"No problem, Doc."

I was wrong to doubt. When Chui saw me, he jumped into my arms and attacked my face like I was a human salt lick. We headed back to our humble abode, both reveling in our mutual love and respect. Almost as good as Hayes holding me… almost.

We enjoyed our dinner together: a microwaved cheese enchilada for me and a bowl of Adult Mini Chicken and Brown Rice kibble for Chui. With our bellies full, we settled down to watch a movie. I could not turn off my brain.

I was concerned about Rhonda's welfare. And what about the whistleblower? Did I want to go down that road? It was a bit personal. After all, a contract had been put out on my life. But we needed to speak with the whistleblower to solve this case. If she were still employed, she could be the person on the inside. There was a law that protected whistleblowers in the pharmaceutical industry. Would the company make up an excuse to fire her? Perhaps Rhonda could ask around without putting herself in danger. There must be an employee list somewhere online. If there was, Rhonda would find it.

With these thoughts racing through my mind, I looked over at Chui who was snoring.

Chui never had insomnia.

Chapter 38

We both awoke to the uproar as Harley entered the kennel room. Everyone wanted to be walked at once, and they were deafeningly vocal about it. Chui joined in with a howl for a few seconds until he realized he was not in the kennel this morning. I stepped outside in my pajama scrubs to walk Chui in his KSU purple pride doggie nightshirt. He hiked his leg on my fake fire hydrant, and we hurried back in so I could hike mine.

Chui rode shotgun with me on today's errands, secured in his doggie seatbelt because he got motion sickness in the back seat. He could still reach the window to stick his nose out. His wild-eyed, spiky-haired look amused me.

Most people who rode in my front seat got that same look. I told him to focus on the horizon.

Our first stop was Target to pick up a few healthy food items: microwave popcorn, Marie Callender's™ chicken pot pies, Lay's™ Baked Potato Chips, frozen cheese nuggets, honey wheat bread, tuna for my brain, and Diet Dr Pepper for my soul. No need to buy toilet paper, soap, light bulbs, paper towels, toilet bowl cleaner, shampoo, or creme rinse. I pilfered those from the clinic.

Today, Chui wore his therapy dog vest. If anybody ever needed a therapy dog, I did. He wasn't allowed into public areas such as hospitals, schools, or nursing homes unless he was 'therapying' someone. Actually, he wasn't cleared for Target. However, no one ever questioned the vest, as I probably looked like I needed an emotional support dog. No shame here. Chui took up his place as the masthead of the red plastic cart.

We both loved how quiet Target shopping carts were.

People waited in a long line for coffee, as the smell of Starbucks dark roast called to me. We called it Tarbucks because of its location. The chalkboard listed Ethiopian Yirgacheffe, my favorite coffee. In Africa, our Ethiopian friends often invited us to join in their coffee ceremony. Now, that was the way to drink coffee—beans freshly roasted, ground, and brewed right before your eyes in a beautiful ritual. Chui pawed in the direction of the barista as if commanding the ship. He knew they had free Puppuccinos, a blob of whipped cream in a cup. I bypassed the coffee for now, much to Chui's chagrin.

Chui was a people magnet. Everyone wanted to take pictures with him and learn about his breed. I had to stop the cart so that they could pet him. He thought he was a celebrity. Sometimes I put sunglasses on him so people wouldn't recognize him.

Full speed ahead, Captain!

We rushed to the back of the store for the food items. I avoided any mirrors. One time, Chui saw his reflection and jumped out of the cart to greet it. He barked his head off as if he'd found his Ancestry.com match. On the way out, we visited the dog toy section. He chose a small KONG Extreme Tires model for himself.

What a macho dog.

He picked out a KONG Cozie Rosie Rhino for Lola. He was thoughtful like that.

Next up, the Sagebrush Savings and Loan. Kelly worked the drive-up window. She saw my Land Rover coming several car lengths away and was ready by the time we got to her window.

"Good morning, Doctor Dakota. How's my favorite vet and her fur baby doing today?"

I winced. Chui hated to be called a fur baby. He thought it was like calling a human baby a skin baby. Just shouldn't do it.

"Chui and I are busier than a cat with one eye watching two mouseholes," I quipped.

Kelly and I had our little ritual. She opened the big money drawer, and I inserted a deposit slip, the check, and then Chui. Whoosh, he was inside the bank. At least I didn't put him in the pneumatic tube.

That would have been traumatic.

I laughed hysterically every time. Chui, not so much, but he got a doggie pop, so he didn't complain. Kelly carried him around to greet the loan department. I was holding up the line. The guy behind me must have thought I dropped my dog off as collateral. Kelly returned Chui, who had a sheepish look. He only tolerated this because he loved me.

Oh, that and the doggie pop.

I'd promised Chui some time at the dog park earlier, but I was uncomfortable with that. Although vaccinated, there was too much doggie flu going around. I believed he had a robust immune system because of his constant exposure to other dogs in the kennel, but I didn't want to take any chances with my family member. Plus, I was keenly aware that someone was still out to kill me.

We headed back to the clinic. I opened the car door for Chui and unfastened his harness. Chui rarely wore a leash. He never wanted to leave my side. With two bounces, he jumped down and headed for the back door, tail wagging. He couldn't wait to give Lola her new toy.

London met us at the kennel. "Hey, Doc. Rhonda called and left a message for you."

"Okay, thanks. I'll call her from my room." London offered to put Chui and the two new toys in the kennel. I would have loved to see Lola's face when Chui gave her the toy.

I dialed Rhonda's number. "Hey, how's the big city?"

"The big city stinks, but the job is promising, and the housing with my cousin is free. I met the other janitor in my section yesterday, Walter Warren. He's been here for a few weeks, but get this. He told me his family has a long history with this company. It appears his father was employed by this company decades ago, when it was known as LifeShield."

"That's fascinating!" I responded. "Was his dad a janitor too?"

"Oh, his dad wasn't a janitor. You're not going to believe this." Rhonda dropped a bomb. "Walter said his dad was a project director."

"No way!" I exclaimed.

What a coincidence. No, strike that. How supernatural. I didn't believe in coincidence.

"He could be a valuable resource. Did you ask him about the Immunovax secretary who secretly recorded the board meeting when they put a hit out on me? Does he know if she's still with the company?"

"I did. Bad news. She's dead. Walter didn't know her, but the rumor is that she committed suicide. Who knows? I wouldn't put it past the board to have her snuffed out, too."

A wave of nausea flooded over me. Good thing I was seated on my bed; I might have fainted otherwise.

Another death. These people were pure evil.

"Thanks, Rhonda. Keep digging, but don't put yourself in danger. Too many questions too quickly could cause angst in high places."

"Gotcha. I'll be careful," she replied and hung up.

We urgently needed information about the current hits ordered on Brock, me, and possibly Jake, but I felt uneasy about Rhonda going undercover. She wasn't the most subtle of investigators. I dropped to the floor on my arthritic knees and prayed.

"Dear Lord, keep your eyes on Rhonda. Surround her with angels to guide and direct her. In Jesus' name, Amen."

There, it was now in His hands. Probably always had been, but I felt better officially turning it over to Him.

Chapter 39

I called Rhonda back in the evening and insisted she Zoom me into her workplace. Her phone rested on her cleaning cart. I'd turned it over to God but was still concerned. I watched as she pushed her giant dust mop down the corridors of Immunovax. She started to sing the theme from "Live PD."

"Whatcha gonna do when they come for you? Bad boys, bad boys." She did this when she was nervous.

Rhonda whispered into the phone, "I have an eerie feeling that someone is watching me, but I can't pinpoint their location."

"Rhonda, if you are uncomfortable, get out of there. Those people are murderers."

Suddenly, a sinister shape separated itself from the wall and walked toward Rhonda. I heard her let out her breath as she recognized him.

"Hey, Walter, I didn't know you were working the night shift," she said nervously.

"Not working, just carrying out a mission that is best done at night," he mumbled.

"What mission?" Rhonda and I asked simultaneously. Walter was unaware I could see him on my computer screen in Hays. Rhonda ignored me and probably hoped I'd keep quiet. My chest spasmed as I realized I couldn't stop whatever might happen next.

At least there would be a witness.

"Rhonda, you ask too many questions," Walter said suspiciously. "You know that, don't you? I suspect you have a hidden agenda for working here."

"Me? No! My agenda is to pay the rent and put food on my table," she replied shakily.

I knew she had a gun on her somewhere. She never went anywhere without a weapon. Surely they didn't run security checks on janitors at that place. Rhonda moved in front of her cart, blocking my view for a second.

Was that intentional? This guy gave me the creeps.

"Rhonda, you don't look, sound, or work like a janitor. Are you here on a mission, too?"

Rhonda moved providing me visual on Walter. His eyes darted to the door, then back to her. He lowered his voice. "If you are, let me help you. I've been surveilling this company since my father died." I could tell Rhonda didn't know whether to trust him.

"Go on, Walter. Let me hear your story," Rhonda said softly.

Walter continued, "Let me get this off my chest. LifeShield treated my dad unfairly years ago. I took this job to vindicate him in some way. For many years, LifeShield struggled with persistent corruption issues. CEO Samuel Jacobson and COO Charles Thomas are responsible for the current troubles. Money is their top priority. People don't matter. My dad and his work didn't matter."

He was on a roll. Rhonda wisely remained quiet.

"Back in the eighties, LifeShield sent my father to Kenya to research sex workers who, though working in risky environments, never contracted HIV/AIDS. They seemed to have an innate immunity. I still have all my father's notes."

I sucked in air. No way! Did we both have notes from

that research? That was incredible! We had to compare them.

"That's interesting, Walter. What else did you learn from his notes?" Rhonda wanted to keep him talking.

"His research focused on discovering why these women were immune and on developing a vaccine to prevent the disease. They never produced a vaccine, but they worked alongside two researchers who were onto something. Not a vaccine, but a treatment of sorts. It would have been revolutionary. My father noted that this couple claimed to possess enhanced immunity when exposed to Ebola in Uganda. Constant exposure to this highly transmissible virus didn't affect them. They were able to work freely among the infected population. My dad suspected this couple performed their own secret research to determine the source of their super-immunity."

Enhanced immunity. Secret research. This couple. That couple was my parents! The phrases bounced around in my brain like a trapped cat in a dog kennel. Is this really happening? Perhaps God was in control.

"Did your father mention the name of this couple?" Rhonda interjected.

"No, he didn't, probably for their security and his. It didn't help, though. Those two researchers turned up dead before they could develop a marketable treatment." Walter paused and seemed to fight back tears. "The company claimed it was a random carjacking, but my father had his doubts. Too convenient. Too close to the date that LifeShield backed out of the vaccine production negotiations with the U.S. government. They reasoned that HIV replicated too quickly and mutated too readily to develop a vaccine. They were willing to wait until technology caught up with vaccine production and didn't want immunotherapy to steal the market in the meantime. They swore my father to secrecy on the project, which he honored. His dying wish, however, was that I get justice for that couple. He knew they had a daughter, and that haunted him the rest of his life."

Uncontrollable weeping came from deep within my soul. I'd never grieved properly over the loss of my parents. I was young, and there was so much to do to get their bodies back to the U.S., plan a funeral, sort out their finances, and finish school. Tears soaked the T-shirt quilt that served as my bedspread. I tried to stifle my sobs so that Walter couldn't hear them.

Hopefully, Rhonda had muted me.

"Wow, that's quite a story, Walter, but why tell me? I'm just a janitor here." Rhonda tried to draw him out. I knew she was as shocked as I was. "Did you ever make any progress on getting revenge or whatever it is you're after?"

"I'm not after revenge," Walter replied calmly. "I do want someone to be held responsible. That story is not the only one where a researcher ends up dead. I'm also concerned about the events of the past few weeks. I believe this company has targeted more people. It must be related to current research on super-immunity. The company may have been renamed, but the evil is still firmly rooted in the board members of Immunovax, specifically with the CEO, Samuel Jacobson."

"Walter, I don't want to be disrespectful, but isn't all this viral research stuff above your pay grade? How do you even understand your dad's research papers or the current research done here?" I knew Rhonda wanted to keep him talking.

"Don't judge a book by its cover, Rhonda. I hold a Ph.D. in both Immunology and Genetics with a specialty in Virology. This job is just a cover to get information."

I was flabbergasted. He sounded credible if a bit unhinged. I hoped Rhonda would follow her gut. That was her God-given gift.

"Well, Walter, what I'm about to tell you will knock your socks off."

Rhonda took a deep breath before she proceeded. She was about to deliver some earth-shattering news to this janitor/virologist who'd been on his hunt for many years. She filled him in on me, my parents, the successful hit on Brock, and the unsuccessful attempts on Jake's life and mine. She didn't introduce me, though. I guessed she didn't want him to know I'd eavesdropped on their conversation.

"Rhonda, you're an answer to my prayers. God brought you here to help me stop this madness and greed. Let's put our heads together and get these scumbags." Walter high-fived Rhonda, almost knocking her phone and me off the cart. They parted equally energized.

With hushed intensity, I said, "Rhonda, are you still there? Rhonda? Did we lose our connection?"

She finally responded. "No, I just had to hit the can. Can you believe what just happened?"

"Believe it, Rhonda! The Bible says, 'The steps of the righteous man are ordered by the Lord.' He directed you to the right place and the right person. Find out how much Walter has accomplished. Get that information on a USB stick and into my hands. I'll take it from there."

We were on the verge of a breakthrough. I could feel it.

Chapter 40

After a good night's sleep, Chui and I were up early, ready to unmask a culprit or two. This wasn't a good day for Chui to tag along. He and Lola were content in their doggie digs with their new toys. I poked my head outside my room and saw Harley sliding a reluctant basset hound over the tile floor to the surgery room.

"Hey, Doc, how's it goin'? This guy is going under the knife this morning. He's getting a facelift and an eye tuck," she laughed. "You wanna be next, Doc?"

Was that an insult?

"I've earned my wrinkles, and I'm hanging onto them. Don't need to go on any reality plastic surgery nightmare shows."

"Okay, just so you know, we're here for you when you decide," she joked.

As veterinarians, we perform cosmetic surgery only when it is medically necessary and would improve the pet's quality of life. Several dog breeds have eyelids that roll in and irritate their corneas, or facial folds so deep that they develop chronic infections. We could help those conditions.

On the way out, I rechecked my face in the mirror and tugged loose neck skin toward the base of my ear. I thought I looked rather good for my age. Maybe Hayes would have a different opinion.

Oh, Hayes, Hayes, wherefore art thou, Hayes?

The night before, I'd set up a lunch meeting with the remaining Belladonnas to discuss Rhonda's new temp job. I'd head over there right after I got a haircut. My stylist, Rachel, had her hands full. My hair was as thick as a horse's tail and just as coarse. I refused to do any curling, straightening, styling, moussing, gelling, or hair-spraying. I didn't even want to waste time blow-drying, but I wanted to look good. She understood me. Low-maintenance hair that looked like I'd spent $300 on it. After about an hour in her chair, she told me she'd done all she could under the restraints I'd given her. I checked it out in the mirror.

It was poofy. I'd never be able to duplicate this look.

As I left the salon, I saw Hayes getting out of his car in front of the hardware store. "Ruby, it's so good to see you! Your hair looks pretty."

"Thanks. I just had it done at Rachel's salon. Did you know she used to be a dog groomer before attending beauty school? I'm always afraid she'll revert, throw me in a sling, shave my whole body, and place bows over my ears."

I actually wanted to say, '…and express my anal glands,' but I thought that would be a little crude for someone I was trying to impress.

"What are you doing for lunch?" Hayes asked.

Oh, dang it. Why didn't he ask me before I scheduled the Belladonna meeting? Did he take me for granted? Should I cancel the Belladonnas? No, that would be too needy. Besides, there were weighty things we needed to discuss about Rhonda and the case.

"Oh, Hayes, I'm so sorry, but I'm already booked for lunch. Maybe another time." I tried to act nonchalant.

The games that almost-lovers played…

He looked surprised. Hah! Take that. I did have other options besides him. Not handsome ones, not ones who wore seductive cologne, but options, nevertheless. He shrugged his shoulders as he entered the hardware store. I climbed into my car and sank into the seat. I thought I'd won, but I didn't feel victorious.

I felt lonely.

Kit and Emily had settled into our booth, which looked off kilter without Rhonda. She was a valuable member of our group, and we loved her.

"Is Rhonda in Kansas City already?" Kit asked.

"Yeah, she's one of us. We have a right to know," added Emily.

I had no idea they'd be so upset. I guessed this went back to when I'd called Rhonda first about my unexpected trip to Manhattan.

"Hey, I apologize. Rhonda and I thought it would be better to keep her travel under wraps until she arrived in Kansas City. She's now undercover at Immunovax."

"I'm having second thoughts about this plan," Kit said with concern in her voice. "It's dangerous! She has no idea what these big pharma companies are capable of. People sometimes disappear or worse."

She was right. We hadn't thought this caper through very well. We all knew Rhonda was fearless, but she often disregarded the cost.

"Rhonda knows what she's doing," I tried to reassure them. "She's already found another janitor gathering information for his own personal vendetta against Immunovax."

I conveyed the history of this new sidekick and his father and informed them of the whistleblower's untimely death.

"Yikes! Now I'm *terrified* for Rhonda!" Kit's voice trembled.

I was scared, too, but I tried to bluff my way through. "It seems this guy has already uncovered some data, and he has his dad's records from Kenya. Emily, you could help by comparing my parents' notes with his father's notes when we get them. It could reveal some clues. Perhaps Rhonda will gain access to them somehow. Rhonda is making nice with this guy. He now knows why she's there, though. Hope we can trust him."

The Belladonnas started to slide out of the booth when the restaurant door opened. I squinted to see who it was. No, I didn't need glasses. Well, maybe I did. Anyway, I could identify that hunk of a man anywhere. I drew a sharp breath as my face heated up.

"Ruby, it's Hayes." Kit pointed out the obvious.

"Do you want us to leave?" Emily asked politely.

"No, that's okay. He may prefer that you stay. Who knows?" Kit and Emily slid back in.

He hadn't seen us yet. He wandered over to the bar, not waiting to be seated. It felt like all eyes in the place were on me. Was I paranoid? Perhaps. I did know I was both excited and terrified to see him. What if he continued to act as if nothing had happened between us? Should I sneak out without acknowledging him? I watched as he ordered a Dr Pepper.

Oh, we were so compatible.

He slowly turned to his left, taking in the few patrons. When his gaze landed on me, I froze. Well, I was already frozen, but I quit breathing.

"Ruby. What are you doing here?"

I lifted my head in acknowledgment. "Hey, Hayes."

Brilliant, Ruby.

"Hello, Kit, Emily. Don't tell me. Let me guess. The Belladonnas are here to solve the mystery of the inaccurate sniper. How's it coming? Mind if I squeeze in beside you, Ruby?"

Duh, no. I moved over just a little, which forced him to press up against me.

"I hope you women have something, because we're at a standstill in the investigation," he confided.

"Oh, we have lots. Rhonda is just about to crack the

case," Kit blurted out. I kicked her under the table. "Ow! You mean you haven't told him about Rhonda?" she asked.

I kicked her again, harder this time. Good grief. With friends like this…

"Yes, Ruby, tell me about Rhonda," he demanded.

Oh, no. This wasn't going to end well… again. I had hoped we could discuss that alone sometime.

I waded in. "Rhonda went to visit her cousin in Kansas City."

True.

"She wanted to pick up some extra money, so she's moonlighting while she's there." Kind of true.

"As a security guard, or what?" Hayes asked.

"No, she took a janitorial job that paid well. That was the position they needed filled. You know Rhonda. She'll do anything for a buck."

Was he buying this? From his knitted eyebrows, I'd say probably not. I should come clean.

"Okay, Hayes, it's like this. We sent Rhonda in undercover." I said it fast, like ripping off a bandage. "We needed someone inside Immunovax to determine who had ordered the hits. Brock's secretary told us that Kendall, the intern at S.I.C., took a job at Immunovax shortly after Brock's death. We thought she might be able to help us get information. Rhonda was going to approach her with what we know and see if she would come on board."

"Are you four women crazy?" Hayes exploded. "Going undercover is extremely dangerous for Rhonda. From what I can tell, these guys are serious about their profits. She could be killed."

"The whistleblower has already met that fate," I confessed.

"What? Are you serious? Your meddling may get Rhonda killed!" Hayes was outraged.

"She's the one who found out the whistleblower's death was ruled a suicide. Which we don't believe. Rhonda is fine. Probably."

Now I felt guilty for putting Rhonda in that position. "I'm sorry, Hayes, but there were no leads, no DNA evidence, nothing. We got impatient, and she volunteered. I'm tired of looking over my shoulder, waiting for the next bullet to strike."

"Ruby Anne, this is not your investigation. You women are not Pinkerton agents. Yes, Rhonda has some law enforcement experience, but this is way above her pay grade. She could lose her position, her pension, and her life. Do you realize how easy it would be for them to make her disappear in that city? I want you to call this Wild West investigation off immediately."

I wanted to stick my tongue out and tell him he wasn't the boss of me, but that would have been immature. My eyes began to well up. It was like my father yelling at me all over again. I bit my lip and pushed through the tears.

"Rhonda has gathered more information in her first few days there than you and the FBI have in weeks. We're tired of waiting."

"What do you mean, more information? Ruby, if you withhold evidence in this case, I swear I'll…" He stopped and took a deep breath. "Ruby, you know I care about you… a lot. I don't want anything to happen to you or the Belladonnas. If something happened to Rhonda, you'd be forced to live with that forever. I don't want you to go through that kind of pain. If you could help me solve this case, I would be so grateful, but you must get Rhonda out of there before she gets hurt. Please, baby."

Did he just call me baby in front of the Belladonnas? Did he have no shame? Oh, I would do anything for this man.

"Okay, come by the clinic, and I'll fill you in. We can figure out how to extricate Rhonda safely and still get the information we need."

Hayes peeled out of the booth and headed for the door. I

sat there gawking at him.

He looked back over his shoulder. “What are you waiting for?” he laughed.

Chapter 41

The devil on my left shoulder would like to brag that we got together that afternoon, but we didn't. That wasn't to say we didn't connect, so to speak. When we arrived at the clinic, he clasped me to his chest and heaved a big sigh.

"Ruby, I was so afraid I'd messed up our relationship. I know I can be a bit hyper-focused on my job."

You think? I kept quiet, enthralled by the way it felt to have him hold me. I knew if I took a breath, I would inhale his scent and helplessly, passionately pass out.

"Ruby, say something. Are you upset?" he asked.

"Do I look upset? I'm clinging to your body like Saran Wrap. Hayes, if I were upset, you'd know it," I flippantly answered.

That wasn't true. I often stuffed my feelings. "I was waiting for you to make the next move. I *am* a lady, you know."

I almost choked on that line.

"I have a confession," he whispered. "I was stalking you this morning. When you entered Hickok's, I thought I'd better take advantage of the opportunity."

I loved this guy. He was as manipulative as I was.

In a few minutes, I mustered the strength to take a deep

breath. “Hayes, if we don’t put some space between us, I’m quite sure I won’t be able to stop this steamroller of seduction pressing us together. I’m not that good at resisting temptation when it comes to you. Lately, my thoughts have been preoccupied with scenarios of us in incredibly hot, passionate embraces in the most interesting places. I know I’m going to regret saying this, but let’s take a break.”

He pulled away slowly and kissed my cheek like a grandpa. That broke the spell.

Mission accomplished.

“Ruby, this relationship is too important to me to become physical too soon. I can wait. Let’s talk about the case. That should cool us off.”

Reluctantly, I pried open the door of my little fridge and pulled out two Diet Dr Peppers. We took our assigned seats in my room, the only seats available: the recliner and my bed. He sat facing me with his knees surrounding mine. Not a neutral position by any means. I tried to focus.

I began, “Let’s start with what we know, like the ballistics information. The bullets from Brock's and my attacks came from the same handgun, a Glock. Jake’s came from a sniper rifle.”

“That’s right, Ruby. But I’m interested in the new information you might have. Tell me what Rhonda has learned that’s relevant.”

“She has befriended the other janitor on her team, but he’s not a janitor. He’s the son of a researcher in Kenya who was doing vaccine research at the same time as my parents.”

“His father knew your parents?” Hayes asked. “What is that connection?”

I filled him in on what Rhonda had learned from Walter.

“Immunovax has been around a long time. They were formerly known as LifeShield. That’s where Walter’s parents and mine crossed paths. LifeShield dropped the vaccine research when it proved ineffective against HIV. They also eliminated any competitors in the market, namely, my parents. Walter's dad's final request was that Walter bring to light my parents' murder. He knew they left an orphaned daughter, and it haunted him."

I knew I would have to tell him why they killed Brock. Hayes needed to know, no matter how guilty I felt.

"I'd kept my parents' research papers from Kenya and shared them with Brock. In those notes, he found that my parents' team was hoping to find a specific gene that protected against viral infection. This science was in its infancy, so there was no way to identify the gene yet."

Hayes's eyes looked like they were glazing over.

"You're losing me, Ruby," he said.

"Stay with me. Brock's company, S.I.C., now possesses those tools. His new research on immunity revealed that individuals with a particular genetic makeup were more than twice as likely to resist viral infections. This protection increased more than eightfold for those with two copies of the gene. I am one of those rare individuals. My genetic makeup could pose a threat to Immunovax's soon-to-be-released vaccine. They want me eliminated. I assume a mole at S.I.C. leaked Brock's research to Immunovax. I'm afraid that research on my blood got him killed. Wait, could Kendall have been that mole?"

Hayes seemed dumbfounded. I didn't know whether it was because civilians could gain that kind of access, or whether he was upset with the Belladonnas for even attempting it.

"Ruby, I should turn you over my knee and spank you," he said.

A dozen snarky comebacks came to mind, each more ridiculous than his empty threat.

Then he added, "Sorry, probably not a good punishment. I see your pupils dilating again. I'm just afraid you Belladonnas are in over your heads. You understand?"

"Yep, I understand, but they killed my parents, and I was a target of an assassin. This is too personal for me to let go."

We finished our drinks still facing each other, he in the chair and I on my bed. "Well, Hayes, we both have things to do. Let's get out of here before they call me up front to advise on some dog that swallowed a pincushion."

He tugged me up off the bed, and we hugged briefly on the way out to his car.

"Ruby, you've given my team and me a lot to go on. I'm glad we were able to sort things out. I'll try to be more sensitive to your needs and less laser-focused on my job."

"Thanks, Hayes, we can do both. I just needed to know I'm not the only one taking cold showers at night."

He gave me that sexy, quirky smile and slid into his unmarked car. I returned to my room for a nap. Since I'd been off work, I'd often enjoyed a guilt-free nap in the middle of the day. I could get used to this. But then I remembered I'd promised to Zoom with Rhonda to see where the investigation was going. She had scheduled lunch with Walter.

"Hello. Hello. Rhonda, are you there?"

I really disliked Zoom calls. I never knew if my microphone was muted or on, or if my face was visible to the other people on the call. The creativity of other people's backdrops, which often featured palm trees or a shelf of literary classics, intimidated me. I usually Zoomed in my bedroom. My backdrop was a shelf stacked with unread medical journals flanked by a poster of the life cycle of the dog tapeworm.

Once I was on a Zoom call with a group of old vets. The person in charge kept all our microphones unmuted. One old guy kept burping, and every time he did, his face would fill our screens without him knowing. His picture would disappear, he'd burp, and there he was again on full display. It was hilarious. But I couldn't laugh, or I'd become the next face across everyone's screen.

"Rhonda, how's it going up there in BBQ central?" I asked, assuming she heard me. I saw her face on the screen, but she seemed distracted.

"It's going good… too good," she whispered. "We've just broken into the server room and downloaded recent emails between board members and Immunovax's CEO Samuel Jacobson. Walter has already accessed old files. It's not easy. They've got a heck of a firewall. Project Immunity, that's what they call it, goes back to when your parents were in Kenya. Why would they keep all this incriminating history?"

"Rhonda, be careful. How did you get in?" I asked.

"It was easy. Walter had the code. There are advantages to being a janitor."

"Yeah, like taking a bullet to the back of your head. Have you located Kendall there yet?" I asked.

"No, no one seems to know who she is. Walter couldn't find her in the employee database. Maybe she's just too new. This place is so big she could be in several labs."

I saw sweat roll down Rhonda's forehead. Walter was striking the keyboard feverishly in the background. He had a couple of USB sticks on the desk beside him.

"Yikes, Dakota. I gotta go. Someone is tapping at the glass."

"Rhonda, are you okay?" I watched her grab her mop and quickly busy herself at a desk, away from Walter. "Rhonda, answer me. Just keep the call on."

The video ended abruptly.

Rhonda didn't respond to texts throughout the night. Walter's last name remained unknown, and there was no way to contact Immunovax. I slumped down in my recliner with Chui by my side.

"Chui, what have I done?"

My Bible lay on my nightstand. It reminded me I wasn't in this alone. It was as if my parents were rooting for me, while a "great cloud of witnesses" cheered me on.

"Dear Lord, this company has hurt so many people. Help me track down the bad guys. Protect my friends who are involved because of me and send angels to be with Rhonda and Walter. Oh, and please put Hayes and me together again soon. I promise to be good. Amen."

I sometimes made promises I couldn't keep.

CHAPTER 42

The next morning, Chui stood over my face. He had a bladder the size of a walnut. It's remarkable that he managed to make it through the night. As every blade of grass in the alley received a thorough sniff and a squirt, the day's plan began to take shape, ways to push the investigation forward while I waited to hear from Rhonda.

Jake's shooting still bothered me. How did the sniper only wing him? I'd been flitting around in my clinic when he failed to kill me, but Jake was an easier target. Was his Tesla truck a factor? I conducted a quick AI search to determine whether Teslas were bulletproof. They had Armor Glass®, which wasn't bulletproof but designed to absorb and redirect impact forces. This could account for the miss. The company also noted that its stainless-steel angled surfaces deflected incoming projectiles.

Perhaps this sniper wasn't as inaccurate as we thought. He had still hit him, just not in a critical body part.

Jake continued to occupy my thoughts. Now that he was repentant, I was concerned about his welfare. How was that for hypocritical? I pulled up Jake the Snake in my contacts and hit the call button.

"Hello, this is Dr. Morgan speaking," he answered. He sounded like he was back to normal, only more pleasant, not with the chest-thumping bravado of old.

"Hey, Jake. How's the shoulder? Ready for a boxing match?"

My father had taught me how to defend myself. I could spar with the best of them, meaning girls under five feet tall.

"Ruby, it's good to hear your voice. My shoulder is mending nicely. Have you discovered any leads on who could have done this to me? Oh, and to you and Brock?" That was a good sign. It was no longer all about him.

"The Belladonnas are on it. We're about to make a break in the case. I can feel it."

"Not that I'm paranoid, but do you and I need extra protection?" Jake asked. "Someone who wants us dead is still out there."

His voice now sounded shaky. He was right, but I didn't answer him. We did need protection. Of course, he felt unsettled, but the old Jake would have shown no fear. Then a thought hit me. Did they want us dead, or were they just trying to scare us? That would explain the poor marksmanship, but not the hitman who chased me down the hall of my clinic. The first shot should have been enough to terrify me.

"Jake, did you ever meet a researcher named Kendall at Brock's facility? She was there when I came to Brock's office, the day when you and I fought."

"Yes, I remember. The security guard stepped in just in time to save you."

Maybe Jake wasn't that much improved.

"I've never met anyone named Kendall. Why?"

"Just following a trail," I answered. "According to the receptionist, she's relocated to Immunovax. However, we can't find any record of her employment there."

"I'm afraid I can't help with that," Jake responded. "I don't have access to Immunovax employee records. Is this matter urgent? I could make some inquiries."

Who stole the old Jake? He wanted to be helpful?

"That would be great. Her name is Kendall Jackson. Could you check it out and let me know what you find? I'd appreciate that."

Working with Jake felt weird, like a rat collaborating with a boa constrictor. It could have had a bad outcome. I cut him off before he replied. "Gotta go. Talk to you later." Click.

That felt good.

Just as I clicked off, my phone rang. It was Rhonda.

"Rhonda! Thank God. Are you okay? I've been worried sick all night. Were you caught?"

"Sorry, I slept in this morning. It was a close call," she confided. "The security guard saw us as he made his rounds. We pretended to clean so he wouldn't catch us accessing the computer. He did see my cell phone, though. He ranted on about us not using phones in this secure area. That jerk took it away and told me I could pick it up at the employee entrance this morning. I wanted to cold cock him, but Walter calmed me down."

"Oh, I am so relieved. Did Walter get the information we needed?" I asked.

"He did. Those idiots left all those emails on the server. He got everything."

"Good. Your job there is done, Rhonda. The Belladonnas and Hayes want you out of there now. Tell Walter thanks from all of us. Would he come to Hays, Kansas, this weekend and bring his father's research papers? Emily wants to compare both copies. They could work together to uncover what happened back then."

"I'm sure he would welcome some time away from this place," Rhonda replied. "It's like a freaking cesspool of sudden death up here, not to mention a bazaar of biohazards. They should post a motivational poster in the boardroom: Collaborate, Innovate, Eliminate. I'll let you know what he says."

"Thanks, Rhonda. Glad you haven't lost your sense of humor. So happy you're still alive."

As I stuffed my phone into my pouch, it started playing "Unchained Melody."

That was now Hayes's ringtone.

"Hey, Hayes. I just got off the phone with Rhonda. She had a close call, but she's fine. I was going to call you, but I didn't want to alarm you."

"You didn't want to alarm me. Are you kidding?" Hayes yelled into the phone. "I am the one you are supposed to alarm. Don't you get that?"

"Yeah, I do, but moot point now. Rhonda and the other janitor have the evidence that could break this case wide open. And get this, he still has his father's old research notes from his time in Kenya. He wants justice for his father, who passed away with untold secrets. Can you believe it? We've asked Rhonda to bring him back to Hays. He can sit down with Emily and compare my parents' notes with his father's."

"That's fine, Ruby, but that doesn't make me feel any better." It sounded like he was speaking through clenched jaws, just like my father used to do. I heard him inhale slowly. As he let it out, he added, "Ruby, I'm worried about your safety."

There was a long pause before he continued.

"I have some interesting data for you as well." There was a dramatic shift from his concerned voice to his detective voice. "We ran a background check on all S.I.C. employees, including Kendall. When her information was flagged, we discovered the photo in her file was fake. We performed facial recognition with no hits. The real Kendall Jackson was a university researcher who died under suspicious circumstances in Kansas City. Looks like someone stole her identity and used it to gain employment at S.I.C. She might have used another alias at Immunovax if she even went there."

"Are you talking about Titer's mother? I can't believe it! She very well could have been the mole at S.I.C., leaking research to Immunovax. Good grief. I usually read people well, but I must have had macular degeneration on this one. I'm waiting for some information from Jake to help you find fake Kendall."

"So, Rhonda is on her way back? She did a heck of a job up there," Hayes admitted.

"That's our Rhonda," I said without rubbing it in. "Hey, I've got another call coming in. We can talk later."

"Sure," Hayes answered. "Let me know when Rhonda gets back."

I didn't usually get this many calls in one day. Of course, I got calls at the clinic, but I meant personal calls.

"Jake, what's up?" I asked.

"I have an accountant friend in Kansas City who works for Immunovax. He has access to employee pay sheets, but there are privacy concerns. He hasn't found any Kendall yet, but he owes me a favor."

"Doing your physical therapy?" I asked.

"Yes, but it's painful," he answered.

"Good." Oops, Freudian slip. "Oh, Jake, I didn't mean I was glad it's painful. Please get back to me if you uncover any further information. Thanks for your help."

"You're so welcome, Ruby."

Chapter 43

I stuck my head outside my room and saw a familiar face down the hallway. "Sadie, you look cute today." I couldn't remember the name of the owner who answered in a squeaky baby voice on Sadie's behalf.

"*I'm just the best wittle dog in the whole wide world.*"

Using her adult voice, she continued, "Dr. Dakota, it's good to see you. Are you okay? Why aren't you seeing patients today?"

"I'm just taking a breather for a few weeks. I hope my replacement is doing a good job."

"Oh, yes. She's fine. I just came in to have Sadie chipped. I never wanted to put her through that, but we'll head to Florida soon. I don't know what I'd do if she ran off at a rest stop somewhere along the way. At least if she has a chip, they could contact us."

The owner's name finally popped into my head. "Mrs. Mintzmeyer, you know that inserting that chip isn't painful. I am so glad you've reconsidered. Sadie will be much safer with that little implant," I reassured her.

As I retreated into my apartment, it hit me.

Microchips. Microchips! An idea came to me from above.

When Kendall brought her cat, Titer, in for vaccination,

Titer had soiled the carrier and himself. Harley and I took him to the surgery room to clean him up. While Harley dried him off, I ran a chip reader over the area between his shoulder blades. It popped up with information from a person with a different name. I didn't know if London ever recorded that in Titer's record.

I rushed to the front desk. London was spraying Ramos with a water bottle. He broke into song. "Raindrops Keep Fallin' On My Head." She must have taught him that second song. I liked it better than "Singin' in the Rain." I begin to laugh hysterically at the outlandishness of a parrot, in a vet clinic, taking a shower, and singing a song from *Butch Cassidy and the Sundance Kid*.

Perhaps I was just high on the possibility that we might soon know the identity of the S.I.C. mole.

"London, could you pull up the records on Kendall Jackson? I need to see if we recorded her cat's microchip information in her file."

"That creepy lady and her cat are embedded in my memory," London said. She screwed up her face like she just smelled a skunk. "It says here, Harley cleaned up the cat and scanned Titer for an ID chip without the owner's permission. When Kendall checked out, I asked her if she needed to update the chip info since the name was different. Suddenly, she erupted at me, shouting that we had violated Titer's civil rights. Then she immediately went into a sickening, sweet voice. She made some comment about adopting him from the humane shelter, and that it must be the previous owner's information. I dropped the conversation but noted the details in Titer's chart just in case she'd stolen him. The interaction just felt weird."

"Good work, London! I'm so blessed to have you working up front. What did the chip say?" I asked.

"Here's the ID number that came up. I accessed the database and recorded the name, phone number, address, and email," London responded.

"Let me see it," I demanded anxiously as I pulled the chart over where I could read it. I squinted. "The owner is Miranda McCullough, and the address listed is Washington, D.C. Now that's interesting."

I debated what to do next. Call Hayes? The Belladonnas also needed this new information. After all, they risked their necks to help me. I could have called an emergency meeting at Emily's house during lunch, but I decided to wait until Rhonda was back in town. A group call with Kit and Emily would suffice. Rhonda had her hands full in Kansas City.

Kit showed up on my phone screen. "What's up, Doc?" This was Kit's usual reply at the pharmacy. She talks to a lot of Docs.

"What's the emergency?" Emily's ear appeared. "Is Rhonda okay?"

"Emily, put the phone in front of your face! Yes, she's in one piece. She's heading home today, hopefully with her new janitor friend," I told them.

"New janitor friend? A boyfriend? That was fast! She's only been up there a few days." Emily was amped up, unlike her usual, steady self.

"Calm down. No, not a boyfriend. He's got some vital information we need to nail these scumbags. There *was* a close call, but they bluffed their way through it," I told them.

"I won't relax until I see the whites of their eyes," said Emily.

"Me either," Kit added.

"The big news is that we might have a lead on the mole," I continued.

"You what? How?" Emily asked.

"When Hayes did a background check on S.I.C. employees, Kendall Jackson came up as a red flag. The picture on her application didn't match the name she provided."

"I know we talked about her at the bar as a possible source of information at S.I.C.," Kit remembered.

"Yes, but it came to me that her cat, Titer, was microchipped. I first met the girl when she brought her cat to my clinic. The information on the microchip wasn't Kendall Jackson, but Miranda McCullough. It listed a Washington, D.C. address. I believe this is her real name."

"That's incredible! Have you been able to confirm it?" Kit was shocked.

"No, but I will get the info to Hayes and let him run it through their databases. I'll let you know as soon as we have an update. Now, we've all got things to do before they get here. Do you think Walter could stay at Rhonda's place? Does she even have an extra bedroom?" I asked.

"And will Rennie even let him past the front door? That's the big question," Emily added.

"For security's sake, perhaps it would be better if they weren't in the same place with all that information," Kit offered.

"Maybe he could stay with Hayes. Does he have an extra room, Dakota?" Emily asked coyly.

Kit and Emily, on separate screens, got knowing looks and began to snort.

"Stop it, you guys. No, I don't have firsthand knowledge of his house's layout. Never been there… yet."

"Emily, gather up any findings on my parents' research that could be helpful," I continued. "List any questions that Walter's paperwork might answer. Kit, you can take the incriminating information off the USB stick that Rhonda and Walter are bringing back. Okay?" They both nodded, and we signed off.

Another run at Hayes was in my future. I was eager to share the information with him.

"Hello, Ruby Anne," he answered my call. "How's my vivacious little vet doing today?"

Ooh, I loved that. "Who is this? I was trying to call

911," I teased him. "Is this how you answer the phone? Not very professional, Hayes."

"Funny, Ruby. I think you've got some dementia going on there."

Okay, that wasn't funny. He could be right.

"I've got some news you're going to love," I said. "What's it worth to you?"

"Are you attempting to extort a police officer, madame? Under the Federal Blackmail and Extortion Law, it is a crime to demand something from me in exchange for information. You could do hard time."

Hayes played along. I could play too.

"Would I do that time in a jail of my choosing? Because I'd choose house arrest... your house. Think of it. You could bring me my meals, frisk me occasionally, perhaps take me to the showers…" I would never say these things to his face. Apparently, distance brings boldness…

As I started to blush, I wondered what *his* face looked like on the other end of the line.

"Ruby Anne, you'd better get to the point of the call, or I'm going to have to make an emergency run to your clinic."

"Okay, okay, Hayes. The good news is that we might have a name for our mole. She may be Miranda McCullough from Washington, D.C."

I filled him in on the backstory. He drew in heavy breaths. Hoped it was because of me and not just the new information. I suspected it was the latter, though.

"Ruby, that's incredible! You are amazing."

"That I am, dude. 'Bout time you realized it."

"Is Rhonda back yet with the janitor?" he asked.

"He's not a janitor. He's a highly qualified researcher, and yes, they should make it here tonight. Maybe we could all go to dinner together," I suggested.

Ah, it was the post-dinner activities I was interested in, though.

"Oh, I was supposed to ask you if Walter could stay at your house."

Oops! That cancelled my nighttime hopes. That was probably God getting in the way of my fun again.

"We should put him in a hotel in case I have company. What do you think?" Hayes suggested.

"Talk to ya later," I squeaked out. I was having tachycardia with occasional PVCs (Passionate Visceral Connections).

Chapter 44

I was curious about Miranda McCullough. Who was she? I did a quick Google search which produced nothing for a Miranda McCullough from Washington, D.C. There was no Facebook page, nothing. I hoped Hayes would have more success.

I knew I should call Mary Hazlett at CEZID, but I was reluctant to trust that place with this added information. I was sure she was upset with me for refusing a security detail, but here I was, still alive… so far.

I hadn't left my room all day. No one had called me to the front to bail them out. I liked this new relief vet. She seemed capable of running the place without me. Did that make me happy? It was bittersweet. On the one hand, I appreciated the release and peace of mind that came with not having to make one decision after another, often under intense duress. On the other hand, I loved the challenges and responsibility that came with the job, and the satisfaction I got from a difficult diagnosis made and a life saved. Nothing was as rewarding as watching a patient who'd been near death a week earlier bounce down the hall to reunite with its owner.

Talking about bittersweet reminded me I hadn't spoken to Darryl and Glenda in a while. I should run over and see them, but they'd have more questions than I cared to answer.

I opted to take a shower instead. Gertrude, the groomer, finished early and no longer needed the tub. I put Chui in with me. He loved to take a shower now and then. I used the clinic dog shampoo and conditioner on both of us. It didn't help him. His hair was still wiry and stuck out everywhere. I toweled off, and Chui shook himself almost dry. We looked at each other in the mirror.

Was that weird, sharing a mirror with a chiweenie dog?

He seemed happy with his appearance. Me not so much.

Perhaps I should elevate my makeup game a bit. That was another thing about getting old—makeup. If you didn't use it, you looked blanched and weathered. If you did, your skin looked crepey. Not creepy, but crepey. Well, maybe creepy too. Like the flappy skin on the underside of your upper arms. Perhaps I'd opt for the old lady's three-step MBM method: Moisturizer, Blush, and a swipe of Mascara. In this case, less was more. I spritzed a bit of "My Way" into the air and twirled through the mist. It might have seemed like a waste of money, but if it affected Hayes like his cologne affected me, it was money well spent.

A knock at the back door interrupted the blessed quiet. Everyone had cleared out for the day. I grabbed the nearest thing resembling a robe, which happened to be a slightly used paper surgical gown, and shuffled to see who was disturbing my peace.

Chui and I padded down the hall barefoot. He was always barefoot. That could be dangerous in a vet clinic. Never knew what you might step in.

"Who's there? I don't open doors for strangers anymore. It's bad for my health."

"Ruby, it's Rhonda. I've brought Walter with me to meet you," she hollered through the door.

Oh, again with the timing. I let them in.

"Are you performing barefoot surgery now?" Rhonda

noticed my gown. I didn't dare tell her I had nothing on underneath.

Walter was surprisingly handsome in a skinny, nerdy, Poindexter sort of way. He wore horn-rimmed glasses and had a shock of red hair sprinkled with gray that fell into his eyes. Somewhere, a twenty-year-old was wearing this look well. This wasn't that guy.

Not the same effect.

Rhonda beamed, as if she were about to nab a criminal, which she might be.

"Where's Rennie?" Rhonda asked.

"He's with Harley," I answered. Her countenance dropped. I knew she missed him.

"I wanted Rennie to meet Walter," Rhonda said.

I wasn't sure Walter wanted to meet Rennie. He didn't look much like a pet lover to me.

He looked allergic.

"Give me a minute to get dressed and let Hayes know you made it. Have a seat in the waiting room." Chui escorted them to the front. He was surprisingly calm, considering he'd just met a stranger. Chui had always been a good judge of character, though. The visitors set the boarders into a frenzy of rude barks as they passed the kennel room. Chui barked back, and immediately, there was quiet. I didn't know what he said in doggie language, but he ruled the kennel room.

I immediately called Hayes, who agreed to meet us at Hickok's in 15 minutes. I threw on my last clean scrubs, a bit wrinkled but still presentable, and reunited Chui with Lola in their cozy kennel. Rhonda and Walter climbed into my Land Rover, and we headed for the bar.

We pulled into Hickok's parking lot just as Hayes stepped out of his unmarked minivan. He looked every bit the detective on a mission. I guessed this *was* police business.

Rhonda made the introduction. "Hayes, I'd like you to

meet Walter Warren. He has a story that will blow your mind. Walter, this is Detective Hayes Wassinger."

As we migrated toward a corner booth, I executed a smooth move to claim the seat next to Hayes. Somehow, I managed to trip over nothing and nearly fell into his lap.

Mission accomplished.

Walter reached into his jacket and cautiously passed the USB drive to Hayes. I assumed it had been burning a hole in his pocket.

"Thanks, Walter. What's on this stick?"

"It's the log of internal email traffic at Immunovax," Walter replied just above a whisper.

"Thank you, Walter," Hayes answered. "We'll have our guys make a copy and go through it for evidence that Immunovax was in on the shootings here in Hays. Rhonda, I'm happy you're still alive, but you know what you both did was illegal and dangerous. I don't want to know how you obtained the information on this USB stick. That said, it was good police work, Rhonda. Thanks for your help."

Rhonda beamed with pride. "You bet your sweet, uh, bippy, it was," she replied.

Oh, no, not a Rowan and Martin reference. That dated her. Poindexter, er, Walter, seemed to get it, though.

"I couldn't have done it without her," Walter piped up. "She's good at undercover work."

My mind went immediately to another kind of undercover work.

Stop that, Ruby, I told myself unsuccessfully. I slid a bit closer to Hayes. He didn't move away.

"Walter, you told Rhonda that your father knew my parents in Kenya. Did our paths ever cross?" I asked.

"I don't think so, Ruby. During my time there, I attended boarding school at Rift Valley Academy. You would have been attending university in the States. My family never met you."

I knew this was going to be difficult for me. I got right

to the point anyway.

"You said your father didn't think my parents died accidentally in a carjacking."

I swallowed a lump the size of a KONG ball in my throat and tried not to cry.

"No, Ruby. The convenient timing and lack of investigation into their death always bothered him, but what haunted him was you, their only daughter, suddenly orphaned. He should have spoken up years ago. He was afraid to stir up trouble back then, so he made me promise I would."

"I'm anxious for my friend, Emily, to comb through our parents' research notes for clues that might substantiate our suspicions. CEOs at Immunovax, or LifeShield, over the years, must have hired contract killers to take out people who threatened their profit margin. Did you make a copy of your dad's notes?" I asked.

"Of course," Walter replied. "I placed a copy in a secure place in Kansas City. Here's your copy. When do I meet Emily?"

"Maybe tomorrow," I replied. "I'll text Emily now. I could drop the notes off at her place tonight so she can get a jumpstart on it."

As we continued with small talk, Rhonda touched Hayes's arm. "Hayes, I have a request."

Oh no, Rhonda. Rhonda, I silently pleaded. She said it anyway.

"Could you keep Walter at your place while Emily compares this research information? I'm afraid he could be in danger. After all, both of us will be absent from Immunovax on Monday. Who's going to empty the wastebaskets? The security guard may put two and two together, which could make Walter a target."

Hayes didn't answer her question about Walter's lodging. Was that a no?

Please let it be a no.

Instead, he continued to fill us in on the details. "We don't know where Miranda is right now, in Kansas City, Hays, or even Europe. Even as we speak, she could be on her way out of the country. Miranda McCullough is a bit of a ghost."

"What databases did you check out?" Rhonda asked.

"We ran her picture through our facial recognition database. Clean criminal record, no known ties to Immunovax, minimal social media presence. But we struck gold on LinkedIn. Miranda created a profile under the name Kendall Jackson to secure the job at S.I.C. It showed experience in industrial vaccine research at several companies. Most of those were fake, but at one place, the HR person remembered her. She recalled that Miranda excelled in her field but did not stay with the company for long, just like S.I.C. She was only there for one month. That seems to be a pattern."

"How did she pull off that charade at the company for a month?" I asked.

"It looks like she has a degree in chemistry," Hayes answered. "Perhaps that was enough to give her credibility. Once she finished her assignment, she moved on. I wouldn't be surprised if we found other incidents of corporate espionage or even shootings in the same cities where she was employed. Although we were unable to locate employment records for Immunovax, she appears to have some kind of association with the company. The FBI's forensic auditor is reviewing Immunovax's books to identify that connection. Miranda could be a gun-for-hire for corporations that need inconvenient people taken out."

Rhonda spoke up. "A professional hitwoman? Now that's a new one on me. That makes me even more nervous. Hayes, you never answered me. Do you think Walter can stay with you?"

I stepped on her toes to no avail.

Hayes glanced at me and replied a little too quickly.

"Sure, Walter can stay with me. Let's go, Walter. I'm anxious to check out this USB stick."

Ugh, his good angel triumphed over his bad boy side. I admired his dedication, but I was also crestfallen. Since I'd brought Rhonda and Walter to Hickok's in my car, I'd have to return her to the clinic. I wouldn't even get to see the inside of Hayes's place. Visualization would have added to my fantasies, but that would have to wait for another time.

My phone dinged. Emily had responded to my text. She wrote, "I'm available to meet tomorrow after church. I'll let Kit know so all the Belladonnas can be there. Bring the information on over. I'm home."

I leaned my head on my car window, watched Hayes and Walter disappear, then nudged Rhonda. We had a delivery to make.

Chapter 45

Hayes had the USB drive, but I needed to see those emails myself. He probably wouldn't give them to his tech guys before Monday. Maybe he'd let Walter show me what was on that stick. Could I insert myself into their sleepover tonight? It would be better than me lying awake all night imagining what's on it. I picked up my phone, then hesitated.

Was this too pushy? No, this was my life, I decided, and proceeded to call Hayes.

"Hayes, could I come over tonight and look at that stick with you? I won't be able to sleep until I know why those guys wanted me dead."

I was unable to hear Hayes ask Walter. He must have muted me because there was silence.

"Walter says that would be okay. He's tired, but he understands how important this is to you. Come on over. Bring Chui if you want."

Yay! I got to have my two favorite guys in the same room at the same time. I grabbed Chui, who was a bit disgruntled that he wasn't invited to dinner with me, but he quickly warmed up when he saw we were going somewhere in the car. It always amazed me how a dog with six-inch legs could leap into a vehicle that towered over his head. It didn't take me long to get to Hayes's place. I might never have been inside his place, but that didn't mean I hadn't driven by.

Again, not stalking, simply curious.

Chui leaped over my lap directly onto the ground. Really? He seemed more excited about this than I was. Hayes held the door open, and Chui walked right in, as if he belonged. I decided to do the same thing. Maybe Hayes would take the hint.

"Hey, Chui, make yourself at home. Ruby, I'm glad you couldn't wait to see me again," Hayes greeted us. I felt a gentle touch of his lips on my cheek. I pulled away and pretended to be unimpressed for some misguided, immature reason.

"You had nothing to do with it. I wanted to see Walter," I replied.

"Okay, then. He's all yours. He's in the dining room, tapping away on his computer."

Hmm, he took that jab well. Rats. I'd forfeited the tour in the interest of appearances. What I could see spoke clearly: Early American Bachelor Pad. Pool table in the living room. Tiki bar along one wall.

Still better than my one-room Art Deco Zoo look.

"Walter, can you pull up the relevant emails?" I asked.

"Already done. I was able to recover these from Immunovax's secure server, the one they keep off their main network. They must use it exclusively for sensitive communications. I searched for any mention of Brock, Jake, or you, either directly or in code. I've put them in their own folder so you can peruse the most pertinent ones tonight. You'll want to examine the emails more thoroughly in case I missed something, but this should be enough for a cursory look. Are you sure you want to read them?" he asked me.

I nodded. "I won't be able to sleep if I don't."

Walter continued. "They talk in a weakly veiled code

sometimes, and other times they say exactly what they mean. You and Hayes can review this while I shower and prepare for bed. I was up at the crack of dawn. That Rhonda is a taskmaster."

"More like a drill sergeant, I'd say, but I understand. She's a great friend," I joked with Walter.

"Hayes, I can't read this without you by my side."

I could see his chest puff up. It was funny how guys rose to the occasion when challenged. Let a woman show a slight weakness, and they were all over it, trying to help.

It was a damsel-in-distress kind of thing.

"I'm here for you," Hayes whispered as he pulled his chair so close to mine that I could feel his body heat. He stretched his arm around my shoulders, and it felt like I was finally safe.

Hayes opened the file and scrolled down the email list. He tapped on the first one.

"Let's start with communications around the time of Brock's murder."

The screen populated with several results. Hayes opened the first one, dated three days before I discovered Brock Benton's body.

From: c.thomas@immunovax.com
To: operations@brownwater-consulting.net
Subject: Containment Protocol Project Immunity

The situation at the Kansas location requires immediate intervention. Asset B has accessed restricted data on the old Kenya trials and appears to have linked it to Asset D's bloodwork. Intelligence suggests he may be developing an immunotherapy that would make our vaccine redundant. Suggest both assets be taken out.

Recommend implementing full containment protocol before end of week. Standard compensation package applies with bonus for discretion and expediency.

Timeline is critical. Board meeting scheduled for next

week requires this matter to be fully resolved.

CT

"Asset B? That's Brock!" I gasped. "And D is Dakota. They're talking about *my* blood samples." My voice trembled. "They must have killed him because he discovered something about my immunity. Does that mean Kendall, I mean Miranda, was the mole at S.I.C.?"

Hayes's eyes narrowed, and his jaw tightened as he scrolled to the response sent the next day.

From: operations@brownwater-consulting.net
To: c.thomas@immunovax.com
Subject: Re: Containment Protocol Project Immunity

Confirmed receipt. Will start implementing within 48 hours. Will take out Asset D first. Will require access codes to research facility. Asset B has enhanced security protocols in place.

Situation will be handled with customary discretion. No traces.

OBW

"This is cold-blooded." Hayes's voice was a combination of controlled anger and emotion. "They're discussing murder like it's just another business transaction."

I pointed at a different email thread. "What about this one from right after the shooting at my clinic?"

Hayes opened the message.

From: c.thomas@immunovax.com
To: s.jacobson@immunovax.com
Subject: Status Update on Kansas Situation

Initial containment efforts failed. Our consultant reports that Asset D remains active, despite multiple opportunities for intervention. The window incident did not yield desired results.

Of more concern is that Asset D has expanded her support network and engaged local law enforcement resources we hadn't anticipated.

Recommend escalating to Protocol Omega. All three primary concerns (RD, BB, JM) must be neutralized before the FDA meeting. The old Dakota immunity profile from Kenya cannot become public knowledge, or our entire U.S. vaccine market share is at risk. The previous attempt on Asset D was clearly insufficient.

Send authorization code when ready.

CT

"RD is you, Ruby, and BB is Brock Benton. JM must be Jake Morgan. They were planning to kill all three of you," Hayes said grimly, his hand instinctively moving to his service weapon. "The 'window incident' was the shooting at your clinic." He scrolled further and opened a more recent email.

From: s.jacobson@immunovax.com
To: c.thomas@immunovax.com
Subject: Re: Status Update on Kansas Situation

Authorization code: ALPHA-5527-PERMISSION

Proceed immediately. Board is concerned about timeline slippage.

Use the Kenyan protocol for RD. Poetic justice seems appropriate.

Eliminate Asset B as soon as possible. Security codes to facility have been sent.

JM's corporate connection with Immunovax and, possibly, S.I.C., provides sufficient cover for an escalation. No connection to company can exist. He must be eliminated.

Full containment must be achieved by week's end.

Additional resources have been allocated to your discretionary fund.

Do not fail again.

SJ

"Kenyan protocol," I whispered. "That refers to my parents, doesn't it?"

Hayes reached for his phone. "We need to get additional protection for Jake immediately. They're planning to finish what they started with him."

"Jake was lucky, I mean blessed, to survive the first shooting," I said. "He's still in a weakened condition. If they try again..." I shuddered at the thought.

Not long ago, I might have relished the idea.

Hayes nodded grimly. "I'll contact the police in Kansas City and have them station an officer at Jake's home. I'll also put a 24-hour detail on you, Ruby. If you move, they move. Don't try to ditch them." He looked at me, his expression softening despite the gravity of the situation. "This is not up for debate, Ruby." The policeman side of him was at odds with the lover in him. "I'm sorry, Ruby. I know this is a lot to process."

I straightened my shoulders; calm determination replaced my initial shock.

"My parents died over forty years ago because of these people. Brock is gone. They tried to kill me once already." I placed my hand over Hayes's. "I'm not hiding, Hayes. We will use these emails to bring Immunovax down, for good."

Hayes nodded, a hint of admiration in his eyes. "That's my Ruby. First, we properly secure these records. Then we notify the FBI—*my* contact, not the one who escorted you earlier. I don't know who we can trust."

I glanced back at the screen. "Wait, scroll down more. I want to see if there's anything about my trip to CEZID.

That couldn't have been coincidental."

Hayes continued scrolling, revealing one more damning message:

From: c.thomas@immunovax.com
To: h.leakey@cezid.gov
Subject: Dakota Specimen Results

Your lab at CEZID has had the Dakota blood samples for two weeks now. The delay in reporting is unacceptable. Our arrangement was clear.

The board requires confirmation that her immune profile matches our projections based on the parental samples collected in Kenya. If verified, proceed with the extraction protocol as discussed.

Remember. Your research funding for the next five years depends on the successful completion of this project.

CT

"They have someone at CEZID, too! I can't believe Dr. Leakey was the leak. He wanted to arrange my protection," I whispered. "This goes deeper than we thought."

Hayes looked up at me, his expression resolute.

"Then we dig deeper."

Chapter 46

Walter snored loudly, asleep on Hayes's couch, while Chui curled up in the crook of his arm.

"I'd better get back to my place," I said reluctantly. "Hayes, I'm glad you were with me tonight. It made the blow a little softer."

I stood on my tiptoes and kissed him gently on the cheek. He didn't settle for that. He drew me in, arms around me, and for a moment, the room, Walter, and every sensible thought I owned simply disappeared. I stepped back before I did something I'd have to explain later.

Walter emerged from hibernation. "Hey, what's happening here?" He sat upright, which slid Chui onto the floor. "Am I interrupting anything?"

We pulled apart like we'd been hit with an electric cattle prod.

"Just saying goodbye to Ruby," Hayes recovered quickly.

"That's one heck of a goodbye. Looks like you two are saying goodbye for a long time," Walter quipped.

"No, no, that's our usual parting ritual. It's our thing. We're just friends with no benefits." Even I didn't believe me this time. I took a deep breath and steadied myself.

"Did you read the emails?" Walter asked.

"We did," I replied, still panting like a retriever waiting for his owner to throw the gundog dummy.

"Are you okay?" he asked. I wasn't sure if he referred to my heavy breathing or the brutal emails.

"I'm a lot of things, but okay isn't one of them. I'll be okay when we catch these guys. Thank you so much for your help, Walter."

"My pleasure, believe me."

"I'm heading out," I told them. "You two behave yourselves. I'll probably see you tomorrow after the Belladonna meeting."

Hayes walked Chui and me to my car. "Little Ruby, when will we get some quality time alone, huh? It seems like the world is conspiring against us."

"Let's get these guys first, Hayes. Then we'll celebrate. Okay?"

Did I just say that? Police work ahead of romance? What just happened here?

Sunday morning, I made my weekly appearance at church. I usually sat in the back row, so I could get out quickly without shaking the pastor's hand. I still felt like he saw right through me. His wife was a doll, though, who loved her two dachshunds, Sugar and Skittles.

Her dogs didn't attend church. Dachshunds don't feel guilty about anything.

I returned to the clinic to grab a quick lunch of cheese nuggets and a snuggle with Chui. He felt a little neglected these days. Couldn't be helped. I was anxious to see what Emily might have uncovered in those old research notes. She probably stayed up all night. That wasn't fair, but she was often up all night with patients.

Emily hosted our one o'clock meeting with the full Belladonna crew, plus Walter. We didn't invite Hayes this time. We needed to work through the evidence first without official constraints. He'd probably spend the day going through the emails again. Did I just pass up a chance to be near him? That said volumes about what was at stake in this meeting for me. Plus, I might not want him to know everything about my past.

He might think I could still be carrying some communicable African disease.

Emily moved to the fireplace mantel and reached out to tap her water glass with her red pen. The laughter died down, and each Belladonna, along with Walter, turned toward her with a sense of anticipation.

“While we've all worked hard, it was Rhonda and Walter who obtained the information that solved the puzzle,” Emily began.

She pulled two notebooks onto her coffee table. One was my parents' research journal, and the other belonged to Walter’s father. She placed her reading glasses on the bridge of her nose and took a deep breath.

“Ruby, I’m certain some of this information will be difficult for you to hear. You lost your parents when you were in your twenties. That’s too young, but the way you lost them made it even more tragic. We’re all here for you. You know that, don’t you?”

I could already feel the tears threatening. I swallowed hard. “Yes, I know that. You Belladonnas are my family, you and Chui. Don’t pull any punches, Emily. Tell it like it is.”

Emily opened both notebooks to the pages marked with sticky pink and lime green tabs. She began, “I spent most of the night comparing these notes. The overlap is incredible. Ruby, your parents and Walter's father were working on something groundbreaking that could have changed disease therapy forever.”

“Can you explain to me what they were studying in layman’s terms?” Rhonda asked, shifting in her recliner.

“I’ll try, Rhonda. Both sets of notes reference a specific group of sex workers in Nairobi regularly exposed to HIV who never contracted the disease. This was unprecedented at the time. The medical community was desperate to understand why."

"My father was assigned to study this phenomenon," Walter explained. "LifeShield was initially developing an HIV vaccine, and these women were of great interest."

Emily continued, "What's interesting is the connection. Walter's father worked for LifeShield, and Ruby's parents worked on a government research project. Initially, they were working toward the same goal. At some point, the government and LifeShield's research paths split, and not amicably."

A light bulb went on in Kit's head. "I get it. The company wanted a profitable vaccine, but Ruby's parents found something even better."

Emily lifted one of the notebooks and tapped on a reference. "Exactly. Ruby's parents identified a genetic pattern, a specific protective gene, in these women."

"Wow, that's huge!" Kit exclaimed.

Emily continued. "This finding wasn't limited to HIV. Using their own blood, as researchers often do, Ruby's parents discovered that each of them had one copy of this protective gene. This helps explain why they were immune to Ebola, which they'd both been exposed to in Uganda. And get this, your parents discovered this same genetic immunity not only in themselves, but also in their daughter in a double dose. Researchers now know that people with two copies of this gene are eight times more likely to remain asymptomatic even after significant viral exposure."

Everybody stared at me like I was a performer in a freak show.

"Ruby," Emily said calmly, "according to these notes, your blood has a unique genetic marker that makes you super-immune to certain viral infections. Your parents called it enhanced natural immunity."

"They called it Bulletproof," I recalled. "So, I'm some kind of new species?" I attempted a joke, but my voice cracked. Emily gave me a compassionate smile.

"You're more like an advanced hybrid, a blend of traits gathered from both parents, a killing machine against deadly viruses," Emily continued. "Your parents tried to develop a treatment, not a vaccine. Even though they didn't have the appropriate technology at the time, they still believed they could isolate this genetic factor. They hoped to eventually develop a therapy to help infected patients fight off the virus after exposure. This was much different than LifeShield's vaccine strategy."

"Ah, a therapy that would render their vaccine less valuable!" Kit got it; her eyes narrowed. "That's one heck of a motive for murder, I'd say."

Walter's jaw tightened. "My father's notes showed that about a week before your parents died, they had a breakthrough. They had successfully isolated the genetic marker and were prepared to publish their findings."

Emily turned to another sticky note. "Ruby, here is an entry from your father's journal dated two days before they died. It reads:

'LifeShield requests that we delay the release of our findings. We denied their request. We are so close. Ruby's immunity profile confirms our theory. Meeting with U.S. officials from the National Institute of Health next Tuesday.' That was the last entry by your father." Emily's voice faded.

My vision clouded. I felt faint, but still croaked out the words, "They never made it to that meeting."

Emily shook her head. "No, they did not. The next notes are enlightening." She flipped to another page. "Three days after your parents died, Walter's father wrote this:

'The carjacking story doesn't hold water. Compound security guards had to have been compromised. No guard to open the gate or push the panic button. No evidence of robbery. Not a crime of opportunity. It was a skilled attack. LifeShield executives tout new vaccine contract with government. Dakota treatment protocol shelved indefinitely.'"

I couldn't breathe. Four decades of grief spiraled into anger. "They killed my parents just like they tried to kill me."

"There's more," Emily said quietly. "Your parents knew they were in danger. They were playing with high stakes. They hid copies of their research findings with trusted colleagues, which is how you ended up with these notes after their deaths. They were trying to protect you, Ruby."

Kit had a theory. "This is why Brock was so excited about your blood work. He must have made the connection between your immune system and your parents' research. He was on the verge of finishing your parents' project!"

"Which is why Jacobson had him killed," I whispered.

"These notes reveal something else," Emily continued. "Your parents' research showed that the protective gene is most effective when inherited from both parents, an extremely rare condition."

"In your case, Ruby, you got a double dose of immunity," Walter added.

Rhonda, ever the sleuth, cut through the technical jargon. "So now we have motive. LifeShield, now Immunovax, protected its vaccine market for years by eliminating threats to its products. First, Ruby's parents, and now, years later, Brock, along with the attempts on Ruby and Jake."

"But why Jake?" Kit wondered. "He was working with them."

"Jake was only an investor in both Immunovax and S.I.C.," I told them. "He might have figured out what was happening, but it's more likely Immunovax wanted to eliminate the chance of Jake continuing Brock's research."

"There's one last crucial piece of the puzzle," Emily said, as she flipped to her final sticky note. "Ruby, your parents made a copy of a specific genetic sequence responsible for your immunity. They encoded that sequence into these research notes. I've transferred all of this onto a USB stick."

Behind his thick glasses, Walter's eyes bulged with excitement. "That's the key! With modern CRISPR technology, we could use this sequence to develop genetic treatments for multiple viral diseases. This technology wasn't available back then, but today, it could revolutionize immunology."

"And destroy Immunovax's vaccine empire," Rhonda added.

"So, they'll keep coming after me," I said flatly. "As long as I'm alive, my blood and my parents' research threaten their pocketbook."

Rhonda stood up, her eyes steely. "Not if we take them down first."

Chapter 47

I was in awe of the Belladonnas, those fiercely loyal women, and Warren, the man who shared my loss. “My parents died trying to save lives. Brock may have died for the same reason.” I dried my tears and squared my shoulders. There was a shift in my resolve. “I'm done wondering. Let's finish what my parents started. That includes your father, too, Walter. He was brave enough at the end of his life to want Immunovax to suffer the consequences of their evil actions.”

Emily reached out and took my hand. “The Belladonnas are with you. All the way.”

Walter nodded in agreement. “So am I, Ruby. For my father, for your parents, and for you.”

For the first time since my parents' murder, I felt something different than grief. I felt purpose. With friends by my side, I might survive long enough to see justice done.

“I have to get this information to Hayes,” I said triumphantly. “Hope it doesn’t bother him that a bunch of old ladies and a virologist-slash-janitor solved this before the police and the FBI.”

Walter and I headed for the police station. At this point, I'd been kidnapped and nearly murdered, but handing evidence over to law enforcement, even if he were my almost-boyfriend, made me nervous. I was still concerned that the IRS could arrest me.

G-men were G-men no matter what uniform they wore.

"You're sure you can make this stick in court?" I asked Hayes as I reluctantly slid Emily's USB stick across his desk like it was my most valuable possession.

I supposed it was.

Walter sat beside me, his father's research notes at his side.

"Ruby, you and Walter have given me enough to take down half of Immunovax's executive board." Hayes carefully placed this new evidence in an official envelope and continued. "FBI forensic accountants found email trails and financial records that connect them to payments made to Miranda McCullough, the shootings, Brock's murder, and now we'll have a direct link to your parents' murder years ago. This is a walk-in touchdown."

"Forty years is a long time to wait for justice," Walter mumbled.

I reached over and squeezed his hand. "Hey, Walter, no regrets. Our parents would be proud. My parents died trying to save lives, and we're finishing what they started."

Hayes tucked the envelope into his jacket. "The Kansas Bureau of Investigation and the FBI will coordinate the arrests. It'll happen simultaneously at multiple locations."

"Will I need to testify against these scumbags?" I asked, picturing myself in a courtroom, explaining super-immunity to a dozen jurors.

"Eventually, but that's months away." Hayes's eyes softened. "At least for now, the threat is almost over."

Almost. I'd learned the hard way not to count on "almost."

CHAPTER 48

The Belladonnas insisted on watching the morning news together at Emily's house. It had been almost a month since we'd handed over our evidence. We huddled in front of her 75-inch Samsung TV like Kansas City Chiefs football fans during a championship game. TV trays held our coffee mugs and chocolate croissants.

At last, the news for which we'd been waiting. "We interrupt this program for breaking news," the anchor announced. "Federal agents are making arrests at pharmaceutical giant Immunovax in what authorities call one of the largest corporate conspiracy cases in recent history."

The camera cut to the company's Kansas City headquarters, where police escorted men and women in suits out in handcuffs.

"Among those arrested are CEO Samuel Jacobson and Chief Operations Officer Charles Thomas, who face the following charges: conspiracy to commit murder, corporate espionage, and obstruction of justice. The arrests stem from a decades-long cover-up involving the deaths of medical researchers in the U.S. and overseas and recent murder attempts in western Kansas."

We pumped our fists simultaneously and let out a

whoop that splashed our coffees right over the edges of our mugs.

"Authorities credit the breakthrough in the case to Detective Hayes Wassinger of the Hays Police Department, working with federal investigators."

"Look at your guy," Rhonda elbowed me as Hayes appeared on screen. He looked professional but uncomfortable as he tugged at his white collar. Several reporters thrust microphones at him.

"This case demonstrates how dedicated law enforcement agencies can work together to enforce the law, even when the trail has gone cold for decades," Hayes said.

He didn't mention us, as agreed. The Belladonnas, Walter, and I remained anonymous. Hayes got the professional accolades; we got to avoid becoming targets again. The screen cut back to the anchor.

"In two related stories, authorities have apprehended a suspected contract killer known as Miranda McCullough at Washington Dulles International Airport as she attempted to flee the country. McCullough is suspected in multiple murders across several states. Also arrested, a researcher, Dr. Hans Leakey, from a government biosecurity facility on charges of Theft of Trade Secrets and Government Property, with more charges to follow."

"We did it," Emily whispered as she slumped back into her recliner. She was as relieved as I was.

Walter's phone rang. He looked at the screen and smiled. "They've arrested my former supervisor at Immunovax. He falsified the employment records, keeping Miranda's name a secret."

"The truth has been muzzled for years, but now it's biting back," Kit said.

I should have felt triumphant, but mostly I felt tired. One morning news report didn't wash away forty years of buried trauma.

But it was a start.

Chapter 49

The Sagebrush Savings and Loan parking lot was practically empty. I was unaccustomed to free time during the week or, actually, anytime. Dr. Valerie Simpson had transitioned from a relief veterinarian to an associate, a role that made me both proud and slightly threatened. Walter waited for me in the lobby, a cardboard box under his arm.

"All set?" I asked.

Walter nodded. "Now that Immunovax's criminal activities are exposed, legitimate research into immunotherapy can continue."

"Yes, using our parents' work as a foundation," I added.

We stepped into the bank vault, where a safety deposit box held copies of my parents' research. Walter carefully placed his father's notes in the box alongside my parents' notes, with a digital backup of everything.

"I'm heading back to Kansas City this afternoon," he said as we exited the bank. "My cover at Immunovax is blown. I wasn't a very good janitor anyway. Jake has offered to make me the head researcher on super-immunity at S.I.C. As soon as I tie up some loose ends, I'll move to Hays."

Oh, that would make Rhonda happy.

"Super-immunity, without the super-assassins," I joked weakly.

Walter continued, "Ruby, I've been meaning to ask, with your genetic profile, would you consider..."

"Donating blood samples for the research?" I finished for him. "Already arranged it with Jake. Under proper supervision, this time, with transparent protocols. Our parents' work will help countless people. Just make sure you name the gene therapy after them, not us."

Walter agreed. "I think the Dakota-Warren Protocol has a nice ring to it."

I laughed as I realized it was the same name, whether we used our names or our parents'.

Walter gave me an awkward hug before he climbed into his rental car. "The Belladonnas are something else," he said through the window. "Keep them close."

"I intend to." Tears welled up in my eyes as I watched him drive away.

I drove back to the clinic, where Jake awaited my arrival. Yesterday, he had emailed me a contract for my future employment with Pets Buy.

"I'm not sure about this," I told him as he greeted me in the now meticulously organized clinic office, the same office that used to trigger my anxiety.

"It's a good arrangement, Ruby," Jake said, his voice gentler than I'd ever heard it. His arm was still in a sling, a reminder of how close we all had come to disaster. "Pets Buy recognizes your importance to the continued success of the business. You will remain as senior veterinarian, with the same compensation package, but with reduced hours and no administrative duties. Dr. Simpson handles the day-to-day operations."

"And if your corporate bosses decide this isn't profitable…?" I challenged him.

I still didn't trust corporate.

Jake shrugged his good shoulder. "I've learned

something these past few weeks. There's more to life than profit margins. I almost died with nothing but spreadsheets to show for my existence."

"Careful, Jake. You're starting to sound almost human," I teased.

"Don't spread that around. I have a reputation to uphold." He stood to leave, then paused. "You know, I always respected your medical skills, Ruby. I just never knew how to show it."

"Being shot at changes people," I observed. "It changed both of us, Jake, but I wouldn't recommend it as a management technique."

After he left, I stayed in the office, looking around at the clinic that had been my entire world for so long. Three days a week now, instead of seven. No more sleeping in a back room. No more missing life because of work.

It was terrifying. It was liberating.

CHAPTER 50

The Belladonnas had claimed our booth at Hickok's. The place was quieter than usual, just a few locals playing darts in the back.

Emily raised her water glass. “To justice served,” she toasted.

“To Ruby's parents and Walter's father,” added Kit.

“To lifelong friends and love,” I said, as I made eye contact with each one.

“To survival,” Rhonda said with her usual bluntness.

We clinked glasses just as the door swung open. Hayes was no longer in detective mode; he wore jeans and his Kansas City Chiefs jersey which made him look athletic and adorable. His eyes found mine immediately.

“Ladies,” he said with a nod to my friends. “Mind if I borrow Dr. Dakota for a moment?”

Three pairs of eyebrows shot up in perfect synchronization. I was never going to hear the end of this.

“Take all the time you need,” Emily said sweetly.

Hayes led me to a quiet corner. “I thought you'd want to know. Miranda McCullough is talking. She's implicated everyone, trying to cut a deal.”

“That's great news!” I said. “Hope they don’t make it too good a deal. She *is* a murderer after all.”

"That's up to the feds. But that's not why I'm here."

I waited, suddenly aware of the pulse in my neck.

"We wrapped up the case! The threat is gone." His eyes held mine. "And I wonder if you might want to have dinner sometime? Not at your clinic. Not because of a murder. Just... dinner."

"Detective Wassinger, are you asking me on a date?"

"I am." He offered a smile that made me feel like I was sixteen again, which was ridiculous at my age. "Unless you're still worried about maintaining professional boundaries."

I thought Hayes owned the professional boundaries for both of us. Mine had sprung more holes than a chain-link fence in a bad neighborhood. Everything churned through my mind—my parents' legacy, Brock's death, my own brush with mortality.

Life was too short for artificial boundaries.

"I'd like that," I said.

His smile widened.

"How's Saturday?"

"Perfect." I paused. "I have a request, though."

"What's that?"

"Could we eat at your house? I've been there once but didn't get the full tour."

The color that flooded his face was truly satisfying.

"Ruby Anne Dakota, you continue to surprise me," he said after he recovered.

"Good," I replied. "I'm finally learning how to live."

We returned to the Belladonnas, who pretended they hadn't been trying to lip-read our exchange with eagle eyes.

"So, Hayes," Rhonda asked, "is there going to be an undercover operation at your place on Saturday night?"

She *had* been reading lips.

"Rhonda!" Emily scolded as she blushed.

Chapter 51

Six months later, Chui and I stood in front of my bathroom mirror in my new apartment, one with a real bedroom, a kitchen with a stove, and a living room where we could entertain guests. No more waking up in the middle of the night to barking boarders. No more showering in the grooming tub.

"My name is Dr. Ruby Anne Dakota," I said as I practiced my presentation. "Thank you for the invitation to speak at this National Immunology Conference."

I adjusted my new navy-blue suit, not my old scrubs, and referred to my notes for the hundredth time. Tomorrow I would speak before an auditorium of prestigious researchers. I would tell them about my parents' work, Brock's sacrifice, and S.I.C.'s genetic breakthrough that could one day save millions of lives.

Last year, I would have called in sick. Now I looked forward to this opportunity.

My phone dinged with a text. Ah, it was Hayes. I smiled as I read: "Give 'em heck tomorrow, Bulletproof. We'll celebrate when you return."

He had given me a new nickname. I smiled and texted, "Don't solve any murders without me."

Just then, the doorbell rang. Chui launched into his

discordant combination of a welcoming committee and guard dog routine. When I opened the door, there stood the Belladonnas. Kit held a bouquet of sunflowers tied to a liter of Decaf Diet Dr Pepper.

"Surprise!" they shouted in unison. "You didn't think we'd let you go to Washington without a sendoff, did you?"

Oh man, I hated stuff like this, but I put on my appreciative face for my friends. "Oh, how sweet of you guys. You shouldn't have."

Ugh.

"We wanted to. You're about to become famous… in the virus world, anyway," Rhonda boasted. "Don't forget to mention our names."

Emily, Kit, and Rhonda bustled into my kitchen… yes, my kitchen. That sounded good, even though I was still learning to cook. I pulled out Science Diet coffee cups from the cabinet as the women fussed over Chui. No fine china yet. Perhaps that would make a great wedding gift in the future.

Nope, on second thought, don't think so. Not the fine china type… or the wedding type. Or am I?

We all settled around the kitchen table. When I looked at these three women, who had helped me find justice and myself, I felt something foreign—a deep contentment in my soul.

"Ruby," Emily said, as she poured Diet Dr Pepper into our coffee mugs, "your parents would be so proud."

At the mention of my parents, I no longer felt gut-wrenching grief. Instead, I felt my parents were somehow part of this moment.

Later that night, after the Belladonnas had scattered to their homes, I went through my packing list one more time. I included a small, framed photograph of my parents, dressed in white lab coats. They held hands as they smiled at the camera. I'd kept this photo hidden for years because it hurt too much to look at it.

"I'll finish what you started," I whispered to the photo.

Chui jumped up on my bed. He always panicked when he saw my suitcase, not that he'd seen it that many times. As I comforted him and smoothed his fur, I realized something had shifted: I wasn't stressed about tomorrow for the first time in a long time.

Instead, I looked forward to it.

The therapy sessions had worked. I hadn't had an anxiety attack in weeks. Hayes's patient cooking lessons had improved my diet, and I had moved forward several rows from the back pew at church.

Maybe I was drawing closer to God, too.

With Chui at my side, Hayes somehow woven into my future, and the Belladonnas surrounding me as my chosen family, I was finally building something that wasn't just a career.

I was building a life.

About the Author

Annie holds a Doctorate in Veterinary Medicine from Kansas State University. From 1981 to 1997, she owned small animal practices in Nebraska and Kansas.

At forty-six, she felt the call of God to sell her clinic, house, cars — everything — and move to Africa. Dragging along a husband and three children (ages 11, 13, and 14), screaming and kicking, they spent the next nineteen years in Kenya doing street outreach, building group homes, and establishing Teen Challenge rehabilitation centers.

Her first book, the memoir *Little Dogs Pee Higher*, was featured on Adriana Trigiani's summer reading list. She and her husband, John, now reside in the beautiful Missouri Ozarks.

Special Request from Annie

If Ruby Dakota made you smile, cringe, or gasp in Not Immune to Death—please post a review online on Amazon or Goodreads. Even a sentence or two matters more than you think, and Chui would appreciate it!

I'd love for you to follow my author page on Facebook: https://facebook.com/anniemooremartin

You'll be the first to know when Ruby's next adventure is released.

GET TO KNOW THE AUTHOR

Annie Moore Martin, DVM

Discover the real Annie as she takes you on her remarkable life's journey in her memoir, *Little Dogs Pee Higher*. Ruby Dakota may be a fictional character, but as you read Annie's memoir, you might just wonder — is Ruby really fictional, or is she Annie? **Available on Amazon** in paperback, e-book, and audiobook.

A Few 5-Star Reviews from Amazon Readers

"Proving once again that laughter is the best medicine, LITTLE DOGS PEE HIGHER is a charming book that inspires you to take risks, be present, embrace challenges, and celebrate the world."

"Couldn't put this book down! Such a great read, loved reading about the adventures in Kenya. Can't wait to see what will be next."

"I found the title got my attention. It was lighthearted humor in so many stories and gut wrenching tales of hard decisions that parents make. Loved the broad spectrum of stories included. Would highly recommend this book!!"

"Hooked from the beginning! As soon as I started the first chapter I couldn't put it down. Found myself smiling knowing that I was in for a ride. I felt I was right there experiencing every moment...the descriptions and writing is amazing! I can't wait to see what's next!"

"This book is a must read! If you've ever wondered what a life of adventure would look like, this story is it! With authenticity, vulnerability and just right amount of humor, the author opens up about the hard circumstances that lead her and her family to make the decision to follow God's leading to Africa. Once there, her story is filled with unexpected twists and turns, danger, setbacks, terror, heartbreak and sacrifice, right along with surprising blessings, joys, hope and miracles. A real page-turner! Just read it! I know you will enjoy it as much as I did."

www.ingramcontent.com/pod-product-compliance
Lightning Source LLC
LaVergne TN
LVHW020705110826
845149LV00012B/2117

* 9 7 8 1 9 7 0 5 6 0 4 0 4 *